FLASK OF THE
DRUNKEN MASTER

FLASK OF THE DRUNKEN MASTER

A HIRO HATTORI NOVEL

SUSAN SPANN

SEVENTH
STREET
BOOKS®

Published 2019 by Seventh Street Books®

Cover image Eric Lafforgue / Almay Stock Photo
Cover design by Nicole Sommer-Lecht
Cover design © Start Science Fiction

Inquiries should be addressed to
Start Science Fiction
101 Hudson Street, 37th Floor, Suite 3705
Jersey City, New Jersey 07302
Phone: 212-431-5455
www.seventhstreetbooks.com

10 9 8 7 6 5 4 3 2 1

ISBN: 978-1-63388-548-6

Library of Congress Cataloging-in-Publication Data available on file.

Printed in the United States of America

For my brother, Rob, a real-life Hiro

CHAPTER 1

"Halt!" The armored samurai stepped forward to block the bridge. "No one crosses the Kamo River without identification. State your names and your business in Kyoto."

Hattori Hiro gestured to the Jesuit at his side. "Father Mateo Ávila de Santos, a priest of the foreign god, from Portugal. I am Matsui Hiro, his interpreter and scribe."

After a pause, Hiro added, "Our business in the capital has not changed since yesterday. As you know, we live just up the road."

The samurai pointed east, away from the bridge. "You live two blocks past Okazaki Shrine, beyond the official boundary of Kyoto. You cannot enter the city without declaring your names and business. That, also, has not changed since yesterday."

Hiro considered pointing out that only a fool asked for identification from men he recognized. However, he didn't bother. Men who followed orders blindly didn't respond to logic, and Hiro, a *shinobi* assassin, didn't waste time on fools.

"You've stopped us every morning for a week," Hiro said, "and yet, our names and business have not changed."

"Surely you remember us—your words suggest you do," Father Mateo said in perfect Japanese.

The Jesuit's skill with the Japanese language often made Hiro wonder why few people questioned the priest's continuing use of a translator. After three years in Japan, Father Mateo spoke and understood the language well.

Fortunately, most Japanese natives believed their language and culture far too nuanced for a foreigner to master. Hiro knew this also—it was one of many factors he depended on to shield his true identity and his mission to protect the Jesuit's life.

"I have orders." The samurai glanced over his shoulder as if expecting to see someone behind him.

Hiro's attitude softened a fraction. Many men obeyed unreasonable orders out of fear, and Matsunaga Hisahide, the *samurai* who controlled Kyoto, inspired well-founded fear in all who served him.

"Noodles," Hiro said.

The samurai's forehead wrinkled in confusion. "Excuse me . . . noodles?"

"Our business in Kyoto," Hiro said without a smile. "Do we have to show a travel pass to eat a morning snack?"

The samurai's cheeks flushed almost as dark as the crimson armor that covered his chest. "No," he said, "but I need not apologize for following orders."

"Not to me," Hiro said. "However, this priest has the emperor's personal permission to enter and leave Kyoto without restriction, and, unless I am mistaken, the emperor outranks Matsunaga Hisahide."

Technically, Father Mateo worked in Kyoto under a blanket permission granted to all the Jesuits, but Hiro hoped his companion would cooperate with the bluff.

The samurai's mouth opened and shut like a fish hooked out of the river beneath the bridge. He bowed. "I apologize, Father-*san*. I did not know."

"If you wish to keep your job," Hiro said, "I suggest you learn to distinguish between genuine threats and imagined ones."

As Hiro followed the priest across the bridge, he considered the irony in his parting words. Despite his current position as the Jesuit's bodyguard, Hiro's shinobi training made him a dangerous threat indeed.

Father Mateo said nothing until they started south on the road that paralleled the riverbank.

"You know what I think of lies." The priest spoke softly to ensure the samurai wouldn't overhear.

Hiro put on an innocent look. "I told no lies."

"Permission to work in Kyoto hardly equates to unfettered movement." Father Mateo frowned at Hiro. "You stretched the truth on purpose to intimidate that young man."

"I wouldn't have had to do it if he exercised discretion." Hiro disapproved of men who flexed their power without cause. "We have tolerated his arrogance long enough."

Father Mateo's lips drew into a disapproving line.

The men walked on in silence.

The clear blue sky and pleasant summer temperature soon lightened Hiro's mood. By the time they turned east on Sanjō Road, the priest's good temper seemed to return as well.

A few minutes later, they reached the road where Hiro's favorite noodle vendor frequently set up his wheeled cart. Shuttered *sake* shops and restaurants lined the narrow street. The last of the patrons would have straggled home just hours earlier, as dawn began to kiss the eastern sky. Fortunately for the hungry shinobi, vendors opened earlier than sake shops and restaurants. Charcoal smoke and the oily odor of roasting fish already filled the air.

Hiro's mouth watered at the thought of handmade noodles in a savory, fishy broth. He spotted the vendor almost at once and had to restrain his pace to keep from hurrying toward the cart. A samurai never hurried. Not even for the tastiest *udon* Kyoto had to offer.

The vendor greeted Hiro with a deep, respectful bow and a happy grin. "Good morning, Matsui-*san*. So nice to see you!"

"Good morning, Kenji." Samurai didn't bow to vendors, but Hiro's use of the merchant's name conveyed respect.

"Two bowls this morning?" Kenji asked as he bowed to Father Mateo.

Hiro nodded and reached for his purse. As he withdrew it from his *kimono*, he heard shouting at the far end of the block.

"Arrest me!" a reedy voice screeched. "I'm the guilty one, not him!"

Hiro recognized the voice. He wished he hadn't.

The shouts continued. "I'm the murderer, you fool! Why won't you listen?!"

Hiro felt his noodles slip away as he turned in the direction of the sound.

Half a block to the south, a samurai stood alone in the narrow street. The man wore a colorful surcoat, cut in the style favored by *yoriki*—the assistant magistrates who supervised lower-ranked policemen known as *dōshin.*

Hiro frowned. If a yoriki left his office before noon, someone was either dead or being arrested.

Possibly both.

A bald-headed monk in a stained brown robe jumped up and down in front of the yoriki. "Listen to me!" he yelled. "I'm a dangerous man!"

The yoriki stepped around the monk as a pair of dōshin emerged from a nearby brewery.

The policemen held the arms of a brewer who walked with a lowered head and sagging shoulders. Hiro couldn't tell if the merchant's posture suggested guilt or merely embarrassment.

Years of training told the shinobi to turn away and ignore the scene.

But Hiro's conscience wouldn't let him do it. He recognized the monk who hopped and danced around the yoriki. More importantly, he knew the brewer walking between the dōshin.

The man was named Ginjiro—and Hiro owed him a personal debt.

CHAPTER 2

Father Mateo looked up the street. "Are the dōshin arresting Ginjiro, the brewer? And did that monk say 'murder'?"

Hiro nodded.

Father Mateo had met Ginjiro a couple of months before, while investigating a murder at the shogunate. Hiro knew the Jesuit would want to help the brewer, even though most Japanese would turn away. The priest cared more for justice than for etiquette.

Father Mateo switched to Portuguese. "We have to help him."

Hiro appreciated the language shift. The noodle vendor didn't need to hear this conversation.

"Not our business," Hiro said, also in Portuguese, though he slipped his coin purse into his kimono as he spoke. He intended to help Ginjiro, too, but hoped an argument would cause the priest to show some caution. "The yoriki could arrest us for interfering."

"That man is your friend," Father Mateo said. "You cannot turn your back on his distress."

"He owns a brewery I frequent," Hiro said. "He's not a friend."

Father Mateo shook his head in disapproval. "Ginjiro helped when you needed him. I think that makes him more than just a brewer."

The time had come to let the Jesuit win.

"Agreed," Hiro said, "but let me lead. We cannot anger the yoriki."

He turned to the noodle vendor and switched back to Japanese. "Regrettably, we will not need noodles after all."

Kenji bowed as Hiro and Father Mateo walked away.

The two men walked toward the brewery at the leisurely pace of samurai enjoying a morning stroll.

Ahead, the balding cleric shouted, "I am the murderer! Listen to me!"

The yoriki ignored the monk's confession.

Hiro didn't believe it either. The monk, whose name was Suke, spent his evenings drinking Ginjiro's sake and mornings sleeping it off in the narrow alley beside the brewery. He might be guilty of vagrancy, but not of murder.

Suke turned to the dōshin who held Ginjiro. "I am a dangerous man!" the monk declared.

The wooden shutters covering the brewery storefront rattled open, revealing Ginjiro's adult daughter, Tomiko, and a tiny, gray-haired woman that Hiro recognized as Ginjiro's wife, though at the moment he could not recall her name.

The elderly woman squinted and blinked like an owl caught in sunlight. When she saw Ginjiro between the dōshin, she clutched at Tomiko's sleeve and whispered something in her daughter's ear.

Tomiko bent her head and whispered back. When the elderly woman released her sleeve, Tomiko bent down and set a pair of *geta* in the street. She stepped down into her sandals, approached the yoriki, and bowed, hands crossed before her body to show respect.

Hiro noted with approval that Tomiko did not tremble. Women rarely showed such courage when addressing the police.

Suke pushed himself between Tomiko and the yoriki.

"You fool!" the monk declared. "Are you deaf, or merely stupid?"

The yoriki turned away.

Suke drew a breath but let it out, the words unspoken, at the sight of Hiro and the priest.

"Hiro-*san*!" Suke ran toward them, long sleeves flapping like a pair of greasy wings. "He wants to arrest Ginjiro, but I'm the killer."

The yoriki met Hiro's eyes and shook his head.

Father Mateo approached and asked, "Has a murder been committed?"

Hiro wondered how the Jesuit always managed to ask the most obvious question possible.

Suke pointed to the narrow space between the brewery and the restaurant next door. "In the alley. He's still lying where I killed him."

The dōshin holding Ginjiro's arms looked around, as if for instructions. The yoriki made a motion for them to wait.

"Good morning, Father." The yoriki bowed.

Hiro wondered whether the yoriki knew that "Father" was a title or whether he omitted the suffix "-san" to slight the priest.

"Good morning." The Jesuit returned the bow. "I am Father Mateo Ávila de Santos, and this is my interpreter, Matsui Hiro."

The yoriki gave Hiro a cautious look. Father Mateo's introduction didn't mention the translator's rank or province of origin, indicating Hiro was *ronin*, a masterless samurai forced to adopt a trade.

"What happened here?" Father Mateo asked in Japanese.

The yoriki looked at Hiro. "Please inform your master we do not require his aid."

Hiro translated into Portuguese, mostly to delay the priest's response. Father Mateo's Japanese was better than his patience.

"We know this brewer," Father Mateo said. "He's not a killer."

Hiro felt a rush of pride as the Jesuit made a Japanese-style gesture toward Ginjiro. The priest remembered that samurai considered pointing rude.

The yoriki scowled at Hiro. "Tell your master he is misinformed."

"I am not misinformed," Suke said, "and I already told you, Ginjiro is not the killer."

"Shut up, old man," the yoriki said in a voice that sounded more bored than angry. "Don't make me arrest you for causing trouble."

"Arrest me for causing a murder!" Suke shrieked.

The yoriki raised his hands in exasperation.

"Who was murdered?" Father Mateo asked. "I see no corpse."

"No one important," the yoriki said.

Father Mateo started toward the alley. "I want to see."

CHAPTER 3

The yoriki looked from the priest to Hiro. "Stop him!"

"Me?" Hiro shrugged. "You're the assistant magistrate. I'm a translator."

The yoriki sighed and made a dismissive gesture. "Then go with him, and make sure he touches nothing."

Hiro raised an eyebrow at the yoriki's unexpected change of mind.

"You think I don't know who you are?" The yoriki lowered his voice. "Magistrate Ishimaki speaks quite highly of the priest and ronin who captured General Akechi's killer a year ago. There cannot be two such pairs of men in Kyoto.

"If I stop the priest, I risk a reprimand. It's safer to let him look, provided he doesn't interfere."

Hiro found it curious—and not entirely pleasant—that the magistrate considered their activities worth discussing. He preferred to remain unnoticed when he could.

Hiro bowed and followed the Jesuit into the alley.

The eaves of the two-story brewery overhung the roof of the neighboring restaurant, leaving the alley in constant shadow. Barrels stood in rows along the brewery wall, while stacks of boxes lined the side of the restaurant. Two people could walk abreast in the space between, but only if they knew each other well.

Beyond the end of the brewery, the alley opened into a yard that served as a communal garden and storage space for the residents of the block. The buildings fronted on different roads, but their occupants considered themselves united by the open space they shared. At the moment, the way to that open space was blocked by a dōshin standing guard at the far end of the brewery. He stood in the gap;

looking bored but alert, ready to stop the neighbors from wandering into the murder scene.

A dead man's body lay on the ground outside the narrow door that served as a private entrance to Ginjiro's storeroom. Customers didn't use that door, but Hiro didn't think this man had come for a flask of sake.

The victim lay on his stomach with his face turned toward the restaurant and his arms splayed out to his sides. The back of his head was covered with graying stubble and spattered blood, while an injury left the base of his skull misshapen and concave.

The dōshin noticed the priest. "You shouldn't be here."

Hiro raised a placating hand. "The yoriki gave us permission to view the body."

The dōshin looked past Hiro as if expecting someone to follow them into the alley. When no one appeared, he said, "All right, you can look, but don't touch anything."

Father Mateo stopped a respectful distance from the body. Hiro passed the Jesuit and leaned down for a closer look. The corpse's close-cropped hair and lack of swords indicated a commoner, and the quality of his clothes suggested a merchant. He wore a faded striped kimono, once expensive but now fraying at the seams. A patch on the back revealed a repair, but the tailor had matched the pattern well, using cloth from inside the hem. Most people would not have noticed it was mended.

"An artisan?" Father Mateo gestured to the corpse's upturned palms. "Those calluses say he worked with his hands."

"Yes," Hiro said, "but the strength of his upper body and the condition of his clothing suggest a merchant. I don't see rice dust on him . . . perhaps a brewer?"

"I'm impressed!" The dōshin took a step forward, but stopped as if remembering he shouldn't discuss the murder, or the victim.

Hiro nodded. "A brewer, then."

The dōshin flushed an embarrassed red. "I didn't say—you didn't hear me say that."

"What killed him?" Father Mateo asked.

Hiro indicated the flattened base of the dead man's skull. "Beaten to death, most likely with something blunt."

A tear in the corpse's scalp revealed shattered bone beneath. Congealed blood spattered the back of the victim's head and shoulders, and a spray of rusty droplets covered the ground around the body as well as the base of the brewery wall.

"We agree." The dōshin nodded. "Killed in a fight—an accidental death."

Hiro looked at the misty droplets around the body and on the wall. "I disagree. This man was murdered."

The dōshin looked suspicious. "How do you know his death was not accidental? Where were you last night when this brewery closed?"

"At home, on Marutamachi Road." Hiro nodded at Father Mateo. "The priest can attest to my presence there. Also, the yoriki told us the man was murdered."

The dōshin waited for Father Mateo's affirming nod before asking, "How do you know so much about his death?"

Hiro gestured to the wall. "Tiny droplets mean the blows were struck with vicious force. Above knee height, the droplets change from round to elongated, and the tails of the droplets all point upward."

"So?" The dōshin frowned.

"So," Hiro said, "that means the victim lay on the ground, unconscious, when those blows occurred. Any experienced warrior would have known that."

"I did know it," the dōshin said. "The yoriki declared the death a murder, probably unintended. He instructed us to call it an accident."

Hiro recognized the bluff. No dōshin would ever admit ignorance to a ronin.

Father Mateo studied the stains as if he might find the killer's name in the pattern. "Do you think the attacker surprised him from behind? This man must not have seen his assailant coming."

"He saw something." Hiro gestured to the dead man's face. "The injury to his eye preceded death."

The right side of the corpse's face lay against the ground. The lower side of the nose and cheek had blossomed into the reddish purple color common in the parts of a body closest to the ground at the time of death. The left side of the face was mostly pale—also normal, for the side of a body that didn't face the ground.

However, the flesh around the man's left eye swelled out in a dark blue lump the size of a chicken egg. Tissues didn't bruise that way unless the victim's heart was beating. Someone punched the dead man's face before he died.

"That's why we think the death, though murder, was unintended," the dōshin said. "Two men fight, one ends up dead. It happens fairly often."

"Indeed," Hiro said. "What makes you suspect Ginjiro?"

The dōshin stepped forward and gestured to something near the brewery wall.

Hiro leaned across the corpse to look.

A piece of broken pottery lay on the ground beside the dead man's shoulder. The circular shard resembled the base of a shattered stoneware vessel—a sake flask.

It was inlaid with Ginjiro's personal seal.

CHAPTER 4

Father Mateo leaned over the body. "Is that the broken base of a sake flask?"

Hiro hoped the Jesuit wouldn't ask about the mark.

"Yes," the dōshin said. "The murder weapon—part of it, anyway." Hiro circled the corpse and examined the shard.

Ginjiro bought his sake flasks from a potter who produced them for the brewer by special order. The flasks had a distinctive color, and each bore the brewer's mark impressed in the base. The markings distinguished Ginjiro's flasks, which never left the brewery, from the ones that customers brought for personal use.

"That is the brewer's mark," the dōshin said.

Hiro straightened. "A broken flask outside a brewery hardly marks the brewer as a killer."

"I agree," Father Mateo said. "Anyone could have stolen a flask or dropped it in the alley."

"More importantly," Hiro added, "delicate pottery would have shattered before causing so much damage to the victim. Unless, of course, the flask was full, but I see no sake on the body or the ground."

The dōshin crossed his arms. "If it's a coincidence, where's the rest of the flask? We haven't found any other pieces here."

"You believe the killer took them with him," Father Mateo said.

Conveniently leaving the one with Ginjiro's seal, Hiro thought.

"Why would Ginjiro kill a man with a flask that bore his seal?" Father Mateo rubbed his chin.

"Arguments happen," the dōshin said. "Angry men don't think before they act."

"That's a lot of assumptions for one dead body and one small shard from a sake flask," Hiro said.

"Ginjiro didn't kill Chikao." Suke's voice echoed through the alley as he entered. "I'm the killer."

Hiro noted the dead man's name and wondered how Suke knew it.

"Shut up, old man," the dōshin said. "Go away before I arrest you."

Hiro raised a hand and said, "We're finished. We'll walk him out."

The shinobi took hold of Suke's sleeve and led the monk back out to the street, where the yoriki stood talking with Tomiko. Ginjiro's wife stood nearby, but her glazed expression suggested inattention.

Hiro looked up the street and saw the dōshin lead Ginjiro out of sight around a corner. The brewer's head hung low, like a man condemned.

Father Mateo followed Hiro's gaze. "Where are they going?"

"To the magistrate," the yoriki said. "The facts are clear and not disputed. Ginjiro argued with the victim yesterday evening. Late last night, Chikao returned, and Ginjiro killed him."

Hiro glanced at Father Mateo, expecting the priest to argue.

Suke struck a fighting pose. "You want guilt?" the monk demanded, curling his fingers into fists. "I'll show you guilt!"

"Calm down," Hiro said. "If you're the killer, explain how it really happened."

The yoriki sighed and shook his head, but Suke lowered his hands and said, "I will. I'll tell you everything."

The monk straightened his shoulders and raised his chin like a child about to confess to a youthful crime. "Last night I sneaked a flask out of Ginjiro's at closing time. I didn't intend to steal it, I just wanted to finish the sake. I would have returned the flask in the morning."

Suke paused as if concerned that Hiro might accuse him of stealing flasks. When the shinobi said nothing, the monk continued, "This morning, when I woke up, my flask was gone. I saw Chikao's body and heard the dōshin say Ginjiro's flask—the one I took—was the murder weapon. Clearly, I am the killer!"

The yoriki made a disgusted gesture. "Clearly, you were too drunk to hear a man being beaten to death beside you. We have listened to your story. Go away."

Suke jumped forward and shoved the yoriki, catching him off guard. The samurai fell backward and sat down hard in the dusty street.

The dōshin, who had followed them from the alley, ran to Suke. He seized the monk by the arms.

Suke bowed his head. "I surrender," he said quietly. "Deliver me to the magistrate for judgment."

The yoriki stood up and brushed the dirt from his clothes. "Arrest him—but the charge is public drunkenness, nothing more."

"Nothing more!" The angry dōshin glared at Suke. "He assaulted you and confessed to murder."

"He's a drunk." The yoriki removed a pebble from his sleeve. "He wobbles like an infant and he smells like a brewery floor. I believe he spent the night in the alley. The rest of his story? Merely a drunkard's dream."

"But . . . the assault!" the dōshin protested as he tied a length of rope around Suke's wrists. "This man attacked you."

"You are mistaken. I stumbled and fell." The yoriki paused to let his words sink in. "Now take him away, and send some bearers to carry Chikao home."

"Don't worry, Tomiko," Suke said as the dōshin led him away. "I'll tell the magistrate what happened. Ginjiro will be home in time to open the shop tonight."

Tomiko smiled weakly, as if unwilling to put much faith in Suke's promise. She laid a hand on her mother's arm and guided the older woman back to the brewery.

Hiro wanted to speak with Ginjiro's family, but first he had some questions for the yoriki. "Where is Chikao's brewery? Did the victim belong to the brewer's guild?"

"Do not mistake my leniency for permission to investigate." The yoriki finished brushing the dirt from his trousers. "The magistrate doesn't need your help—or his." The yoriki glanced at Father Mateo.

"What if we disagree with your assessment of the crime?" the Jesuit asked.

Hiro stifled a nearly overwhelming urge to drag the priest away from the scene by force. As usual, Father Mateo didn't know when to hold his tongue.

The yoriki smiled, but his eyes were devoid of warmth. "Then you will keep your disagreement to yourself."

"Have I misunderstood the samurai code?" Father Mateo asked. "I thought honor required noble men to seek justice and act with mercy."

"That argument might work with a samurai from the ruling clans," the yoriki said. "But I see crimes, and criminals, every day. Justice does not mix with mercy where commoners are concerned."

The yoriki started toward the alley, paused, and turned back to Hiro. "I expect cooperation—and discretion—from you both. Murder is a matter for the magistrate alone, especially now, with the city on alert. If you speak of this to anyone, I will ensure you share the killer's fate."

Hiro doubted the yoriki could carry out his threat, but knew better than to challenge him in public.

Father Mateo called after the yoriki, "Why insist on privacy? Unless, of course, you don't intend an honest investigation."

CHAPTER 5

The yoriki stopped and slowly turned toward Father Mateo. Hiro shifted his weight to his toes and prepared to fight. No one accused a yoriki of corruption without consequence.

To Hiro's surprise, the assistant magistrate didn't draw his sword.

"The details of Chikao's murder might cause violence within the brewers' guild," the yoriki said. "The shogun's recent death has the samurai clans on the brink of war. I do not need a war among the artisans as well.

"Chikao died in a fight. Anyone who says otherwise will be punished."

"The family will guess the truth," Father Mateo said. "No one will believe those injuries came from a simple fight."

"That is not your problem," the yoriki said. "I allowed you to see the body as a courtesy. Do not repay my kindness by causing trouble."

"We have no wish to cause trouble," Hiro said. "We didn't even know Chikao."

"But you know Ginjiro." The yoriki looked down the street and frowned. "Fools! I told them to send Ren to the Lucky Monkey."

His gaze shifted back to Hiro and Father Mateo. "The dead man's business partner is coming. One word out of place, and I'll have you flogged."

Hiro understood the yoriki's wish to avoid more violence but disagreed with forcing Ginjiro to bear the blame. Not without more evidence of guilt. Hiro didn't normally involve himself in other men's business, but couldn't abide a yoriki who blamed the innocent just to close a case.

Father Mateo's chagrined expression suggested the Jesuit also had no intention of letting the matter drop. For once, Hiro agreed with the priest. They would conduct an investigation, with or without the yoriki's permission.

Hiro just hoped that Father Mateo was smart enough not to say so.

He turned as footsteps approached behind him. Hiro stood several inches taller than Chikao's business partner, but the sake brewer weighed substantially more. Muscled arms bulged the sleeves of the brewer's striped kimono, and his waist was thick, but not with soggy fat. His slicked-back hair had a slight green tinge, suggesting its deep black color was not natural.

The brewer bowed to the yoriki. "A dōshin came to my home. He mentioned an accident and sent me here. Why are we at Ginjiro's?"

"Thank you for coming so quickly, Ren." The yoriki's tight-lipped expression promised an unpleasant afternoon in store for the dōshin who delivered the incorrect message. "There has, indeed, been an accident, but I intended for you to meet me at your brewery, not this one. Unfortunately, the dōshin delivered my message incorrectly."

After an awkward pause the yoriki added, "I need you to break the news to Chikao's widow."

"Widow?" Ren's forehead wrinkled. "What happened to Chikao?"

"A fight—" the yoriki began.

Before he could finish Ren exclaimed, "Ginjiro killed Chikao?"

"We do not know that," Father Mateo said.

The yoriki cut the Jesuit off with a glare.

"Ginjiro must be involved," Ren said. "There's no other reason to send me here, and I know they argued yesterday. Ginjiro hit Chikao and threatened worse. Where is my partner's body? I want to see him."

"The bearers have already carried him off," the yoriki lied, his words surprisingly convincing. "Ginjiro is under arrest and will be punished, though the evidence shows the death was accidental."

"Chikao is really dead?" Ren's eyes reddened. "This will devastate Mina."

The yoriki nodded. "All the more reason for her to hear the news from you and not a dōshin. Will you accept the responsibility?"

Ren dipped his head in consent. "Of course." He clenched his jaw and looked away, fighting to keep his emotions under control. "How did this happen? How did he die?"

"The details remain under investigation," the yoriki said. "I cannot tell you any more."

"Would you like me to accompany you?" Father Mateo asked the brewer. "Often, a priest can make these burdens lighter."

Ren looked at Father Mateo. "Thank you, but Mina would prefer a Buddhist priest." He bowed to cover the need to wipe his tears. "Please excuse me, I have sad news to bear."

He straightened and walked away.

Hiro doubted Chikao's family and friends would accept the yoriki's explanation quite so easily after the initial shock wore off. Still, grief came first. Questions would follow later.

When Ren had left, Father Mateo turned to the yoriki. "I trust your familiarity with the victim and his family didn't influence your decision not to investigate the crime."

Hiro stared at Father Mateo. Even a fool knew not to accuse a yoriki a second time.

The yoriki narrowed his eyes at Hiro. "Translate my next words with exceptional care.

"I need not defend myself to any man. However, I will explain— once more—because the magistrate respects this foreign priest.

"I know Chikao because I arrest his son on a regular basis, usually for fighting and public drunkenness. I know Chikao's partner, Ren, because the profits from their brewery often go to pay young Kaoru's fines. I assure you, I do not consider either man a friend. In truth, I regret it was the father—not the son—who died today."

At the end of the Portuguese translation Hiro added, "Do not antagonize him further."

Father Mateo held Hiro's gaze just long enough to make the shinobi wonder if the priest would ignore the instruction. Finally, the Jesuit nodded. "Will the magistrate punish Ginjiro's wife and daughter?"

The yoriki shook his head. "The brewer's guilt will not extend to his family unless they played a role in the crime. Based on the facts, that seems unlikely. I will tell the magistrate they are innocent."

Hiro's attitude toward the yoriki softened slightly at those words, though he disagreed with the man's conclusions about Ginjiro.

"Please excuse me," the yoriki said, "I must report to the magistrate."

"What about the body?" Father Mateo asked.

"The *eta* will see to the corpse." The yoriki indicated a trio of men approaching from the north. They walked unusually close together, heads low and faces bowed to the ground. Strips of cloth around their heads identified them as members of the untouchable caste.

The yoriki walked away. He paused to give instructions to the untouchables, who nodded in understanding but did not speak or meet his eyes.

Father Mateo watched the silent men walk past and enter the alley. "Are they outcastes?" he asked with interest. "I've never met one, until now."

"You won't now, either," Hiro said. "Not even beggars converse with their kind."

Father Mateo looked disappointed. "No man is untouchable to God."

"If you want to help Ginjiro, you will leave them unmolested." Hiro started toward the brewery. "Besides, we need to speak with Ginjiro's family."

The shutters across the storefront rattled open as Hiro approached. Tomiko stood alone in the doorway. Despite her reddened eyes, she shed no tears. Instead, she gave Hiro the even look of a competent merchant. Unlike a samurai woman, she had no need to act demure.

"Good morning, Tomiko," Hiro said in formal Japanese. "Please accept our condolences."

"My father did not kill Chikao," Tomiko said. "I need your help to prove it."

Father Mateo joined Hiro at the door. "We will help in any way we can."

"Have you evidence to prove your father's innocence?" Hiro asked.

Tomiko's shoulders drooped. She shook her head. "We were sleeping when the murder happened."

"The yoriki claims your father argued with Chikao last night," Father Mateo said. "Did you hear it? Do you know what happened?"

Tomiko shook her head again. "I didn't work in the shop last night."

"Don't worry," Hiro said. "I was here. I saw the argument."

CHAPTER 6

Father Mateo frowned. "You told the dōshin you stayed home all night. You let me confirm a lie."

Hiro shrugged. "I stepped out during your prayer meeting, had one flask of sake, and returned. After that, I did stay home all night."

"So you heard Chikao and Ginjiro argue?" the Jesuit asked.

Hiro found it surprising that the priest had not said more about the lie. Father Mateo's love of truth, and Hiro's selective honesty, had caused the two men problems more than once.

"I heard the argument start," Hiro said. "Something about an unpaid bill and Ginjiro's support of Chikao's petition to join the brewers' guild. After that, they went into the alley, along with a third man, likely Chikao's son."

"The alley?" Father Mateo asked. "The one where Chikao died?"

"Yes," Hiro said, "but they all came out again a short while later. Ginjiro returned to the brewery. The others went down the street."

"The bill belongs to Kaoru—Chikao's son," Tomiko said. "He owes us money and hasn't paid."

She paused, as if debating whether she should speak her mind. At last she said, "Forgive me this request. I know you've solved other murders . . . helped the families. You owe us nothing, but I have no one else to ask . . ."

She trailed off with a distant look in her eyes, as if remembering someone else—someone she might have asked under different circumstances. Hiro suspected she thought of Kazu, Hiro's clansman and former drinking companion. Tomiko didn't know that either man was a shinobi. Like everyone else, she believed that Hiro was only an interpreter and Kazu merely a clerk at the shogunate. Also, like everyone else of her gender, Tomiko had fallen for

Kazu, despite the fact that she was an artisan's daughter and could never marry a samurai.

Hiro wondered how much Ginjiro's daughter knew about the recent shogunate murder and Kazu's subsequent disappearance from Kyoto.

He would never ask.

Father Mateo took Tomiko's silence as a question. "We will investigate this murder, too."

"However, you must understand," Hiro said, "if your father killed Chikao, our investigation will condemn him."

"It will not." Tomiko straightened. "You will prove his innocence. I know it."

The *noren* that separated the shop from the rooms beyond pushed open. Ginjiro's wife shuffled into the room and joined her daughter at the door. She blinked in surprise at the sight of the men in the entrance.

"Matsui-*san*," Tomiko said, "I believe you know my mother, Yoka. Mother, do you remember our friend Matsui Hiro? His companion is a priest of the foreign god."

Yoka's wrinkled face and graying hair reminded Hiro of Father Mateo's housekeeper, Ana, but the similarity went no further. Where Ana had a slender build, Ginjiro's wife resembled an ancient Buddha, wrinkled and pale, with a swollen belly.

Yoka's left eyelid drooped almost fully closed. Her lips pulled down on that side as well, and a bead of drool pooled at the side of her mouth. She tilted her head to the side and looked at Hiro like a puppy attempting to understand its master's words. "Where is Ginjiro?"

"He went with the dōshin, remember?" Tomiko asked in a gentle voice. "To help them understand why Chikao died."

The question, and Tomiko's answer, made Hiro suspect that Yoka had suffered the fainting illness, which killed many elderly people and left the survivors weak in body and mind.

Yoka's right eye opened wide. The left one didn't flicker. "Chikao is dead?"

"He died this morning," Tomiko said, "before the dōshin came."

Yoka nodded slowly. "I remember. He died in the alley." She raised a trembling hand to her mouth. "Why did he die? Should we worry about his ghost?"

"No, Mother," Tomiko said. "His ghost won't harm us."

Yoka lowered her hand. "Would you like some sake, Matsui-*san*?"

"No, thank you." Hiro smiled. "It's still early in the day."

"Mother, could you measure some rice?" Tomiko gestured toward the rooms behind the noren. "I will help you wash and cook it when I finish here."

"Measure rice?" Yoka's forehead wrinkled, then smoothed. Her good eye took on a happy glow. "I can measure rice. I don't need help. I remember how."

She turned away and shuffled off, murmuring, "measure the rice, wash the rice," as if to fix the task in her mind.

After she disappeared through the noren, Hiro asked Tomiko, "When did it happen?"

"The fainting illness?" Tomiko glanced over her shoulder. "About a year ago." She smiled, though her lips stayed tight. "You may have noticed we keep her out of the shop."

"I knew only that I hadn't seen her." Hiro saw no point in belaboring the obvious.

"It happened in the night," Tomiko said. "She woke up paralyzed. She couldn't speak or even move. The physician said she wouldn't live, but we cared for her as best we could and gradually she recovered. That is, her body recovered. Her mind is not the same.

"Until today, the changes made me sad. But now—is it cruel to say I'm glad she doesn't understand what happened?"

"Not at all." Father Mateo looked at the wooden counter where the customers sat in the evening. "Can you manage the shop with your father gone? Will your patrons allow a woman to serve them sake?"

Tomiko smiled. "Most of them buy more when I watch the counter. It lets them talk to a woman without paying teahouse rates." After a thoughtful pause she continued, "Please forgive my boldness, but I would like to hire you—to pay you for finding Chikao's real killer."

"I am sorry," Hiro said. "We are not for hire."

"You've solved other murders. I know you helped Kazu—" Tomiko stopped abruptly, as if sorry she said the name. Her eyes widened with understanding. "I apologize. It is because my family is not samurai."

"Your status makes no difference," Hiro said. "We simply do not offer ourselves for hire."

"Could you make an exception?" Tomiko bit her lip as if fighting tears. "If they execute my father, we'll lose everything. Mother and I will have nowhere to go. Matsui-*san*, I beg you. I have nowhere else to turn."

She bent forward in a bow.

"He didn't mean we wouldn't help," Father Mateo said. "He meant we will not take your money."

Hiro said nothing. The priest's interpretation was correct.

Hiro admired Tomiko's dedication to her parents. In addition, he owed her father a debt of honor. A month before, Ginjiro had bought the shinobi time to solve a murder and prevent an unjust execution. It seemed only fair to return the favor now.

Unless, of course, Ginjiro was the killer.

Hiro did not consider investigating Chikao's death a conflict with his duty to guard the priest. Unlike the previous murders, this one seemed unlikely to create any special danger for Father Mateo. The Jesuit's words or actions might offend a touchy samurai, but Father Mateo often did that anyway.

Moreover, Hiro liked the thought of catching another killer.

Hiro didn't object to killing, under proper circumstances. He had done it more than once, with no regrets. That said, he never tried to blame his assassinations on someone else. Hiro believed a killer had the right to escape, or at least to try, but not to blame an innocent person for the crime.

"We will help," Hiro said, "as long as you understand we cannot promise to save your father."

"I understand," Tomiko said, "and thank you. Now, if you will excuse me, I must help Mother."

Hiro stepped away from the door as Tomiko slid the shutters closed. When he heard the latch click into the locked position, he started toward the alley.

"Where are you going?" Father Mateo asked. "Do you think they'll let us examine the body again before they move it?"

"I don't know," Hiro said, "but I intend to try."

CHAPTER 7

When Hiro and Father Mateo entered the alley, the three men standing around the corpse knelt and bowed their cloth-wrapped heads to the ground.

Hiro started toward the body without comment.

Father Mateo paused in front of the outcastes. "I am Father Mateo Ávila de Santos, a priest, from Portugal."

The men didn't move or speak. In fact, they didn't acknowledge the words at all.

Hiro frowned at the priest and shook his head. Men of rank didn't speak to outcastes, except to deliver orders.

Father Mateo waited for almost a minute. As Hiro expected, the outcastes didn't answer and didn't move. Finally, the shinobi took pity on the cowering men.

"Leave us," he ordered. "We wish to examine the body without you present."

The outcastes scrambled to their feet and fled the alley, bowing as they went.

"Why did you do that?" Father Mateo asked.

"They wouldn't have answered you," Hiro said. "I told you, it's not permitted."

"Why haven't they moved the body?" the Jesuit asked.

"Probably waiting for a priest." Hiro knelt beside the murdered man. "They believe a special blessing will keep the dead man's ghost from seeking revenge on those who touch the corpse."

Chikao's outstretched arms gave Hiro pause. The position suggested the victim hadn't tried to block his fall.

Hiro wondered whether a pair of assailants had cornered the man in the alley. While one distracted the victim, the other could have struck him from behind. Bandits sometimes did that, but the crushing blows to the skull seemed inconsistent with a robbery. Thieves took a victim's money and escaped as fast as possible. They didn't stick around to abuse the corpse.

"How does a man get a bruise on his eye and end up lying face down in the street?" Father Mateo asked. "Shouldn't that blow have knocked him backward?"

Hiro examined the dead man's face more closely.

Chikao's left eye looked grossly distended, the skin swollen tight with bruising beneath the surface. That kind of swelling took at least an hour to develop, sometimes more.

"Yes," Hiro said, "but I don't believe that blow is the one that felled him. Look at the blood on his head and shoulders. What do you see?"

"There's a lot of it," Father Mateo said.

Hiro nodded. "True, but I meant the pattern. It's all spatter. If the cut on his scalp had occurred before he died, blood would have flowed down over his neck and shoulders. This wound oozed but didn't bleed, which means his heart stopped beating before it happened. All this blood was driven out when the murderer smashed the skull with a solid object, over and over again."

Hiro pantomimed striking the corpse.

"I get the idea." Father Mateo raised a hand in protest.

Hiro stopped the reenactment. "The force of the killer's strikes sent blood all over the body, the wall, and the ground, but the lack of a bloody pool beneath Chikao reveals he didn't bleed much after he hit the ground.

"A strike to the eye is rarely fatal. It probably wouldn't even cause a fall. The blow that knocked him out came from behind."

As Hiro finished, a voice shouted, "Do not disturb the dead!"

Hiro turned. A Buddhist monk, far younger and cleaner than Suke, stood at the alley entrance near the street.

"We haven't touched him," Father Mateo said.

The monk approached. When he reached the body, he asked, "Do you know what happened?"

Hiro opted for the yoriki's explanation. "An accident. He died in a fight."

The monk bent down and examined the wounds. "Crushing blows to the head. What cut his scalp?"

Hiro wondered how a cleric recognized the cause of death.

However, he also enjoyed the reversal—usually, it was Hiro's understanding that startled others.

"I don't think it's a cut," he said. "The skin tore open under the force of the killer's blows. The fractured skull created an edge that split the skin."

"Interesting," the monk replied. "He didn't defend himself?"

Hiro debated the best response. The yoriki told them not to discuss the crime, but Hiro didn't want the monk to become suspicious and question their authority to view the murder scene.

Before he could make a decision, Father Mateo said, "The first blow knocked him senseless. When he fell, his opponent beat him to death."

The monk shook his head. "This killer had an angry soul."

"How do you know that?" Father Mateo asked.

The monk gestured toward the bloody wall. "Only an angry man strikes so many times, or with such force." After a pause he added, "Also, I would guess the killer was not samurai."

The statement put Hiro's curiosity over the edge. "What makes you say so?"

The monk smiled. "I was a physician before I renounced the world. I cannot forget the man I was, or the things I saw, when I lived that life. A samurai kills a man with a sword. He doesn't use his hands."

Though accurate, it wasn't the reason Hiro would have given.

"Also," the monk continued, "a samurai would have stopped when the man was dead."

Hiro disagreed. Furious samurai rarely showed much self-control. The shinobi leaned forward and laid two fingers on the dead man's neck.

"Why check for a heartbeat?" The monk inquired. "We already know he's dead."

"I'm feeling his temperature," Hiro said. "His skin seems cool, but pliant. He died within the last few hours. Some time after midnight, before dawn."

The monk nodded. "You are a physician also."

It wasn't a question, and Hiro saw no need to correct the error. He stood up and looked at Father Mateo. "We've seen what we need to see."

The monk bowed. "I will care for his needs from here."

Hiro and Father Mateo left the alley and headed north, but not toward home.

"I want to speak with Ginjiro before the hearing," Hiro said. "That is, if we still have time."

The magistrate's compound lay north and west of the brewery, in the southern end of the administrative ward. Hiro and Father Mateo arrived to find the compound gates wide open.

Commoners filled the yard. They spoke in whispers as they waited for the magistrate.

Hiro bowed to the pair of stern-faced samurai guarding the compound gates. "Good morning," he said. "I'm looking for a brewer named Ginjiro."

"If you want a brewer, look in the sake district," the taller samurai said with a grin.

His companion snickered at the joke, though neither Hiro nor Father Mateo smiled.

"The man I seek was arrested this morning," Hiro said.

The samurai's smile faded. "No one remembers a criminal's name. The dōshin bring them in by the dozen."

Father Mateo stepped forward. "This man is not a criminal.

He was wrongfully accused. He has graying hair, and was wearing a blue kimono."

The guard considered the Jesuit's words. "I did see such a man. He's accused of murder."

"Wrongfully accused," the priest repeated.

"I doubt it," the guard replied, "but, innocent or not, he isn't here. The dōshin brought him, briefly, to lodge his name and case with the magistrate, but his case will not be heard until this afternoon."

CHAPTER 8

"**N**ot until the afternoon?" Father Mateo repeated. "Why?"

"Shogun's orders," the tall guard said. "The magistrate hears all capital crimes in public, at the afternoon session."

"The afternoon hearing is public?" Father Mateo asked.

The tall guard turned and gestured toward a bed of white sand on the opposite side of the courtyard. Behind the sand, a wooden dais rose several feet above the ground. Neither the wood nor the sand showed signs of weathering.

"The shogun ordered the change a month ago," the guard explained. "All serious cases must be heard, and the sentences carried out, in public. To help the common people understand the consequences of their crimes."

"Shogun Ashikaga gave that order?" Father Mateo asked.

"Shogun Matsunaga gave the order—after Shogun Ashikaga's *seppuku*," the guard replied.

Hiro didn't miss the veiled challenge in the words. Rumors questioned the former shogun's "suicide," which took place in the night and under the eye of Matsunaga Hisahide, though no one dared to challenge Hisahide's version openly.

No one who valued his life, at any rate.

"I apologize," Father Mateo said. "I did not hear that the emperor had granted Matsunaga-*san* the shogunate."

"He has not made the formal announcement," the samurai said, chin high and shoulders squared, "but he will, when the mourning period for the former shogun ends. Wise men will not wait to recognize Shogun Matsunaga's status."

On the contrary, Hiro thought, wise men won't commit

themselves before the proper time. Aloud, he said, "Forgive the foreigner's ignorance. He does not understand our culture well."

The samurai nodded. "The magistrate ordered the criminals taken to prison until this afternoon. You will find the man you are seeking there."

Hiro and Father Mateo left the magistrate's compound and turned south on a street that led to the commercial ward.

"Aren't we going to see Ginjiro?" Father Mateo asked.

"We need to speak with Chikao's family," Hiro said. "Preferably without Ren present."

"Without Ren?" Father Mateo asked.

Hiro nodded. "Chikao's business partner has the physical strength to commit the crime, and though he seemed upset by the news, emotions can be faked."

"He cried real tears," Father Mateo said, "and physical build means nothing. Any person of reasonable size could have beaten Chikao to death."

"Yes," Hiro said, "but Ren will gain from Chikao's murder in ways another man will not."

"Won't Chikao's son inherit his father's share of the business?" Father Mateo asked.

"Normally, yes," Hiro said, "but until we know for certain, we must consider everyone a suspect."

The Jesuit nodded. "Do you know how to find the Lucky Monkey brewery?"

"No," Hiro said, "I'm hoping Tomiko does."

"Today?" Tomiko asked when Hiro told her about the hearing. "But that's too soon. We need more time to prove my father's innocence."

Rustling sounds from the opposite side of the indigo noren suggested Yoka was working in the kitchen.

Tomiko lowered her voice. "I want to attend the hearing, but I cannot leave my mother alone. I cannot take her with me, either. Since the illness, unfamiliar situations scare her. If she sees my father kneeling like a criminal . . ."

Tomiko pressed her lips together, unwilling to continue.

"Can you tell us where to find Chikao's family?" Father Mateo asked.

Hiro added, "Magistrate Ishimaki might delay your father's hearing, if the victim's family consents."

"They live at the Lucky Monkey," Tomiko said, "in an alley south of Shijō and east of Kawaramachi Road."

"An alley?" Father Mateo asked.

"The address is on Shijō Road," she said, "but the brewery has no frontage. The building sits behind an old apothecary's shop. Look carefully, it's hard to find."

"Have you been there?" Father Mateo tried to hide his surprise, but failed.

"Once, with my father," Tomiko said, "about a month ago. We stopped by on our way to a meeting in Fushimi. A visiting relative stayed with Mother so I could go along."

Hiro noted Father Mateo's confusion. "Fushimi is the sake brewers' ward."

"Isn't this the sake district?" the Jesuit asked.

"This ward has many businesses," Tomiko said. "My father chose to open a brewery here because of the traffic and because we offer food as well as sake. Those who sell only sake usually set up shop in Fushimi, because of the water. Also, the guild has greater influence there."

"Why did you visit the Lucky Monkey?" Hiro asked.

"To ask about the debt." Tomiko raised a hand to her mouth in sudden embarrassment. "Oh! Matsui-*san*, I'm so sorry! I forgot to give you a message. A man came looking for you last night, shortly after you left."

She bowed. "Please forgive my forgetfulness."

Hiro's hopes rose. A message from Iga would confirm that Hattori Hanzō, head of the Iga *ryu*, had learned about the shogun's death. The message might also contain the name of Hiro's new shinobi contact in Kyoto. Kazu had filled that role until the shogun's "suicide" two months before. Since then, Hiro had awaited new instructions from the clan. He doubted the shogun's death would affect his orders to guard the priest, but Hiro put no faith in such assumptions.

"I do not blame you," Hiro said. "You've had a difficult morning. Did the man leave his name?"

"Ozuru," Tomiko said. "A carpenter, I think? He said he would return tomorrow night to discuss the job you wanted done."

"He will return tonight, then?" Hiro maintained a neutral tone, but the message made his stomach churn. Ozuru worked as a carpenter in much the same way Hiro served the Jesuit. Neither man was truly what he seemed.

"Yes," Tomiko said, "I believe he will."

Hiro nodded. "I will do my best to meet him."

The shinobi and the Jesuit left the brewery and headed south.

"Have we time to get to the Lucky Monkey and back to the magistrate before the hearing?" Father Mateo asked.

"We have to," Hiro said. "We need Chikao's family to grant us extra time to find the killer."

"Can they do that?" Father Mateo asked. When Hiro gave him a sideways look, the Jesuit added, "I said so to Tomiko, but I didn't know for certain."

"Magistrate Ishimaki cares about justice," Hiro said. "I think he will grant us extra time unless the victim's family objects."

"Will he release Ginjiro until the trial?"

Hiro shook his head. "No magistrate would set a killer free."

"Do you believe Ginjiro killed Chikao?" Father Mateo asked.
"No," Hiro said, "but murders turn on evidence, not belief."

CHAPTER 9

Despite Tomiko's warning, Hiro and Father Mateo walked right past the narrow alley on Shijō Road. When they reached the Kamo River, they retraced their steps until they found the unnamed alley, little more than a gap between an ancient apothecary and a brothel too low-class to afford a space in nearby Pontochō.

"I never would have looked for a brewery here," Father Mateo said.

As they entered the alley, daylight dropped to twilight, blocked by the buildings' eaves and faded laundry hanging overhead. Mildew and rotting garbage perfumed the air.

Father Mateo coughed and raised a hand to his mouth.

Hiro stifled the almost overwhelming urge to follow suit. The odors burned his sensitive nose and set his eyes to watering. Only the lowest sort of drunk would patronize a dismal place like this.

A pair of sake barrels stood outside the narrow entrance to a building that shared a wall with the apothecary's shop. A faded indigo noren hung in the entrance. Blocky characters on the barrels and the noren read LUCKY MONKEY, but the door beyond the noren was closed and locked.

"That's strange," Hiro said.

"Hardly surprising," Father Mateo answered. "It's early yet."

"Yes," Hiro said, "but a hanging noren indicates the shop is open."

Trailing fragments of spiderweb dangled from the noren's edges, capturing dust and dirt instead of flies.

"Then again," Hiro said, "this one may never come down at all."

He reached between the panels and knocked hard on the wooden door.

"Perhaps we shouldn't disturb them," Father Mateo said.

Hiro glanced over his shoulder at the priest. "Mourning rituals can't begin until they wash and dress the corpse. I'm sure that hasn't happened yet."

Father Mateo ran a hand through his hair. "I may not share this family's faith, but I do respect their grief. Imposing on their sorrow—"

"—seemed a good enough idea when we left Ginjiro's half an hour ago." Hiro finished the Jesuit's thought with different words. "If we do not interrupt them now, the magistrate may execute Ginjiro prematurely."

Hiro turned and knocked again.

Footsteps approached from the other side. The door swung open, revealing a barrel-chested youth with greasy hair and wrinkled trousers. He wore no shirt, his feet were bare, and he smelled like yesterday's sweat and stale sake.

Hiro recognized the man as Kaoru, Chikao's son.

"What do you want?" The young man frowned at Hiro with no sign of recognition. He squinted at Father Mateo and added, "You're not Japanese."

The Jesuit started to bow, but a look from Hiro turned the gesture into an awkward nod. "I am Father Mateo Ávila de Santos, a priest, from Portugal."

Kaoru drew the door open farther. He stepped back as if inviting them to enter. "Mother said she sent for priests. She hasn't returned from the temple, but you can wait inside if you want to."

Father Mateo opened his mouth, but Hiro shook his head and stepped inside. Wise men didn't explain mistakes until the host had missed his chance to slam the door.

Father Mateo followed without comment.

Kaoru led the visitors through the entry and into a twelve-mat room. Medium-grade *tatami* covered the floor. Cheap wooden backrests along the walls and a counter along the left side of the room identified the space as the Lucky Monkey's drinking room.

Decorative scrolls adorned the walls, but their uneven strokes betrayed a novice hand. The monochromatic ink bled away from the images in jagged lines, like unwanted vines growing wild into a wall.

Three large barrels stood in a corner behind the wooden counter, and a line of lacquered sake flasks stood like soldiers on the countertop. In places, the lacquer had worn away, revealing a black undercoat beneath. The choice of lacquered wooden flasks, instead of expensive stoneware, came as no surprise in a place like this.

The smell of last night's grease in the air diminished Kaoru's personal odor slightly. The lack of adequate ventilation, combined with a low, slatted ceiling, gave the room an oppressive feel. Hiro resolved to leave as soon as possible.

Kaoru walked to a sliding door on the far side of the room. He paused. "My father lies through here."

Hiro shook his head. "We are not the priests your mother summoned."

"Then who are you?" Kaoru asked.

"We have business with your mother," Hiro said.

"Who are you?" Kaoru repeated. "Why have you disturbed a house of mourning?"

Hiro gestured to the Jesuit. "Father Mateo introduced himself already. I am his translator, Matsui Hiro."

After a pause just long enough to allow the youth to absorb the information, Hiro added, "The Jesuit carries the rank of samurai."

Kaoru should have bowed. He didn't.

"May I ask your name?" Father Mateo asked in a quiet voice.

Hiro recognized the Jesuit's attempt to ease the tension.

"I am Kaoru," the young man said.

"We hoped your mother would grant us a favor," Father Mateo said.

Hiro considered the overture ill-advised. He didn't know Kaoru well, but the young man's appearance and reputation didn't suggest a helpful nature. The Jesuit should have waited for the widow.

Kaoru squinted at Father Mateo and then at Hiro. "I can't understand the foreigner. He needs to speak Japanese."

"I am speaking Japanese," Father Mateo said.

Kaoru raised a hand to his forehead. "I have a headache. What is he trying to say?"

Hiro didn't expect most people to bow and scrape because of his samurai status, but Kaoru's arrogance went too far in the other direction. This came as no surprise. Kaoru had acted just as rudely the few times Hiro saw him at Ginjiro's.

It was time to make Chikao's son behave.

Hiro straightened his shoulders and laid a hand on the hilt of his sword. "I know you, Kaoru, though clearly you do not remember me."

Kaoru rubbed his eyes and squinted, lips apart and breathing through his mouth. At last he said, "Ginjiro's. I saw you there."

Hiro nodded. Since they had never spoken, he had not expected Kaoru to remember.

"What are you doing here?" Kaoru demanded. "I said I would pay the bill."

Before Hiro could follow up on this revealing comment, Father Mateo said, "We haven't come about your debt, but if you grant our favor I am sure Ginjiro will show leniency."

"I don't need a murderer's leniency," Kaoru snapped.

"But Ginjiro and his family do need yours," the Jesuit said.

Kaoru looked at Hiro. "What did he say? I don't understand his foreign talk."

Hiro's frustration rose. "You understood him fine just now."

"I didn't." Kaoru rubbed his temple. "I cannot understand a word he says."

Hiro stifled a sigh and repeated Father Mateo's words. Arguments only wasted precious time.

Kaoru considered the offer. "Ginjiro will cancel my debt if I agree to your request?"

"I said he would show leniency," Father Mateo said, "I cannot promise cancellation."

Kaoru looked at Hiro until the shinobi translated the words.

"What help do you need?" Kaoru asked.

Father Mateo continued, with Hiro "translating" each sentence as he finished. "Ginjiro didn't kill your father. We need the time to prove it. We wish you to ask the magistrate to delay Ginjiro's trial so that we can find your father's real killer."

"You are mistaken." Kaoru scowled. "Ginjiro is guilty. Ren told me so when he brought the news—not that I needed his opinion. Just last night, Ginjiro made a threat to kill my father."

Kaoru stared at Hiro as if trying to force a memory through the fog of his sake headache. "That's why I know you." He pointed at Hiro. "You were there. You heard the threat!"

CHAPTER 10

Father Mateo gave Hiro a look of alarm.

"You were there," Kaoru repeated, jabbing his finger at Hiro. "You heard everything."

Hiro ignored the young man's pointing finger. Such an insult gave a samurai the right to kill a commoner, but Hiro didn't think Chikao's wife should lose her husband and her son in a single day.

"I did not hear Ginjiro threaten anyone." Hiro spoke in a tone he reserved for disobedient animals and fools. "If you continue this disrespect, you'll learn what happens when brewers forget their station."

Kaoru lowered his hand. "I apologize." He bowed, though his voice and face revealed no remorse. "Ginjiro threatened to kill my father. You may not have heard, but others did."

"Tell us what happened," Father Mateo said.

This time, Kaoru didn't wait for a translation. "Yesterday evening, I went with my father to buy a barrel of sake from Ginjiro. My father offered a reasonable sum, but Ginjiro tried to cheat us. He claimed I owed him money and refused to sell us anything until we paid in full.

"My father refused to pay, so Ginjiro said he would get his money one way or another, no matter what he had to do to get it."

"That doesn't sound like a serious threat," Hiro said.

"Did Ginjiro try to hurt you?" Father Mateo asked.

"No," Kaoru said, "but he wouldn't have, with witnesses around. He waited 'til my father returned, alone, when the shops were closed."

"Why did your father return to Ginjiro's?" Hiro asked.

Kaoru scowled. "He didn't mention his plans to me. He must have gone to pay the bill, because he feared Ginjiro."

"Why didn't you go with him?" Father Mateo asked.

"I was sleeping," Kaoru said. "Why does a foreigner want to help a killer like Ginjiro?"

"I don't believe Ginjiro killed your father," Father Mateo said. "I want to help because my faith requires me to practice mercy, and seek justice, for all men."

"Most interesting," said a female voice behind them. "You don't look like a Buddhist priest."

Father Mateo startled, but Hiro had heard the creak of the door and feminine footsteps in the entry.

Both men turned.

The woman had silver-gray hair and an unlined face that looked far younger than her voice suggested. She wore a pale kimono of creamy silk and a dove gray *obi*. The hem of her dark blue inner kimono peeked above the neckline of the outer garment, emphasizing her ruddy complexion. The aftermath of tears still gave her eyes a glossy cast.

She bowed. "I am Mina, wife of Chikao."

Father Mateo bowed in return. "Father Mateo Ávila de Santos." He gestured to the shinobi. "My interpreter, Matsui Hiro."

Men of samurai rank didn't normally bow to a merchant's wife, but Hiro didn't mind the gesture. Father Mateo's foreign status overcame the breach of etiquette, and his courtesy might inspire cooperation.

Mina crossed her hands and bowed again, more deeply than before.

Hiro nodded but didn't bow.

"How may I assist you?" Mina asked.

"We are deeply sorry for your loss," Father Mateo said.

"Thank you," Mina said. "But a man cannot avoid his karma."

"Karma?" Father Mateo asked.

"Does he know the word?" Mina addressed the question to Hiro.

"I recognize it," the Jesuit said. "I don't understand why you think your husband's karma caused his death."

Kaoru scowled. "It was not my father's destiny to die in the street like a dog."

Mina looked at her son. "Does your disbelief change what happened?"

Kaoru did not answer.

Mina's gaze returned to the priest. "Do not mistake my acceptance for lack of emotion. I deeply regret my husband's death. I will miss him as long as I live. But, as a Buddhist, I must strive to sever worldly attachments and to accept the things I have no power to change."

Tears welled up in her eyes but did not spill over. "I confess, I find this obstacle more difficult than most."

I find it odd that you refer to your husband's death as an "obstacle," Hiro thought.

"Forgive me," Mina said. "You did not come to watch a woman mourn. How may I help you?"

"Ginjiro's family hired us to find your husband's killer," Father Mateo said.

Kaoru sniffed. "The dōshin already arrested the guilty man."

"Perhaps they did," Mina said. "Perhaps they didn't. Bandits rule this city after dark, and your father was carrying money to pay your debt. A thief does seem more likely than Ginjiro."

"Bandits carry knives," Kaoru said. "My father wasn't stabbed."

Mina turned to Father Mateo. "Do the facts support Ginjiro's innocence?"

"We need time to investigate," the Jesuit said. "We need your help to delay Ginjiro's trial."

"You are not dōshin," Mina said.

Father Mateo nodded. "True, but we are men who care about justice, and also mercy."

Hiro struggled to hide his frustration. Overblown statements of moral purpose rarely persuaded anyone, especially people who had to work for a living.

To his surprise, Mina asked, "How much time do you need?"

Kaoru threw his hands in the air. "This is pointless. Ginjiro killed my father!"

"Did the police recover the money Chikao took with him to pay the debt?" Mina asked.

"Of course not," Kaoru said. "Ginjiro took it."

"Someone took it," Mina said. "We need to get it back, to pay the debt."

Kaoru opened his mouth to object but his mother continued, "We owe Ginjiro money, and this murder does not change that fact."

"It does if Ginjiro did it!" Kaoru glared at Mina. "My debt was nothing compared with the value of my father's life."

Mina returned the glare with an even look. "A man who does not pay his debts will never join the brewers' guild. You know this."

"Don't you already belong to the guild?" Father Mateo asked.

"Not yet," Mina said, "our shop remains unlicensed. We petitioned for admission, but the *za* has not yet ruled on our application. We hoped Ginjiro would plead our cause—he did agree to help us—but that was before our son ran up a bill and did not pay."

"That's not the truth," Kaoru said. "Ginjiro inflated the bill in order to bribe us for his support."

"Forgive my son for his lack of tact." Mina shook her head at Kaoru. "His anger will not bring his father back, or find the murderer.

"I wish to know the truth about my husband's death. I will ask the magistrate to give you four more days to find the killer."

CHAPTER 11

Father Mateo looked confused. "Four days? Why only four?"

"After seven days of mourning we commit my husband's body to the flames," Mina said. "At that time, his spirit has to face the Heavenly Judges. If we know his killer's name by then, our prayers can intercede on his behalf. Four days for you leaves three for the magistrate to find the answer if you fail."

Kaoru frowned. "I will not carry that petition to the magistrate for you."

"I hadn't planned to ask you," Mina said. "Ren's word will carry greater weight than yours."

She shifted her gaze to Hiro. "I will ask the neighbor's son to carry a message to Ren this morning. Ren will take my request to the magistrate."

"Speaking of Ren," Hiro said. "Where can we find him?"

"He went home," Mina said, "to change into mourning garments. After that, he intended to speak with the coffin maker."

Mina cast a sidelong glance at Kaoru. "Ren offered to make the arrangements since my son was . . . indisposed. I only hope we can afford a reasonable coffin, since the moneylenders will not give a loan."

Again, she looked at Kaoru, and an awkward silence followed.

"Could you tell us where Ren lives?" the Jesuit asked. "We'd like to find him."

Mina nodded. "He rents a place on Shijō Road, three buildings west of the apothecary. His room is fourth from the street, as you count the doors."

"Thank you," Hiro said.

"Did Ren work last night?" the priest continued. "Did he leave the shop at any point?"

So much for not revealing our suspicions, Hiro thought.

"He worked all night, as did Chikao," Mina said. "My husband left to see Ginjiro in the early evening hours. He returned with a bruise on one eye and fear in both. Ginjiro struck him, and threatened worse, if we didn't make an immediate payment toward Kaoru's debt."

Hiro looked at Kaoru. "Where were you last night?"

"Me?" the young man asked. "That's not your business."

"Kaoru," Mina admonished. "This man is samurai, and our guest." She turned to Hiro. "Please forgive my son's behavior. He went out for an hour or two in the evening and then returned. He helped us close the shop and went to sleep."

Hiro knew the woman lied, but let it pass. He asked the question to change the topic and take suspicion off of Ren.

From Hiro's perspective, Chikao's family didn't need to know any details of the investigation or the names of any suspects. Not until the evidence revealed someone's guilt.

Hiro and Father Mateo left the alley and turned west on Shijō Road. The wind had shifted, filling the air with smoke from the nearby charcoal sellers' street. The pungent aroma of smoldering pine filled Hiro's nose, overwhelming every other smell.

Given the lingering scent of the alley, Hiro didn't mind.

West of the apothecary, rows of rental dwellings filled the block. Property taxes were based on frontage, so most of the buildings presented only their narrow ends to the street. Passageways between the structures led to twisting alleys where the renters lived like soybeans pressed together in a fermentation pot. Each room had a private entrance, but thin walls and tiny spaces meant the residents enjoyed no real privacy.

"I'm glad Mina told us to count the entries," Father Mateo said, as he looked down the passage at the unmarked doors. "We'd never have found the place."

Hiro didn't argue but knew otherwise.

Every dwelling house had an elderly person, usually female, who considered it her duty to keep track of the other residents. These unofficial guardians knew everyone and everything and, in most cases, also loved to gossip.

Hiro and Father Mateo approached the fourth room down. The door slid open before they knocked.

Ren's surprise revealed he hadn't seen the two men coming.

The brewer wore an unadorned kimono over white *hakama*, a color normally reserved for family in mourning.

He bowed to Hiro and then to Father Mateo. "May I help you?" His forehead furrowed as recognition registered in his eyes. "Pardon me, but didn't I see you this morning, outside Ginjiro's?"

Hiro exercised the samurai right to ignore a commoner's question. "We need to know some things about Chikao."

"Pardon me," Ren said, "you don't look like dōshin."

"We are looking into the matter as a favor." Hiro kept his answer vague and hoped the priest would do the same.

"I see," Ren said. "I wish I could help, but I wasn't there when the murder happened."

"Yes," Hiro said, "we understand. Where were you?"

"When it happened? I don't know." Ren thought for a moment. "I came directly home from the Lucky Monkey after closing."

"Of course," Hiro said. "Did you know Chikao intended to visit Ginjiro late last night?"

"No." Ren looked from Hiro to Father Mateo. "Are you a priest?"

"I am," the Jesuit said, "a Christian priest, from Portugal."

"What did Chikao tell you about the debt he went to pay?" Hiro asked.

Ren sighed. "He told me about the argument, the one they had in the early evening hours. I knew he went, because I watched the shop while he was gone. When he returned, he said Ginjiro insisted on payment, immediately, or the debt would impact our petition to join the guild.

"I told Chikao that Kaoru needed to get a job and pay the debt himself—we've taken care of Kaoru long enough."

"This wasn't the first time?" Hiro asked.

"No, and it wouldn't have been the last." Ren exhaled sharply and shook his head. "I told Chikao many times. Kaoru will never learn until he has to deal with consequences. Still, Chikao kept throwing money into a fire and expecting it not to burn."

"So you disagreed with paying this debt," Father Mateo said.

"Wholeheartedly," Ren agreed. "We needed that money to pay for admission into the brewers' guild." He slid open the door, revealing a tidy space. "Would you like to come in? May I offer you tea?"

"No, thank you," Hiro said. "How do you plan to handle your new partnership with Kaoru?"

"What does that have to do with Chikao's death?" Ren asked.

"Investigations always start with heirs," Father Mateo said. "They gain the most from a murder victim's death."

"I doubt Kaoru considers his inheritance a gain," Ren said.

"Nonetheless," the Jesuit said, "he benefits from the tragedy, as do you."

Hiro wished the priest would stop revealing information.

"I? Benefit?" Ren raised a hand to his chest in surprise. "I as sure you, I do not benefit. Before last night, Kaoru was Chikao's problem—his alone. Now, he's mine, at least until I divest myself of the lazy, wasteful dog who is now my partner."

"You do not intend to continue running the Lucky Monkey?" Hiro asked.

"I do not want to see Mina destitute," Ren said, "but I have no intention of continuing to run a shop with Kaoru."

"What will become of the brewery?" Father Mateo asked.

"A complicated question." Ren's artificial smile revealed discomfort. "I cannot tell you. I haven't exactly had time to consider my options."

"Who killed Chikao?" Hiro asked.

"How would I know?" Ren countered. "I wasn't there."

"What about Kaoru?" Father Mateo asked. "Could he have done this?"

"Kaoru?" Ren repeated. "As I said, I don't believe he wanted his father dead. If you want to know what happened, ask Ginjiro."

"Why Ginjiro?" Father Mateo asked.

"The police arrested him for the crime," Ren said. "Though, I admit, I do not think he actually killed Chikao."

CHAPTER 12

"You don't believe Ginjiro killed Chikao?" Hiro asked.

"I think he was involved," Ren said, "however, I don't think he did the killing."

"How could he be involved but not responsible?" Father Mateo asked.

"Do you know what debt collectors do to debtors who refuse to pay?" Ren asked. "I wouldn't want one catching me in an alley late at night."

"You think Ginjiro hired someone to harass the money from Chikao?" Hiro asked.

"Perhaps," Ren said, "or possibly a guard to protect his brewery. Kaoru has vandalized some buildings in the past."

"The yoriki claims that when Chikao returned, he fought with Ginjiro personally," Hiro said.

Ren shook his head. "Chikao knew how to fight. He wouldn't let Ginjiro beat him. No, Ginjiro must have hired someone else to watch the alley. When Chikao returned, that person killed him."

"Why wouldn't Ginjiro mention a guard to the yoriki?" Hiro asked.

"It makes no difference to his liability," Ren said. "The law considers Ginjiro responsible either way. But as long as he doesn't tell the truth, both he and the guard have a chance of escaping justice. Ginjiro blames an unknown bandit. The guard disappears entirely."

"Maybe it was a bandit," Father Mateo said.

"Not even a desperate gambler would take those odds," Ren told the priest. "Kaoru owed Ginjiro money. They argued yesterday evening, and the argument ended in threats. A reasonable man in

Ginjiro's position would make arrangements to protect his family."

"I'm confused," Father Mateo said. "Do you believe the yoriki arrested Ginjiro properly or not?"

"The yoriki made the right decision. I think Ginjiro hired someone who killed Chikao, which makes Ginjiro responsible for my partner's death."

"Even if the death was accidental?" the Jesuit asked.

"The law does not distinguish between accidents and murder in these situations," Ren replied. "A man must answer for his hirelings' actions, as a father must pay the debts of dependent sons. Perhaps in your country the law is different, but this is the law in Japan."

"Speaking of debts," Hiro said, "why did Chikao continue paying Kaoru's debts without complaint?"

"Who said he didn't complain?" Ren asked. "Every father objects to a spendthrift son. But Chikao's other children died in infancy. Kaoru alone survived. For that reason, Chikao refused him nothing. Not until recently, anyway.

"Chikao and I wanted more than an unlicensed brewery hidden away in a low-class alley. We wanted to join the brewers' guild and move to a new location. A few months back, we started saving money toward that goal."

"Until Kaoru ran up a debt," Hiro said.

Ren shook his head. "He didn't want to sacrifice. He wanted women, new kimono, gambling, and sake. I should not criticize the dead, but Chikao's indulgence ruined his son completely."

"If Kaoru killed his father, he will forfeit his inheritance," Hiro said. "The Lucky Monkey will belong to you, and you alone."

"Forgive my lack of tact," Ren said, "but I could not hope for such good fortune. Kaoru is a worthless dog, but not a killer."

Hiro couldn't verify Ren's claim of sleeping through the murder, but the idea of a guard in Ginjiro's alley fit the facts and made some sense. Ginjiro didn't take risks with his family's safety.

"May we speak with you again, if we need more information?" Father Mateo asked.

"Of course," Ren said, "though, I admit, I consider investigations a waste of time. The dōshin already arrested the man who should bear the blame for my partner's death, whether or not he actually killed Chikao."

Tears filled Tomiko's eyes when Hiro and Father Mateo explained that Chikao's family agreed to petition the magistrate.

"Four days is so much time," she said. "I know that you will find the real killer."

Hiro knew the time would pass more quickly than she thought but saw no reason to destroy her slender hope.

"If we don't, the magistrate could still conduct his own investigation," Father Mateo said.

Hiro's stomach sank. So much for hope.

"Please—no," Tomiko's eyes widened with sudden fear. "My father won't survive interrogation."

"Interrogation?" Father Mateo asked. "What do you mean?"

Hiro avoided looking at Tomiko as he answered. "The law allows the magistrate to obtain a confession by any effective means."

"You mean he can torture Ginjiro until the brewer says what the yoriki wants to hear." Father Mateo raised his hand but stopped just short of running it through his hair.

"My father will not lie, and won't confess to a crime he did not commit," Tomiko said. "They'll torture him until he dies because he will not break."

Her hands began to tremble. "Please, Matsui-*san*, I beg you. You must find the killer. It's the only way to save my father's life."

As they left Ginjiro's, Father Mateo asked, "Where do we go from here?"

"To the prison." Hiro glanced at the priest. "We need to hear Ginjiro's side of the story."

"Could Ren be right about the guard?" the Jesuit asked. "We should have asked Tomiko what she knew."

"She would lie to protect her father," Hiro said, "and I don't blame her. It's Ginjiro's place to tell us what he's done."

"Or hasn't done," Father Mateo said.

Hiro nodded. "Trust me, I don't want to learn Ginjiro hired a guard who killed Chikao. If he hired the killer, even just to guard the brewery, Ginjiro's life will answer for the crime."

CHAPTER 13

A pair of dōshin stood on guard outside the prison gates. Despite their samurai swords and topknots, they had little else in common with the well-dressed nobles strolling through the city. The cuffs of their hakama trailed, threadbare, to the ground, and their tunics showed the signs of cheap repairs. One dōshin looked too old to work, his hair more white than gray. The other's wrinkled hands and sagging eyes revealed that he, too, approached retirement age.

Hiro and Father Mateo stopped at the gates but did not bow.

"We have come to see a prisoner named Ginjiro," Hiro said. "We were told that he is here awaiting trial."

"Ginjiro?" the white-haired dōshin repeated. "Yes. I will ask if he can see a visitor."

The dōshin entered the gates and locked them again from the opposite side. His companion, who remained behind, watched the priest with the mute alarm of a Japanese man who had never seen a foreigner.

Father Mateo nodded to the guard but didn't speak. Hiro noted the behavior with approval. The lowest-ranking samurai drew the assignment to guard the prison gates. No man of rank would engage them in conversation without need.

After several awkwardly silent minutes, the ancient dōshin returned. This time, he didn't lock the gate.

"You may see the prisoner," he said, "but only briefly."

"Acceptable," Hiro replied, "we don't need long."

"And thank you," Father Mateo added, to Hiro's minor disapproval.

"Follow me." The elderly dōshin led them into the prison yard.

The ammonia-rich scent of human waste assaulted Hiro's

nostrils with the force of a physical blow. He coughed but stifled it quickly. Coughing showed weakness. More importantly, coughs required deep inhalation, which renewed the assault on Hiro's senses.

The acrid smell rose up from puddles in the dozens of wooden cages that lined the yard and ringed the compound walls. The cages measured three feet across and as tall as Hiro's shoulder—too short for a man to stand erect and not quite wide enough to sit or kneel. Some of the cages stood empty, but most held a single, miserable prisoner. Without a nightsoil bucket, the prisoners' waste ended up on the ground, creating puddles that even the flies avoided.

"How long do they keep these men in those tiny cages?" Father Mateo asked in Portuguese.

"Until the magistrate hears their cases," Hiro replied in the Jesuit's language, glad to keep the conversation private.

"And after that?" the Jesuit asked.

"Fines, or flogging, or execution, depending on the crime."

Near the middle of the compound, three wooden posts stood upright in the center of an open space. Each post measured as tall as a man and almost a foot in diameter, and had a pair of shackles secured to the top by a length of rusted chain. Dark red spots on the whipping posts attracted swarms of iridescent flies. Hiro didn't need to get close to know the spots were blood.

Just in front of the whipping posts, the dōshin took a left and led the visitors to a row of cages near the compound wall.

Ginjiro crouched in a wooden cage near the end of the row, feet half buried in mud and human waste. He kept his eyes on the ground as the jailer approached, in part because of the cage's height but also, no doubt, in shame.

The dōshin stopped and called, "Ginjiro, identify yourself!"

The brewer raised his head. "I am Ginjiro." His mouth fell open in shock, eyes wide, at the sight of Hiro and Father Mateo. He struggled to bow, but the narrow cage made courtesy impossible.

"Matsui-*san*," Ginjiro said, "I am honored, and shamed, by your visit."

"You have five minutes," the dōshin said.

"May we approach him?" Father Mateo asked.

"If you choose," the dōshin said. "I wouldn't. The prisoners throw filth if you get too close."

Hiro and Father Mateo walked to Ginjiro's cage as the dōshin departed.

"Tomiko asked us to help you," Hiro said.

Father Mateo added, "—to prove your innocence."

Hiro wished the priest wouldn't promise results when the truth remained uncertain.

"We have asked the magistrate to delay your hearing," Hiro said.

Father Mateo looked up and down the row of cages. "Chikao's family granted us four days to investigate."

"After that, you answer to the magistrate," Hiro said. "So if you know who killed Chikao, tell us now."

"I didn't kill him. I don't know who did." Ginjiro shifted position as if trying to find a more comfortable one. It didn't seem to work.

"Tell us about the argument," Hiro said.

Ginjiro coughed, likely due to the acrid fumes rising off the puddle in which he stood. "Chikao's son, Kaoru, owes me a debt. He promised his father would pay, but the debt has gone so long, and grown so large, that I demanded payment."

"Did you ask Chikao before you extended credit to his son?" Father Mateo asked.

"No." Ginjiro shook his head. "Why would I? Sons don't use their fathers' credit without permission."

"Kaoru did," Hiro said.

Ginjiro nodded. "So I discovered. At first, Kaoru denied the debt and accused me of cheating his father, but his attitude changed as soon as I showed my ledger. Chikao requested a chance to pay the debt down over time. I agreed, but told him I wouldn't support his application to join the brewers' guild until he paid the debt in full."

"This happened last night?" Hiro asked.

"No." Ginjiro scratched his ear. "That happened about a week ago. After that, I considered the matter closed. Then yesterday, around midday, Kaoru tried to buy a cask of my sake for the Lucky Monkey."

"Kaoru alone?" Hiro asked. "His father wasn't with him?"

"Not the first time," Ginjiro said. "Kaoru explained that his father wanted a better grade of sake, to serve along with the one they brew. I refused to sell, because of the debt, and Kaoru started making threats. He said I'd lose my daughter, my shop, and everything else I owned."

"That's a serious threat," Father Mateo said. "Did you call the police?"

Ginjiro raised his hands. "If I reported every drunk who threatened my business, the magistrate would need to post a dōshin outside my shop on a permanent basis. Kaoru is rude and obnoxious, but matters like this are better resolved in private.

"After Kaoru's visit, I sent a message to the Lucky Monkey, warning Chikao that he needed to keep his son away from my brewery." Ginjiro paused. "Chikao sent a message back, begging me not to involve the guild. He promised to make a payment toward the debt that very night. I didn't believe him, but yesterday evening he showed up as promised, along with Kaoru.

"Chikao started to make a payment, but Kaoru objected. Once again, he claimed that I inflated the bill unfairly. When I produced the ledger, he tried to snatch it from my hands. That's when Chikao pulled Kaoru back and asked me to speak with them privately."

"That's not what I heard," Hiro said. "You told Chikao to go into the alley, not the other way around."

"I named the place," Ginjiro said, "but only after Chikao asked to speak with me in private."

"Why did you wait to report the debt and the threats to the brewers' guild?" Hiro asked.

"The za will not admit a man whose sons or apprentices act in a shameful manner," Ginjiro said. "Chikao is a hardworking man with a spoiled son. It seemed unfair to punish him—and also Ren—for Kaoru's indiscretions."

"What happened in the alley?" Hiro asked.

"Chikao pulled out his purse, but Kaoru snatched it from him." Ginjiro looked at the ground. "At that point, I lost my temper."

After a pause so long that Hiro doubted the brewer would finish the story, Ginjiro said, "The argument escalated. Kaoru wouldn't return the purse, no matter what his father said. Eventually, he left the alley, taking the money with him. Chikao pursued him down the street. I followed only as far as the mouth of the alley."

Ginjiro looked at the ground as if ashamed.

Hiro said, "You yelled something after them."

Ginjiro nodded. "Yes. I said, 'You will regret this foolishness. I'll get my money, no matter what I have to do.'"

CHAPTER 14

Ginjiro turned pleading eyes on Father Mateo. "You must believe me, I didn't intend the words as a threat to Chikao. I meant that I would report this to the magistrate."

Hiro found it curious that the brewer appealed to the priest. "Did Chikao respond to the threat?" Hiro asked.

"No," Ginjiro said. "What could he say? I didn't expect to see him again for a while. Not until he raised the money to pay off Kaoru's debt."

"But he returned to speak with you again when the shops were closed," Hiro said.

Ginjiro shook his head. "He didn't. Well, he must have, but I didn't know he had until this morning."

Five or six cages down the row, a gnarled hand extended through the bars and started waving.

"Hiro-*san*! Hiro-*san*! It's me!" Suke the monk gripped the bars and pressed his nose through the opening. "Make the police release Ginjiro. He didn't kill Chikao."

"Make them release me too," said a ragged man in a nearby cage.

Suke turned to the speaker. "Shut up. You're guilty. You told me so."

The ragged man shrugged. "It was worth a try."

Hiro asked Ginjiro, "Did Suke kill Chikao?"

"I doubt it," the brewer said.

"Then why does he claim he's guilty?" Father Mateo asked.

"Who knows why Suke does anything?" Frustration crept into Ginjiro's voice. "He's a drunk, with a drunk's imagination."

"If you know he's a drunk, why do you serve him sake?" the Jesuit asked.

"He wouldn't go away if I refused," Ginjiro said. "Besides, he doesn't drink that much and doesn't cause a scene."

Hiro redirected the conversation. "Where did Suke go last night when your brewery closed?"

"Into the alley, as always," Ginjiro said. "He did take one of my flasks. I saw him slip it into his sleeve. He's done it before and always returns them. That's why I let him think I didn't notice."

"Do you let other customers take your flasks away from the shop?" Father Mateo asked.

"No. They bring a private flask when they want to take sake home," Ginjiro said.

"So the broken flask in the alley was the one that Suke took?" the Jesuit asked.

"Has to be," Ginjiro said. "I'm not missing another."

"I think I'll talk with Suke." Hiro looked at Father Mateo. "You stay here. He'll talk more freely if I go alone."

As Hiro approached, Suke's mouth gaped open in a nearly toothless smile. Hiro wondered how the monk remained so happy with his feet sunk ankle-deep in stinking filth.

He bent down to look Suke in the eyes. "Why do you proclaim Ginjiro's innocence so firmly?"

A drop of drool glistened on Suke's lower lip.

"Because I am guilty." The monk raised a hand to his head. "Can you get me some sake? I have a terrible headache."

"You have a headache because of sake," Hiro said.

"Exactly," Suke said, "because there isn't any here!"

Hiro couldn't help but smile. "Why did you kill Chikao?"

Suke straightened as much as the cage allowed. "Self-defense—he tried to steal my sake flask."

"You killed a man over half a flask of sake?" Hiro asked.

"The flask was empty." Suke's smile disappeared. "I am a dangerous man."

"Apparently so," Hiro said. "Tell me, how did you kill him?"

"I hit him with the flask, of course." Suke pantomimed the

acton. "Don't ask how many blows it took. I did it in my sleep. When I woke up, the flask was gone and the man was already dead."

"That doesn't prove you killed him," Hiro said. "In fact, it implies you didn't."

"It was me," Suke insisted. "I am a monk but trained as a warrior. I can kill by instinct, even when sleeping."

"That's some instinct," Hiro said.

Suke nodded solemnly. "As I told you, I'm a dangerous man."

Hiro raised an eyebrow. "Dangerous enough to kill a man for stealing an empty flask? I thought monks took vows to cherish life."

"I never claimed I was a good monk," Suke said. "Between us— and this goes no further—I might drink more sake than I should."

Hiro struggled to find a nonsardonic response and failed.

Fortunately, Suke didn't seem to expect an answer.

"You're right that I wouldn't kill a thief on purpose," the monk continued, "but since I killed him in my sleep, I couldn't stop myself. It was me, and also not-me. Understand?"

"Do you really believe you killed a man while sleeping?" Hiro asked. "I think the killer stole the flask without your waking."

"Not possible," Suke said. "I sleep like a cat."

Hiro wondered how much experience Suke had with sleeping cats. "If that's true, why don't you remember someone trying to steal your flask?"

Rippling furrows appeared on Suke's brow. "I killed Chikao. I know I did. Ginjiro had already locked the shop, and he never leaves the brewery after closing."

"Never?" Hiro asked. "You're sure of that?"

Suke tipped his head to the side. "I sleep in the alley. If he ever left the brewery, I would know."

The way you know you killed a man in your sleep. Hiro's patience, like his time, was running out.

CHAPTER 15

"One last question," Hiro asked. "Did you see anyone else in the alley?"

"Anyone else?" Suke looked confused. "Like a vagrant?"

"Anyone at all," Hiro said.

Suke looked at the ground and scratched his cheek with a filthy hand. "I don't remember."

"Thank you, Suke," Hiro said. "I'll try to persuade the magistrate to release you as soon as possible."

"He won't release me." Suke smiled cheerfully. "He'll order me hanged and display my head on a pole as a warning to others. I don't mind. Death will free me to enter my next incarnation. This time, I hope I return as a cat."

"A cat." Hiro had to ask. "Why do you want to become a cat?"

Suke's lips curled into a knowing smile. He raised a hand to wipe the tendril of drool that started down his chin. "Cats catch mice. Mice eat grain. Grain makes sake. As a cat, I'll find a brewery and kill its mice. The grateful owner will give me a bowl of sake every day!"

"Cats don't drink sake," Hiro said.

"I would," Suke said.

Hiro had nothing to say to that. Knowing Suke, he probably would.

Hiro returned to Ginjiro's cage and gestured toward the monk. "He doesn't know anything at all. He claims he murdered Chikao in self-defense, and in his sleep, while defending his precious sake flask."

Ginjiro glanced toward Suke. "Did he mention that he's 'a dangerous man'?"

"Once or twice," Hiro said. A wave of stench from the filth on the ground erased his urge to smile.

Ginjiro sighed. "Please persuade the dōshin to let him go. They shouldn't punish a silly old man for something he didn't do."

"I doubt they intend to punish him long." Hiro remembered the yoriki's words. "They only arrested him to prevent a scene."

"Still," Father Mateo said, "we will speak to the dōshin on his behalf. Is there anything more you can tell us about the night of the murder before we go?"

Ginjiro shook his head. "At closing time I locked the shop and went upstairs. My wife and Tomiko were already sleeping. I went to bed and didn't wake up until the dōshin came to arrest me."

"Did you leave anyone downstairs when you locked the shop?" Father Mateo asked.

Ginjiro stared at the priest but didn't answer.

After a moment that lasted a little too long, Ginjiro asked, "Like a customer? No, they had all gone home."

"Nobody else?" the Jesuit asked. "Nobody guards the brewery at night?"

"Why would I need a guard?" the brewer asked. "We live upstairs."

Hiro admired the Jesuit's effort, but Ginjiro's answers were exactly as expected. If the brewer hired a guard who killed Chikao, he wouldn't say so.

Hiro started to turn away but paused when Father Mateo said, "Thank you. We appreciate your answers."

The brewer did his best to bow despite the cramped conditions. "On the contrary, I am in your debt. You owe my family nothing, yet you help us. I hope I live to repay your generosity."

"We just hope you live," Father Mateo said. "No thanks required."

Hiro nodded, grateful that the foreign priest could speak the words that etiquette denied a Japanese.

As Hiro and Father Mateo left, they found the elderly dōshin waiting near the whipping posts.

Hiro gestured toward Suke's cage. "Why is the monk imprisoned?"

"Him?" the dōshin asked. "He's just a drunk. Word has it, he embarrassed the yoriki. We have orders to keep him until this evening and then release him. No additional punishment. A few more hours in the cage, and he'll go on his way."

The dōshin looked at Father Mateo. "Does the foreigner speak Japanese well?"

"A little," Father Mateo said.

The dōshin looked impressed. "Your Japanese is very good. Are you new to Kyoto?"

Father Mateo smiled. He had spoken only two words, but most Japanese seemed highly impressed to hear a Westerner say any words at all.

"Thank you," the Jesuit said. "I fear my Japanese is poor, and badly spoken."

Hiro approved of the priest's response, which followed the proper self-deprecating manner for answering compliments. He also noted that Father Mateo passed over the question about his time in Kyoto.

With good reason.

The Jesuit mission in Kyoto catered to the samurai ruling class. Nobles would have disapproved of Father Mateo's work among the commoners, so the Jesuit worked alone from his home on Marutamachi Road instead of living with the other priests. Father Mateo's mission wasn't secret, but the priest knew better than to draw unwanted samurai attention.

"Are you enjoying the capital?" the dōshin asked. "Where are you visiting from?"

The Jesuit smiled. "Kyoto is a beautiful city. I have never seen a nicer one."

"Excuse us," Hiro said, "we have business to attend to."

"Of course." The dōshin bowed. "Any place is better than downwind from the prisoners' cages."

As they approached the gates, Father Mateo stopped. Hiro walked past the priest and turned, eyebrows raised in a silent question.

Father Mateo nodded toward the entrance. "Isn't that Akechi Yoshiko?"

To Hiro's surprise, the Jesuit was correct.

A little over a year before, Hiro and Father Mateo solved the murder of Yoshiko's father, retired samurai general Akechi Hideyoshi. The general had raised his only daughter as a samurai warrior, allowing her to dress—and act—like a man.

Yoshiko hadn't changed her appearance since her father's death. If anything, she looked more masculine now than she had before. She wore a blue kimono bearing the five-petaled bell-flower *mon* that symbolized the Akechi clan. With her hair drawn back in a samurai knot and a pair of swords at her side, only her unshaven pate revealed her gender.

Yoshiko stood talking with the samurai guard at the gate.

Hiro approached and bowed. Yoshiko returned the gesture instinctively, but as she straightened her eyes widened with recognition. She smiled a genuine smile.

"Matsui Hiro," Yoshiko said. "A pleasant surprise."

"Good morning Akechi-*san*," Hiro said. "I trust you also remember Father Mateo."

"Of course." She bowed to Father Mateo. "Please, call me Yoshiko."

The woman's tone seemed a bit too friendly, her smile a bit too bright. Worst of all, her eyes had a sparkle that made Hiro fear her interest in him went beyond professional courtesy.

Before Hiro could find a way to avoid further conversation,

Father Mateo said, "It's nice to see you, Yoshiko. If you've finished your business here, we can walk together."

Her smile widened into a grin. "As it happens, I've just finished." She looked at Hiro. "I would be delighted to walk with you."

Hiro fought the urge to turn around and return to the cages. He had seen a smile like that on a woman's face before. Given his aversion to Akechi Yoshiko, Hiro already knew this walk would end in an awkward scene.

CHAPTER 16

"What brings you to the prison?" Father Mateo asked Yoshiko as they walked along the narrow street. "I hope nothing has happened to your relatives?"

"I went to the prison on business," Yoshiko said. "After we finished mourning my father, I went to work for the Sakura Teahouse."

Hiro tried to imagine the samurai woman dressed as a painted entertainer from Kyoto's floating world. His mind refused the image.

Father Mateo looked even more disturbed.

Yoshiko laughed at the priest's confusion. Amusement softened her features, but not enough to make her attractive.

"Not as an entertainer," she said. "I collect the teahouse debts. I also handle collections for several merchants."

Hiro found it odd that she spoke so openly of her work. Most samurai considered a job a humiliating necessity. Worse, most debt collectors were commoners, making collections a shameful occupation for samurai.

Then again, Yoshiko's very existence flouted the rules of samurai conduct. Her choice to live an independent life should not surprise him.

Hiro respected that independence, even though he found the woman personally repellant.

"You're a debt collector?" Father Mateo asked.

Hiro caught the surprise in the Jesuit's tone.

"Yes." Yoshiko glanced at Hiro. "I find it pays quite well."

"Does your mother object to your employment?" Father Mateo asked.

Once again, the Jesuit had blundered into a social error. Family conflict wasn't a permitted topic of conversation among the Japanese. Not for people outside the family, anyway.

Hiro gave the priest a warning look.

"Mother doesn't know," Yoshiko said, "and I would appreciate your discretion, if you see her in the street."

Hiro found the answer surprising—not for its content, but because Yoshiko spoke the words aloud.

"After my father's death," she continued, "the shogun terminated our stipend. We had bills but no income with which to pay them."

Yoshiko paused and looked at Hiro. "It appears I, too, am ronin now."

"Doesn't your mother ask where the money comes from?" Father Mateo asked.

"That is not our business," Hiro said. "Forgive my employer. He forgets his manners."

"His questions do not offend," Yoshiko said. "I am different from other women. It is normal for men to wonder."

"Do you visit the prison often? I haven't seen you there before."

Hiro glanced at Father Mateo, giving the priest permission to answer.

"No," the Jesuit said, "I've never been there before today."

"Visiting a friend?" Yoshiko asked.

Father Mateo nodded. "Ginjiro, the brewer."

Hiro closed his eyes and stifled a sigh. Yoshiko had set a trap and the priest didn't see it coming.

"Of course," Yoshiko said. "He doesn't seem the type to commit a murder."

Hiro wondered how she knew the nature of the brewer's crime.

"We don't believe he's guilty, either," Father Mateo said. "In fact, Matsui-*san* and I are trying to help the family prove his innocence."

"As you identified my father's killer?" Yoshiko held Hiro's gaze a little longer than necessary.

"Nothing that complicated." Hiro forced a smile and glanced at the priest. "In fact, it's not important enough to discuss."

The conversation flagged, but Yoshiko didn't leave as Hiro hoped. Instead, she matched the shinobi's pace, in what she seemed to consider friendly silence.

Tension crept up Hiro's back. Yoshiko's bearing indicated an interest that transcended mere acquaintance. He hoped he misinterpreted her bearing and proximity, but Hiro had seen—and refused—too many women's advances to be wrong.

He wondered how to free himself of Yoshiko before they reached Ginjiro's. Hiro needed to talk with Tomiko, but didn't want to give the female samurai information—especially since she already knew far more than a stranger should.

At Sanjō Road, they found a pair of armored samurai standing guard in front of the fire tower that marked the boundary between the wards. The samurai guards wore bamboo armor over kimono marked with the five-leaved Matsunaga mon. *Wakizashi* hung from their obis, and sheathed *katanas* jutted up behind them like the tails of angry monkeys.

The shorter samurai held up a hand, palm outward. "Halt! State your names and business."

Hiro fought the urge to laugh. The guard's broad girth and bamboo armor made him look like a sake barrel impersonating a samurai.

Yoshiko stepped forward. "I am Akechi Yoshiko, eldest child of General Akechi Hideyoshi. My business is none of yours."

The samurai woman looked relaxed, but Hiro noted her dangling hands and the way she planted her feet exactly shoulder width apart. If the guard provoked Yoshiko, she would fight.

"State your business, or you will not pass." The guard stepped sideways, into Yoshiko's path.

Hiro couldn't decide if the guard intended to start a fight or simply didn't believe the samurai woman would attack.

Yoshiko laid a warning hand on the hilt of her katana. "By whose authority do you speak so rudely? Only the shogun commands the Akechi clan."

The samurai flushed red. Before he could answer, the other guard said, "Our apologies, Akechi-*san*. Matsunaga-*san* suspects that enemy spies have infiltrated the capital. Until they are captured, no one passes certain points without identification."

"I needed no identification here an hour ago." Yoshiko nodded at Father Mateo. "Does this foreigner look like a spy to you? Do I?"

"We were delayed—" the guard began.

His heavyset companion said, "Who knows where a foreigner's loyalty lies?"

"I know the priest's allegiances," Hiro said. "He is no threat."

"And who are you to make such claims?" the portly guard demanded.

Hiro fixed a withering glare on the man. "I am Matsui Hiro, a special investigator, appointed by order of Magistrate Ishimaki. What is your name? The magistrate will want to know who tried to delay my progress."

The taller guard gave his portly companion a nervous look. When the sake barrel didn't respond, the tall guard said, "Again, sir, we apologize. We will not delay you further."

The shorter guard scowled but stepped aside to let them pass.

Once they left the guards behind, Yoshiko turned to Hiro and asked, "Why didn't you tell me you'd entered the magistrate's service?"

CHAPTER 17

Hiro had no intention of telling Yoshiko that his claim was mostly bluff. The magistrate's decision to delay Ginjiro's hearing gave the shinobi permission to investigate, though only by implication.

Before Hiro could respond, Father Mateo said, "I'm afraid we cannot tell you more. You may remember, a year ago, Magistrate Ishimaki ordered us not to discuss the details of your father's death with anyone outside the investigation. Unfortunately, the same restrictions apply to our current duties."

"I understand." Yoshiko stopped at the end of the block where Ginjiro's brewery lay.

Hiro wanted to keep on walking, but manners required a pause.

Yoshiko bowed. "Forgive me. I must leave you here. It is nice to see you, Matsui-*san*. Perhaps we will meet again?"

Her smile made Hiro's stomach clench.

"We'd like that." Father Mateo bowed, oblivious to the fact that Yoshiko intended the words for Hiro. "Please give my regards to your mother. Would she allow us to visit her at home?"

"She would enjoy that." Yoshiko looked at Hiro. "As would I. Perhaps you could join us for a meal tomorrow evening."

"We would consider it an honor," the Jesuit said.

"The honor is ours. We look forward to seeing you, perhaps at sunset?" Yoshiko bowed and walked away without awaiting a response.

Hiro started south with Father Mateo.

After glancing over his shoulder to confirm Yoshiko's disappearance, Hiro said, "I can't believe you offered to visit. What were you thinking?"

Father Mateo looked surprised. "Yoshiko's mother must be lonely since her husband's death. Yoshiko seemed quite pleased that we wanted to come."

"It's not the 'we' that pleased her," Hiro said. "She's after me."

"That's an assumption," Father Mateo said, with a hint of a smile.

Hiro frowned. He hated assumptions almost as much as he hated being caught in one.

"Consider Yoshiko's mother," the Jesuit said, "an aging widow. Visiting her is a charitable act."

Hiro didn't answer.

"You don't have to go with me," Father Mateo said. "I'm sure I can find my way alone, at night, in a city filled with overanxious samurai hunting spies."

Hiro's frown deepened into a scowl. "I will go, but just this once."

The sun stood high overhead when Hiro and Father Mateo reached Ginjiro's. Tomiko had opened the shutters and stood behind the wooden counter, cleaning the countertop with a clean white cloth. She didn't look up, but Hiro saw the shift in her posture that indicated awareness of their presence.

He paused at the edge of the brewery floor, unwilling to enter without permission. Samurai didn't have to ask, but Hiro's notion of courtesy didn't hinge on formal etiquette.

"Good afternoon, Tomiko," he said. "May we speak with you?" She looked up and bowed. "Of course. Please come inside."

Hiro stepped out of his sandals and knelt up onto the knee-high brewery floor. Father Mateo followed suit. They crossed to the counter, though Hiro didn't hand his katana across the countertop. The rules about swords did not apply when the shop was closed.

Tomiko wiped her hands. "Have you seen my father?"

"He seems unharmed," Hiro said. "He asked us to tell you he trusts you to care for the brewery, and your mother, in his absence."

Ginjiro hadn't said any such thing, but Tomiko would benefit from believing he had.

As Hiro expected, Father Mateo didn't confirm the lie but didn't deny it. The Jesuit seemed to understand that certain deceptions furthered a moral goal.

Tomiko inhaled deeply and exhaled slowly, as if struggling to keep her emotions in check. "Thank you. I will try to make him proud."

"Can you truly manage alone?" Father Mateo asked.

Tomiko looked down at the counter. "Forgive my directness, but you are a man of samurai rank. My problems are not an appropriate topic of conversation."

"Your personal safety is," Hiro said, "and I think you underestimate the danger. Someone committed a murder here. The killer may return."

"Why would Chikao's death endanger me?" Tomiko asked. "Do you think his son might try to avenge him?"

"Do you?" Hiro asked. Kaoru wasn't his first concern, but Tomiko's comment made him curious.

"I don't know." Tomiko considered the question. "He has a terrible temper, but I don't believe he would try to hurt us."

Hiro wondered how much Tomiko knew about her father's business, particularly Ginjiro's habits when it came to hiring guards or debt collectors. The woman had clearly inherited her father's talent for keeping secrets, and Hiro doubted she would admit to incriminating facts. He would need to approach the topic of private guards another way.

"What if Chikao's death was accidental?" Hiro asked.

"In our alley?" Tomiko looked confused. "What kind of accident would happen there?"

"Did your father owe anyone money?" Hiro suspected he knew

the answer, but wanted to broach the topic of debt collectors without hinting at his ultimate objective.

"We have no debts," Tomiko said. "My father spends no money before he earns it."

"What about debtors—aside from Chikao—or debt collectors your father hired to work on his behalf?" Hiro kept the questions light, as if they stemmed from random thoughts. "Had your father mentioned any trouble?"

"Only the argument with Chikao and Kaoru," Tomiko said. "We don't have many debtors. Father has hired collectors, from time to time, but I do not think he hired one to deal with Kaoru's debt. Not yet, at least."

She paused.

"No," she continued, "I'm sure he would have told me if he had hired one. But this does give me a helpful idea. I think I'll hire a debt collector to guard the shop until Father returns."

Hiro didn't like the thought of Tomiko dealing with debt collectors, many of whom had flexible attitudes toward personal honor. Her idea surprised him, too. Ginjiro's daughter seemed too wise to risk her safety with an unknown man.

Tomiko smiled at his concern. "Do not worry, Matsui-*san*. The debt collector I intend to hire is a woman."

CHAPTER 18

"Not Akechi Yoshiko?" Hiro asked.

"Yes," Tomiko said. "Do you know her? My father says she works quite fast and gets results."

"Your father knows her?" Coincidences started lining up in Hiro's mind.

"He hired her to collect a debt about a month ago. She brought the money quickly, but I'm not sure he would work with her again." Tomiko paused. "Last week, I heard him talking with Bashō—a merchant who sells the rice we use for sake. Bashō had an injured eye and claimed Akechi-*san* had struck him."

"Over a debt?" Hiro asked.

"She hit him hard enough to bruise his eye?" Father Mateo gave Hiro a look of alarm.

"That's what he claimed," Tomiko said. "My father didn't like it, but I'm glad I heard him say it. I'll feel safer hiring a guard who uses violence when necessary."

Hiro felt a sudden need to meet Bashō.

"That reminds me," Father Mateo said, "Ana said we're out of rice."

Hiro said nothing. The housekeeper had made that comment days before, and Father Mateo had already purchased rice to fill their barrel.

"Does Bashō sell rice for eating or just for sake?" the Jesuit asked.

A smile lit Tomiko's face. "Both. We use the highest quality rice for our sake."

"Will he sell to a foreigner?" Father Mateo asked. "And if so, where can we find him?"

"Bashō has fifty feet of frontage at the end of the Sanjō rice market, west of Karasuma Street and east of Muromachi Road. You can't miss it—it's the largest shop on the block. Tell him Ginjiro sent you. You will get a better price."

"Thank you." Father Mateo turned to Hiro. "Shall we go?"

Hiro considered warning Tomiko not to trust Akechi Yoshiko. Unfortunately, he didn't know if Ginjiro's daughter had told them all she knew about the night Chikao died. If Ginjiro had hired a guard—Akechi Yoshiko or someone else—Tomiko would know. She would probably also know if the guard had killed Chikao.

If Hiro wanted to learn the truth, he couldn't assume that anyone was an ally.

Fortunately, Hiro doubted Yoshiko presented any real threat to Ginjiro's family. Not as long as Ginjiro kept his silence, anyway.

As Hiro stepped down into the street, a familiar balding figure approached the brewery at a rapid trot.

"Hiro-*san*!" Suke raised a hand in greeting.

Prison hadn't done the monk's aroma any favors. The pungent odor of human waste mingled with the sake fumes that rose from Suke's robes, giving the monk the distinctive smell of a man who had bathed in a brewery's nightsoil bucket.

Hiro fought the urge to back away.

Suke grasped the shinobi's arm. "I'm glad I found you." He started toward the alley, dragging Hiro by the sleeve. "I need to speak with you right now."

Hiro started to object, but Father Mateo raised a hand. "No—please—go with him. I will wait for you right here."

Hiro scowled at the Jesuit's amusement. They had no time to cater to Suke's addled needs. Still, he went along with the monk. It was always faster to let Suke speak his mind.

Shadows lurked in the narrow alley, as if daylight avoided the scene of the recent crime. Hiro looked for threats but didn't see anything out of place.

The monk led Hiro far enough from the street to ensure their privacy. They stopped just short of the place where spattered blood still rusted the ground and wall.

"Hiro-*san*," Suke said, "I need your help to free Ginjiro."

"I'm trying to find the killer," Hiro said. "It may take time."

"We have no time." Suke leaned forward. "We need to free Ginjiro now."

"What do you mean?" Hiro had a nasty suspicion he knew what the monk intended.

"You and me," Suke whispered. "We'll sneak him out of prison."

"That won't work," Hiro said. "The dōshin will catch us and throw us into the cages too."

"You're right. We need a diversion." Suke thought for a moment. "The foreign priest could make a scene outside the gates! Will he help us?"

"I don't think so," Hiro said. "He tends to disagree with plans that lead to our arrest."

"No reason to get upset," Suke said. "You're the one who suggested we use the priest."

Hiro opened his mouth to object but realized it wouldn't help. "Why did the dōshin set you free?"

"They told me I'm not guilty." Suke shook his head. "They wouldn't even let me speak to the magistrate. Stupid fools!"

Hiro eyed the monk. "That makes you angry?"

"Of course it does!" Suke crossed his arms. "They plan to punish Ginjiro for my crime."

"You truly believe you killed Chikao," Hiro said.

Suke's eyebrows threatened to launch themselves from the top of his balding head. "It isn't a matter of what I believe—I killed him!"

"You were asleep when the murder happened," Hiro said.

"I'm a dangerous man," Suke replied. "Lethal, even in slumber."

"Maybe so," Hiro said with a sigh, "but the evidence says you're not the killer."

Suke's arms fell down to his sides. "You're sure it wasn't me?"

Hiro gestured to the bloodstains on the wall. "Chikao didn't die from a sleepwalker's blow. I respect your martial prowess, but the killer continued striking the body after Chikao was dead. A sleeper would have woken up and seen the situation."

Suke's jaw dropped open. "That is true. This changes everything! But how did my flask end up in a killer's hands?"

CHAPTER 19

"The murderer stole your flask without you waking," Hiro said.

"Impossible." Suke shook his head. "I'm a dangerous man. No one steals my flask without me knowing. I must have killed him after all. I have to make the dōshin understand."

Hiro realized, with the dismay that accompanies nasty truths, that the only way to stop Suke from interfering with the case was to let the monk believe he was helping solve it.

"How about this?" the shinobi asked. "If the evidence proves you killed Chikao, I'll make the dōshin listen to your story. However, until we know for certain, you keep quiet and help my investigation."

Suke's mouth split into a startled grin. "You'd let me help?"

"Yes, but secretly," Hiro said. "We can't let anyone know. The killer thinks he's safe because you confessed."

"Of course! Of course!" Suke nodded vigorously, sending waves of noxious odors rolling off his robe. "I will help you, Hiro-san! Together, we'll find the killer."

His smile faded. "Even if the killer turns out to be me."

"Listen carefully," Hiro said. "I need you to watch Ginjiro's brewery. Listen to the patrons. Someone might say something about the murder."

"I understand. The killer might get drunk and confess the crime." Suke paused. "I don't suppose you'd give me money to buy a flask of sake—purely to preserve the illusion, of course."

Hiro removed a couple of silver coins from his purse. "Remember," he said as he dropped them into Suke's waiting palm, "your job is to listen without revealing you've joined the investigation. Do not call attention to yourself."

Suke nodded and scurried out of the alley.

Hiro followed, reflecting on his decision. He doubted Suke would prove any help but hoped the assignment would keep the monk out of trouble and out of the way.

Father Mateo met Hiro in the street. As they started south the Jesuit gestured over his shoulder and asked, "What did you tell him? He seems much happier."

Hiro glanced over his shoulder at Suke. The monk had settled in the street to wait for the brewery to open. "I gave him a job, to keep him out of trouble."

Father Mateo smiled. "Let me know how that works out."

"If it doesn't, we'll both know." Hiro saw the Jesuit wince and slowed his pace. "Does your injury bother you?"

Father Mateo looked down at his hands, which were covered in angry scars from an attack two months before. "A little. Is it obvious?"

"Only to me," Hiro lied. "Why did you want to see Bashō?"

"To learn how far Yoshiko's violent tendencies might go," the Jesuit said. "It doesn't take much skill to suspect a connection between Ginjiro and Yoshiko. After all, she knew about the crime. Do you think she might be the guard Ginjiro hired?"

"We don't know, for certain, that he hired one," Hiro said. "Until we do, we must explore all options."

"It's hard for me to believe Yoshiko would kill Chikao," Father Mateo said. "Not with her own father murdered a year ago."

"Yoshiko's father was samurai. Chikao is a merchant. Their deaths are not the same."

Hiro doubted the priest would understand.

"They are to me, and they are to God." Father Mateo paused. "Could a woman beat a man to death?"

"You've seen Yoshiko," Hiro said. "If a man could do it, she could."

Father Mateo sighed. "This investigation seems more difficult than the others. Chikao didn't have any enemies. We don't even have good suspects."

Hiro noticed a noodle vendor and headed toward the cart. As he did, he switched to Portuguese. "On the contrary, we have three: Kaoru, Ren, and Ginjiro."

He switched back to Japanese and ordered two bowls of udon.

"The second two I understand," Father Mateo said in Portuguese, "but why the son? He doesn't want to work. Also, won't he share his inheritance with his mother?"

Hiro smiled at the Jesuit's use of general terms instead of names. "A wife inherits only when the husband leaves a will that names her heir."

Father Mateo watched Hiro pay the vendor. "I can't believe you're hungry."

Hiro accepted some copper change. "I can't believe you're not."

The vendor handed each man a bowl of steaming noodles in pungent sauce.

Hiro inhaled deeply. His stomach grumbled. As he hoped, the chewy noodles had just the right combination of onions, fish, and savory broth.

Father Mateo ate, but slowly, and fumbled with his chopsticks. His injured hands had not regained their full dexterity.

All too soon, Hiro's chopsticks clattered against the empty bowl. He returned them to the vendor. Father Mateo returned his, too, though he hadn't finished his noodles.

The vendor gave the Jesuit's half-filled bowl a worried look. "I'm sorry you didn't like the flavor."

"I enjoyed it." Father Mateo gave the vendor an apologetic smile. "I am not very hungry this afternoon."

Hiro glanced at the Jesuit's hands. He saw no sign of infection but reminded himself to keep an eye on the priest.

Father Mateo switched to Portuguese. "It's not my hands. I suppose I should tell you—I really don't like udon."

A samurai in lacquered armor guarded Sanjō Road at Karasuma Street.

Hiro wasn't surprised. Prosperous rice merchants often served as moneylenders, too. Their storehouses held not only coins but samurai heirlooms left as collateral for loans. With the city on alert, Matsunaga Hisahide would protect them. No man who wanted the shogunate would risk the loss of so much valuable treasure—or the tax revenue that accompanied it.

Despite his understanding, Hiro bristled at the thought of yet another interruption.

The guard stepped into the road and blocked their path. "State your names and business in this ward."

Hiro felt his patience wane. "Surely the shogun has more important business than keeping honest men from theirs?"

"From their what?" The samurai tipped his head to the side, confused.

"Their business," Hiro said.

"My business is to protect this ward." The samurai stepped forward until his chin was only inches from Hiro's chest. "Do not challenge my authority. I speak with the voice of Shogun Matsunaga."

Hiro raised an eyebrow. "Matsunaga-*san* is taller than you and also better looking."

"How dare you!" The samurai's hand moved to the hilt of his katana.

A second armored samurai emerged from a nearby shop, cheeks bulging with an enormous bite from a bun. When he saw the situation, he swallowed quickly, stashed the bun in his armor, and joined his partner in the street. "What's going on?"

"Your friend believes himself the shogun's equal," Hiro said, consciously overlooking the fact that Matsunaga-*san* was not yet shogun. "I chose to disabuse him of that notion."

The second samurai sighed. "Yujiro, let them pass. We're only supposed to stop saboteurs and spies."

The comment revealed these guards hadn't worked together very long, or very often. Regular partners would not contradict one another in public.

Yujiro nodded at Father Mateo. "The foreigner looks suspicious to me, and everyone knows you cannot trust a ronin."

Hiro ignored the insult. Men promoted above their abilities often resorted to bullying.

Father Mateo stepped into the samurai's path. "Indeed, I'm quite suspicious. Best arrest me before I carry out my devious plot . . . to purchase a sack of rice."

Yujiro's cheeks turned purple. "Did you insult me?"

Father Mateo squared his shoulders. "I treat a man as he deserves, and you deserve no better."

CHAPTER 20

Yujiro bared his teeth and took a threatening step toward Father Mateo.

Hiro laid a hand on the hilt of his katana and stepped between them. "We want no trouble."

Yujiro looked at Father Mateo. "Your friend's behavior indicates otherwise."

Hiro agreed. He wondered why the priest insulted the samurai so openly. Father Mateo had never done that before.

The shinobi felt the moment slip toward violence. His limbs relaxed, prepared and almost longing for a fight. Just before he decided to release his martial instincts, training and better judgment took control.

Hiro bowed his head to feign regret. "Please forgive the foreign priest. In his country, a noble man must always return an insult or face permanent dishonor."

"In Japan, he faces death."

Yujiro's sword slipped from its sheath with a whispering ring. In an instant, Hiro drew both of his swords. He crossed them in front of him, blocking the strike. Stepping backward, he lowered the wakizashi. He held the katana level, expecting Yujiro to back away.

Instead, the samurai leaped forward, raising his sword for another aggressive blow.

Hiro blocked with his katana. Deflecting his opponent's sword, he counterattacked with the wakizashi.

Yujiro parried and stepped away.

Hiro struck with his katana. Yujiro backed away again and parried a second time.

Hiro advanced, alternating overhand katana strikes with slashing blows from the wakizashi. Yujiro deflected every one.

To Hiro's surprise, the arrogant samurai was a talented swordsman.

After several flurries of attacks and counterattacks, Hiro sensed his opponent tiring.

Yujiro launched a counterattack with the desperation of a man who knew he must win or die. Hiro was forced to back away, parrying and deflecting. He focused on his opponent's eyes, watching for the chance to kill the samurai and end the fight.

Just as he started to wonder whether Yujiro had only faked exhaustion, the samurai stumbled over an uneven spot in the road.

Hiro leaped sideways, slipping his wakizashi under the samurai's chin. By the time Yujiro regained his balance, Hiro's blade was at his throat.

The samurai bowed his head and lowered his sword.

Hiro raised his katana high to strike the fatal blow, but Father Mateo's expression stayed his hand. Miraculously, the priest didn't seem to want this man to die.

"What are you waiting for?" Yujiro demanded, without looking up.

Father Mateo shook his head.

Hiro looked at the Jesuit. *Killing this man is the right thing to do.*

Father Mateo met Hiro's gaze without faltering.

With a sigh of frustration, Hiro lowered his sword. "My master chooses to let you live."

"The foreigner insulted me." Yujiro straightened and scowled. "His life is forfeit."

"You are mistaken," Hiro said. "It is you who lost the fight. By rights, your life belongs to the priest—"

"—and the priest has given it back to you," Father Mateo finished.

Yujiro looked confused and angry. By law, and by the samurai code, Hiro should have killed him. Survival would leave a permanent stain on Yujiro's personal honor.

Unfortunately, that also increased the chance of a second fight. At this moment, Yujiro had nothing to lose.

Yujiro's partner found his voice. "This is over. Let them pass. The fight was fair."

"The foreigner should fight for himself," Yujiro said, though he sounded more like a petulant child than a samurai.

"Why do you think he hired a ronin?" the other samurai asked. "Everyone knows a foreigner poses no more threat than a woman. Not unless he's carrying a firearm, anyway."

Hiro decided not to mention that, in his experience, women were far more deadly than Portuguese firearms. He had scars on his shoulder and inner thigh—and more on his heart—that proved it. Other injuries faded to memory once the wounds had healed, but the pain of a woman's betrayal—that betrayal—had eased far less than Hiro liked to admit.

Yujiro scowled. "Get out of my sight."

Hiro bowed to the second guard. "We seek a merchant named Bashō. Perhaps you know his shop?"

Yujiro scowled, but the other samurai nodded. "I do. I buy his rice myself."

The samurai turned and pointed west along the market street. "Head that way. It's three blocks down. The noren says 'Bashō.' You cannot miss it."

In the rice sellers' street, the distinctive thump and swish of hulling machines competed with the sounds of merchants calling out specials to passersby. Indigo noren fluttered in doorways, ruffled by a summer breeze laden with the dusty-sweet scent of rice.

"What's that thumping?" Father Mateo asked.

Hiro nodded to the pounder on display in front of the nearest shop. "Hulling machines. Have you never seen one?"

"Not like that," the Jesuit said. "But then, I buy our rice from a cart."

They paused for a moment before the store. Hiro tried to see the hulling machine through foreign eyes.

The pounders featured a round wooden beam, about twelve feet long, with a wooden support in the middle that allowed the beam to pivot up and down. One end of the beam had a flattened place for a person's foot to rest. At the opposite end, a wooden post protruded downward into a bucket filled with rice. When a laborer stepped on the flattened beam, the post rose out of the bucket. When the laborer stepped back off again, the post fell down with a swish and a thump, pounding the rice and shedding the fibrous hulls.

Father Mateo gestured toward the pounder. "The merchant I buy from hasn't got room for one of those on his cart. I wonder where he keeps it."

"If you don't see the machine, he hasn't got one," Hiro said. "Smaller merchants pay to use a larger shop's machine or arrange for a mobile pounder to hull their rice."

The Jesuit nodded. "The machines do look expensive."

"Smaller shops and carts don't always need them," Hiro said. "Many commoners buy their rice unhulled. It's cheaper, and the husks make up in bulk what they lack in taste."

Clouds of rice dust rose from the pounders and floated into the street. The noren fluttering at one side of the open storefront read BASHŌ—FINEST RICE IN KYOTO. The characters flowed down the indigo banner in skilled calligraphy. Bashō had paid a handsome price for his sign.

Hiro noted the heavy wooden shutters folded back on either side of the entrance. Bashō's appreciation of quality extended to security as well.

Despite the size of Bashō's establishment, so many people clustered inside that Hiro and Father Mateo had to wait their turn in the street. As they waited, they watched the customers leave the shop. Some carried bags of rice, while others left empty-handed.

"I wonder why he didn't buy anything," the Jesuit murmured as a well-dressed samurai stepped into the street and strolled away. "He looks like he could afford it."

"No warrior carries a parcel," Hiro replied in Portuguese. "A shop will always deliver a nobleman's purchase."

"Would you truly have killed that man?" Father Mateo asked in his native tongue.

It took Hiro a moment to realize that the priest referred to the samurai guard, Yujiro.

"He intended to kill you," Hiro said. "Did you think I would let him do it?"

"I . . ." Father Mateo trailed off. After a moment, he continued, "I didn't intend to cause violence. Sometimes I forget how quickly words can escalate in Japan."

"Especially now, and especially here." Hiro watched a bird swoop down and peck at fallen grains of rice.

Eventually, their turn came and they stepped inside. Barrels of rice lined the walls on either side of the entrance. Some had covers, but most sat open, displaying the various grades of rice. A *koku* of grain, five bushels by Father Mateo's Western measure, was considered enough to feed an adult person for a year. These barrels held hundreds, or possibly thousands, of koku, the kernels as valuable as silver and indicating the merchant's enormous wealth.

Hiro's mouth watered at the thought of fluffy grains, nicely steamed and mounded in a bowl. His stomach still felt pleasantly full from the recent bowl of noodles, but no one could resist the aroma of plump, high-quality rice.

A clerk approached and bowed to Hiro. His limbs had the gangly look of adolescence; they protruded from his tunic like sticks in a snowbank.

An apprentice, Hiro thought, and, from his skinny state, a new one. "How may I help you?" the young man asked.

"We have come to see Bashō," Hiro said.

"I apologize," the young man said. "My master is not here. I am his apprentice, Jiro. May I help you?"

"We would rather see Bashō," Hiro said. "Do you expect him soon?"

"One moment, please." Jiro bowed and hurried toward a cloth-covered doorway at the back of the shop.

He returned with a middle-aged woman in his wake.

A layer of rice dust covered her clothes and enhanced the gray in her hair. Her eyes surveyed the shop with a confidence born of ownership. The set of her lips suggested little tolerance for fools.

Jiro murmured something to the woman. She nodded, shifted her gaze to Hiro, and started toward the shinobi as Jiro turned to another customer.

The woman bowed to Hiro and then, with equal deference, to Father Mateo.

"Good afternoon," she said. "I am Hama, Bashō's wife. May I ask your business with my husband?"

She studied Hiro and then the priest as if sizing up bags of rice. If she came to any decision, she didn't show it.

"We wish to speak with Bashō," Hiro said.

"He isn't here." Hama's eyebrows drew together. Her lips turned into a frown. "In fact, I don't even know where he is, myself."

CHAPTER 21

"You don't know where your husband is?" Father Mateo asked.

"No," Hama said. "He went to a teahouse with friends and didn't return."

"A teahouse?" Hiro asked. "Does he sleep there often?"

Hama's frown deepened. "My husband doesn't frequent the kind of teahouse that lets patrons stay the night."

As far as you know, Hiro thought.

"Have you spoken with your husband's friends?" Father Mateo asked.

Hiro wished the priest had waited longer before asking. Too many questions in quick succession allowed for accidental omissions as well as conscious evasion.

"They haven't seen him," Hama said. "At least, that's what they told me."

Hiro thought it strange that Bashō's wife showed only frustration, and not distress, at her husband's absence.

"Has this happened before?" he asked.

"What did you say you needed?" Hama gave them a searching look. "I reported the disappearance to the yoriki, but you don't look like dōshin."

"That is true," the Jesuit said, "we haven't come from the yoriki's office."

"And you haven't come for rice."

Hama's pause demanded an answer.

"Not exactly," Father Mateo said, with a dip of his head that suggested an apology. "I'm new to Japan and trying to learn about life in Kyoto. I hoped Bashō might help me sample all

SUSAN SPANN

the grades of rice. I will buy them, but I need to learn about them first.

"You see, in my homeland, we only have one kind."

Hiro wondered when Father Mateo had changed his position on telling lies. He also wondered how the priest lied so well with so little practice.

"One grade of rice?" Hama shook her head. "Can't imagine such a thing. Unfortunately, my husband has disappeared and cannot help you."

"May we help you search for him?" Father Mateo asked.

"Wouldn't know where to start," Hama said.

"Was the teahouse in Pontochō?" Hiro asked.

"He didn't go to a brothel," Hama said. "Bashō does not waste money on prostitutes."

Father Mateo's eyebrows raised in surprise. Hiro gave the priest a look that warned against further questions.

"Thank you anyway," Hiro said. "When Bashō returns, would you let him know that Father Mateo, who lives on Marutamachi Road, would like to ask him questions about rice?"

"Why does he want to learn about merchants' work?" Hama spoke as if the Jesuit wasn't there.

Hiro shrugged. "Foreigners are curious—and in his land, any man can become a merchant."

"Truly?" Hama stared at Father Mateo. "I'd heard foreign lands were strange."

"Will she consider it odd that I haven't offered to let her teach me?" Father Mateo asked in Portuguese.

"On the contrary," Hiro replied in the Jesuit's language, "she would consider it strange if you did."

Hama smiled with a hint of discomfort, as people often did in the presence of languages they didn't understand. "I will give my husband the message—when, and if, I see him."

"I hope he comes home soon," Father Mateo said.

"Soon enough." Hama folded her arms across her chest. "And

when he does, he'll spend more time on business and far less on expensive sake."

Hiro thought, in Bashō's place, he might not come home at all.

"If you know he's coming home," the Jesuit asked, "why report him missing?"

Hama uncrossed her arms and rested her hands on her hips. "I wanted the dōshin to bring him home. He deserves it, for trying to escape a scolding by leaving me here to worry. The first time, yes, but I'm wise to his tricks by now."

Hiro and Father Mateo headed home along the path that paralleled the Kamo River.

"Why do you think Matsunaga-*san* has so many samurai guarding the city?" Father Mateo asked. "Shogun Ashikaga never used this many guards."

"Matsunaga-*san* has controlled the city for only two months," the shinobi said. "You heard the guards. He is looking for spies."

"Spies would justify guards at the city boundaries and the gates, not samurai at the entrance to every ward." Father Mateo thought for a moment. "Do you think the Ashikaga clan will challenge Matsunaga Hisahide's claim to the shogunate?"

Hiro found the Jesuit's guess surprising but not startling. Father Mateo paid attention to local Japanese politics, and generally remembered what he learned.

"The Ashikaga blame Matsunaga-*san* for the shogun's recent death." Hiro offered a simpler truth in place of the deeper problem. "They do not believe the shogun committed suicide."

"I wondered," Father Mateo said. "It struck me as odd that Hisahide announced himself as the shogun's chosen successor. Matsunaga Hisahide serves the Miyoshi *daimyō*. Why would Shogun Ashikaga name another lord's retainer to succeed him?"

Hiro knew the truth about the shogun's reported suicide, but he would not break an oath to satisfy the Jesuit's curiosity. Not when the words would cost the priest his life.

Instead, he focused on the larger issue. "The Ashikaga no longer possess the strength to defend Kyoto against Lord Oda. Matsunaga Hisahide has the power, and the allies, to keep the city safe."

"Provided the Ashikaga do not rebel." Father Mateo nodded. "These samurai guards are a show of force. Matsunaga Hisahide wants to send a message to the Ashikaga clan."

"Yes," Hiro said, "and also to Lord Oda. Hisahide will not tolerate threats to his bid for the shogunate."

Father Mateo stopped walking. "We made a mistake. We forgot to ask the names of the friends who went to the teahouse with Bashō."

"You forgot," Hiro said. "I decided not to ask. Hama would not have remembered the names."

The Jesuit gave the shinobi a cautious look. "You mean, she would have lied."

"She lied already," Hiro said. "No woman shows so little concern about her husband's disappearance."

"Unless she caused it," Father Mateo said.

Hiro gave the priest a disbelieving glance. "Especially if she caused it. No, I think she knows where Bashō went."

"Then why say otherwise?" Father Mateo asked.

Hiro smiled. "Because she doesn't want us to find him."

CHAPTER 22

Father Mateo hurried along the path to catch up with Hiro. "Why would Bashō's wife not want her husband found? Do you think he was involved in Chikao's murder?"

"His disappearance raises suspicions," Hiro said, "but, so far, no facts connect him to Chikao."

"Except that one is dead and the other is missing," Father Mateo said.

Hiro didn't answer.

"I don't think Ginjiro killed Chikao," the priest continued, "and I do not think Yoshiko killed him either. Both of them would want him alive, because he paid Kaoru's debts."

"Perhaps," Hiro said, "but remember, Chikao might have died by accident."

"Accident?" Father Mateo raised his hand and pantomimed a downward strike. "You don't beat an unconscious man to death by accident."

"No," Hiro said, "but accidents happen. Perhaps Yoshiko confronted Chikao in the alley and threatened to hurt him unless he paid the debt. Chikao refused. Yoshiko struck him in the face, the way she apparently did Bashō. Chikao might have threatened to report her—the magistrate frowns on violence in collections—and Yoshiko may have struck him again as he turned to walk away."

"But why would she kill him?" Father Mateo asked. "That seems unlikely."

"True," Hiro said. "She probably struck in anger. Either way, if her second attack knocked Chikao senseless, Yoshiko would have a serious problem."

Father Mateo shook his head. "The woman is a samurai. She

wouldn't murder an innocent man to prevent a report to the magistrate. Everyone knows the magistrates favor nobles."

"Angry samurai make foolish choices," Hiro said, "and a commoner turning his back on a samurai is a grievous insult."

"Grievous insults do not justify murder," Father Mateo said.

"There is another option," Hiro offered. "What if Yoshiko struck Chikao several hours before he died, but he didn't succumb to his injuries until later?"

"You mean, he just dropped dead in the alley?" Father Mateo squinted in disbelief. "That happens?"

"It can happen," Hiro said. "I've seen it once before. A blow to the head can cause a man to bleed inside his skull. If he bleeds enough, he just drops dead, sometimes hours later."

Father Mateo started to speak, but Hiro raised a hand for silence. Someone was approaching on the path.

Hiro turned to see Jiro, the clerk from Bashō's shop, hurrying toward them along the river road. The clerk slowed to a rapid shuffle when he saw the shinobi turn, but his red face and heaving shoulders indicated he'd been running hard.

"Is it wise to let him approach?" Father Mateo asked in Portuguese.

Hiro replied in kind. "A man who intended harm would never make so much noise."

He had barely finished speaking when Jiro reached them.

The young man bowed from the waist—an awkward gesture made much worse by Jiro's skinny arms and heaving chest. Hiro nodded, granting permission for the clerk to speak.

"I wanted to tell you . . . not to waste time . . . looking for Bashō," Jiro panted. "He left Kyoto yesterday."

"Left the city?" Father Mateo asked. "Where did he go?"

And why did you run to tell us? Hiro wondered.

The skinny clerk looked eastward as he fought to recover breath. "Up the travel road . . . to Edo. Hama believes . . . he was drinking in Pontochō, but that isn't true."

Jiro gave Father Mateo an apologetic bow. "I am sorry. He won't be able to answer your questions now."

"Pardon my inquiry," Father Mateo said, "but why did he leave the city?"

Hiro didn't mind the Jesuit's question. Bashō's apprentice would surely lie, but Father Mateo might ask about something Jiro wasn't prepared to answer, and the clerk might accidentally say something useful.

Jiro looked at the ground and mumbled, "He owes a debt he cannot pay."

"To someone in Pontochō?" Hiro asked.

Jiro shook his head.

"It's all right," Father Mateo said. "You can tell us. We'll keep your secret."

Hiro smiled. "Hama doesn't know where Bashō actually spent his evenings, does she?"

Jiro's head whipped up. He gave the shinobi a pleading look. "Please don't tell. She'll fire me the moment she learns I knew . . ."

"Then why did you come to tell us where he went?" the Jesuit asked.

Hiro suspected he already knew the answer.

"I was afraid," Jiro said. "You are a foreigner, an important man. If you ask, the yoriki will investigate. The dōshin will learn about the debt, and Hama will be so angry . . ."

"Tell us the name of the teahouse," Hiro said, "or we tell Hama everything."

Jiro's eyes grew wide. "No! Please . . ."

"Then give me a name," Hiro growled.

"The Golden Buddha." Jiro wrung his hands. "Lately, Bashō went to drink at the Golden Buddha in Pontochō. Until last month, he preferred a house on the other side of the Kamo River—a nice one, the Sakura. Those are the only two I know."

Hiro had never heard of the Golden Buddha in Pontochō, but the Sakura was Yoshiko's house—and the name he expected to hear.

"How do you know Bashō was headed for Edo?" Hiro asked.

"He told me." Jiro glanced over his shoulder. "The Sakura's debt collector started making real threats. Bashō couldn't pay. He thought if he disappeared, the debt collector would leave his wife alone."

"You know that will not happen," Hiro said. "Bashō would know it, too. The law does not distinguish between a husband and his wife regarding debts."

"Yes," Jiro said, "but magistrates show mercy on a woman when her husband runs away."

That, at least, explained why Bashō hadn't told his wife where he was going. Hiro didn't want to be the one to tell her, either.

"Please," Jiro said, "do not tell Hama. My master isn't an evil man. He made a mistake, and he didn't want his family to suffer."

"We understand," Father Mateo said.

Jiro bowed and walked away. Every few paces, he turned around and gave them a pleading look.

"That explains Bashō's absence," Father Mateo said as they watched the apprentice leave.

"Really?" Hiro asked. "Do you believe that boy sneaked out of a crowded shop without Hama knowing? Or that your status scared him into the truth?"

"Why would he lie?" Father Mateo asked. "That makes no sense."

"It makes as much sense as the lie you told to Hama," Hiro said. "Speaking of which, when did lies become acceptable to you?"

"Lies are not acceptable." Father Mateo paused. "I do want to learn about rice."

"And I'm really a woman dressed up as a man," Hiro countered.

"Yoshiko does it better," the Jesuit said.

"That isn't funny." Hiro turned around and started south along the road.

"Where are you going?" Father Mateo followed. "I'm sorry—I didn't mean to insult you."

Hiro looked over his shoulder at the priest. "I'm not upset—I felt a sudden need to see a dead man."

Father Mateo fell in step. "Back to the Lucky Monkey?"

"Yes," Hiro said. "We need to talk with Mina."

The Jesuit looked uncertain. "She's in mourning and probably praying."

"Exactly," Hiro said. "She also knows more than she's told us. Now that she's had some time to consider the consequences of her husband's death and impending judgment, she may listen when you tell her that your god has mercy when a person tells the truth about a crime."

Father Mateo stopped walking. "No. I will not use God's love to trick a woman."

CHAPTER 23

"It's a tactic, not a trick," Hiro said. "We need to learn what Mina knows."

"God has already judged Chikao," Father Mateo said. "His wife's confession cannot save his soul."

"Your god, perhaps," the shinobi said. "Mina's have not decided."

"That isn't how it works." Father Mateo ran a hand through his hair. "There is only one God, one judgment."

Hiro recognized the agitated gesture. He needed to take another tack, and quickly, or the priest might not cooperate at all. "Do you feel sad that Chikao died before you could tell him about your god?"

"Of course," Father Mateo said. "I don't want any soul to suffer."

"Then when we arrive, you can ask to pray in the room where Mina's husband lies. Use the time to tell your god how sorry you feel about Chikao—or whatever it is you say to him about the things that make you sad. Mina won't know the difference, and, no matter whose gods will judge Chikao, it can't do any harm."

Hiro tried to evaluate the success of his words, but Father Mateo's expression revealed nothing. However, the priest didn't turn away, and Hiro was willing to take the Jesuit's silence as consent.

As they entered the stinking alley off Shijō Road, shouting echoed from the Lucky Monkey's entrance.

Kaoru stood in the brewery doorway, facing someone farther inside. "It's my money," he yelled, "the least you can do is leave something for me to inherit!"

He yanked the door closed with a thump and stomped down the alley away from Hiro and Father Mateo.

The Jesuit paused. "We should leave and come back later."

The Lucky Monkey's noren parted. Mina appeared in the entrance. She stood in the doorway and watched her son disappear into the space beyond the buildings.

Mina turned and noticed Hiro and the priest. "Good afternoon." She bowed to cover her embarrassment. "Once again, I must apologize for my son's behavior."

"May we speak with you inside?" Hiro asked.

"Of course." Mina stepped aside. "That is, if you do not object to entering a house of mourning. May I offer you tea?"

"Thank you," Hiro said. "We would like some tea."

Crossing the threshold, Hiro heard the sound of rhythmic chanting somewhere farther inside the building. Male voices rose and fell in the cadence of funeral prayers. The monks had arrived, and formal mourning for Chikao had started.

The chanting grew more noticeable as Hiro and Father Mateo followed Mina into the brewery's drinking room.

She paused and gestured. "Sit wherever you like. I will make the tea."

When she left the room, Father Mateo said, "I can't believe you asked for tea while she's in mourning."

"She offered." Hiro settled himself on the floor. "Preparing tea gives her something to do, and normalcy offers distraction in difficult times. Also, I thought it would please you, since the tea gives us a different way to start the conversation. We may not need your god's help after all."

Father Mateo gave the shinobi a disapproving look as Mina returned.

She carried a tray with a steaming teapot, three ceramic cups, and a plate of sweetened rice balls. She set the tray on the floor and knelt beside it, but instead of pouring the tea she asked the Jesuit, "Would you like to pray?"

Mina smiled at Father Mateo's startled look. "I have a friend who worships your Jesus god. She prays before accepting food and drink. If you wish, you may offer your prayer aloud. Honest gratitude insults no one, whether or not we pray to different gods."

She laid her hands in her lap and bowed her head.

Father Mateo offered a prayer, asking God to bless the house, and Mina, and the food. Hiro appreciated the Jesuit's keeping the prayer short. Tea tasted better hot, and questions, too, retained more palatability without a liberal helping of foreign faith.

Mina poured tea for Hiro and Father Mateo. She had brought a cup for herself but didn't fill it.

"May I pour you tea?" Father Mateo offered.

Mina leaned back in surprise. Guests never poured the tea for female hosts, especially male guests of samurai rank.

"Unless, perhaps, you are fasting," Hiro offered.

Mina's face relaxed with sudden relief. "I am, to atone for my husband's sins. Thank you for understanding."

"How long will you fast?" Father Mateo asked.

"For Chikao, until his funeral," Mina said. "After that, I will fast on my own account."

Father Mateo leaned forward slightly. "Why do you need to fast?"

Mina shifted the plate of rice balls toward her guests. "I intend to become a nun, after I finish mourning for my husband."

"A nun?" Father Mateo looked surprised. His features softened with understanding. "Oh, a Buddhist nun. I apologize—my religion also allows for female nuns."

"Really?" Mina asked. "And do the widows of your faith elect this path?"

"When God calls them," Father Mateo said, "and, sometimes, when they have no other method of support."

Hiro caught the not-so-subtle hint but didn't mind.

"Sometimes Japanese widows also make this choice for economic reasons," Mina said, "though I do not."

"Forgive me," the Jesuit said, "but you mentioned that the moneylenders wouldn't give you loans . . ." He trailed off.

Hiro had hoped the priest would remember Mina's comment about loans. A samurai could never ask, but Father Mateo's status as a foreigner, and a priest, created an excuse for intrusive questions.

"Chikao and I attempted to obtain a loan to pay off Kaoru's debts," the woman said. "But the moneylender knows my son and wouldn't take the risk. Not without a licensed brewery to secure the loan."

Father Mateo looked concerned. "Then how . . ."

Mina smiled. "I don't need money. Chikao's death has freed me to pursue the path I chose many years ago."

She paused. After allowing sufficient time for Hiro and Father Mateo to change the subject if they wished to, she continued, "I grew up near Tofuku-ji, and my father often took me for walks on the temple grounds. Even as a child, I wanted to become a nun and spend my days in meditation, seeking peace."

Her eyes took on a distant look.

The monks' voices rose and fell in the background, chanting prayers.

"And yet, you chose to marry," Father Mateo said.

Mina's eyes refocused on the priest. "As duty required. Obedient children place their parents' hopes before their own."

Hiro wondered what Mina thought of Kaoru's selfish choices.

"Now," she continued, "my husband's death releases me to pursue my heart's desire."

"What will become of the brewery?" Hiro asked.

Mina sighed. "I do not know. I hoped my son would choose to learn his father's trade, but he refuses. Kaoru says he wants to sell our share of the brewery to Ren. My son will squander the money, but what can I do? He is adult, and male. I can't control him."

"Does Ren want to purchase the interest?" Hiro asked.

"I am ashamed to ask him," Mina said. "It seems unfair to shackle Ren with debts, especially now. If my son would only accept his duty . . ."

She trailed off into silence.

Hiro sipped his tea and waited.

Eventually Father Mateo asked, "Did your husband know about your wish to lead a religious life?"

Hiro wished the priest hadn't spoken. People shared more information when the burden of silence reached a certain weight.

"Chikao felt guilty for keeping me tied to the world," Mina said, "but, as I often told him, I never regretted my choice to marry. I loved Chikao and enjoyed our life together."

"Does Kaoru know about your plans to become a nun?" the Jesuit asked.

Mina gave the priest a searching look. "My son did not kill his father."

CHAPTER 24

Father Mateo blinked in surprise. Even Hiro barely managed to keep his reaction covered. Neither man expected Mina to broach the topic of Kaoru's guilt.

"That is what you came to ask me," Mina said, "is it not?"

"I—we—" Father Mateo stammered.

"We did not expect you to guess it." Hiro opted for the truth.

Mina smiled. "All too often, people assume detachment from the physical world derives from a lack of intelligence or perception. They are mistaken.

"I will answer your questions, but first, please tell me why you suspect my son."

Hiro saw no point in pretense. "We have learned that Kaoru has a temper."

Mina lifted the teapot and refilled the shinobi's cup. "I do not doubt my son could kill a man when drunk and angry. But I do not think he killed Chikao, and that opinion doesn't stem from a mother's blinded love.

"Kaoru doesn't consider his father's death a benefit. They argued often, over money, but Chikao always conceded in the end. With his father dead, Kaoru will have to work—to support himself—which is the last thing he would ever wish to do.

"This is a terrible thing for a mother to say about her son, but Kaoru is far too selfish to kill his father."

"But he does inherit the brewery," Hiro said.

"Our half of it, yes, but that will not support his habits long." Mina paused as if unwilling to finish her thoughts. At last she continued, "I've said this much, I will say the rest. My son is a coward. He lacks the courage to take his father's life."

"Perhaps," Hiro said, "but we would prefer some evidence of his innocence. Do you know where Kaoru went last night?"

Mina considered the question. "He wasn't here. If I had to guess, I would say the Sakura Teahouse, east of the Kamo River on Sanjō Road, or else at the Golden Buddha in Pontochō. Before you ask, I do not know what time Kaoru returned. He said he was here all night, and sleeping. I found him asleep and still too drunk to pay attention when Ren arrived this morning with the news of Chikao's death. Kaoru claims he returned before the brewery closed last night. He may be telling the truth. He may be lying. I don't know."

"What about Ren?" Hiro asked. "Do you know where he was last night?"

"Ren worked here all evening with Chikao," Mina said. "After the brewery closed, I cannot tell you, though I doubt that he went anywhere but home. Ren didn't believe in wasting money on women or entertainment. He wanted to join the brewers' guild and invest in a larger shop. To my knowledge, all his money went to savings."

"That must have caused some conflict with your husband," Hiro said.

"Not with Chikao." Mina smiled. "But Ren and Kaoru didn't get along."

"Ren admitted to arguing with Chikao about the decision to pay off Kaoru's debt," Father Mateo said. "Did you know they argued?"

"The argument involved my son. Of course I knew about it." Mina refilled the Jesuit's cup. "Ren threatened to leave the partnership and join the brewers' guild alone if Kaoru's actions stopped the za from approving Chikao's part of the petition."

"Did that create bad blood between them?" Hiro asked.

Mina smiled sadly. "Chikao and I did not want Ren to bear the burden of Kaoru's . . . disappointing choices."

The monks' chanting rose and fell.

Hiro considered Chikao's body—so close, and yet impossible to reach. He wondered whether Mina would grant permission for a viewing. Doubtful, since the funeral prayers had started. Still, a request could do no harm.

"Would you grant us a favor?" Hiro asked.

"You want to see my husband's body," Mina said.

The comment left Hiro momentarily speechless. He forced his surprise away and said, "We believe a closer examination will help us find his killer."

Mina nodded. "I wondered when you would get around to asking. I didn't think the yoriki would let you view him at the murder scene. I will allow it, if you don't abuse his body in the process."

"We will treat him with respect," the shinobi said.

Mina led Hiro and Father Mateo across the room to the *shoji* that separated the common room from the space beyond. The sound of chanting increased as they reached the door.

She laid a hand on the door frame. "Please wait here while I offer the monks some tea. I would prefer they leave the room before you enter."

"You truly don't mind?" Father Mateo asked.

"I do not," Mina said. "The dead may defile the living, but we cannot harm the dead."

An unusual attitude for a Japanese woman, but in character with Mina's perceptive nature.

She drew open the door and stepped into the room beyond.

The chanting stopped. Moments later, a line of elderly priests filed out of the room, followed by two boys in saffron robes.

Mina paused in the doorway as she left. "If you touch my husband's body, leave no sign."

"May I ask why you chose to allow this?" Father Mateo seemed confused.

"I respect every living creature, including the man accused of my husband's murder." Mina glanced into the room where Chikao lay. "I wish to know, with certainty, that the person who dies for this crime is guilty of it."

She gestured toward the room. "You have ten minutes."

Hiro and Father Mateo entered the tiny room. Mina slid the shoji closed behind them.

A pattern of barrel-sized rings on the bare wooden floor suggested a former storage room converted to a far less pleasant purpose. The odors of *sugi* wood and straw still lingered beneath the incense in the air.

Chikao lay face up on a narrow futon at the center of the room. A cone of incense smoldered in a ceramic burner near his head. One of his arms lay stiffly akimbo. The other reached out, as if grasping at something only the dead could see.

Father Mateo looked from the corpse to Hiro. "Is that normal?"

"You mean the arms?" Hiro asked.

The Jesuit nodded. "Why are they sticking out like that?"

"The body must have gone rigid before they retrieved it," Hiro said. "The muscles will loosen tonight or tomorrow. After that, he will look more normal."

Hiro stepped to the side of the futon.

Father Mateo followed. "Only half his face is purple. Did it look that way before?"

Purple mottling covered the right side of Chikao's face from halfway across his nose to the side of his jaw. The left side of Chikao's face was deathly pale, except where swollen bruises blossomed around his eye.

"How did the killer bruise an entire side of Chikao's face?" the Jesuit asked. "And why is the right cheek bruised, and not the left one?"

Hiro gestured to the mottled purple color on the right. "The killer didn't cause this part. The parts of the flesh that lie toward the ground will always discolor shortly after death."

"Always?" Father Mateo asked.

Hiro nodded. "It takes a few hours, but yes, it always happens. The blood settles into those parts of the body, turning them purple, though the parts that actually touch the ground stay pale." He indicated the strip of bloodless skin on Chikao's right cheek and along the jawline. "See? That's where he rested on the ground."

"So, dead people bruise on the underside?" Father Mateo asked.

"It's not exactly bruising," Hiro said. "I think it has to do with the way the blood runs downward after the heart stops beating. That also explains why you see less discoloration when the victim dies from bleeding, because the blood ends up on the outside, rather than trapped beneath the skin."

"I didn't need to know that." Father Mateo stared at the patch of waxy skin along Chikao's jaw. "Why does the part that touches the ground stay pale?"

"That, I can't explain," Hiro said, "but it happens every time."

"Interesting," Father Mateo said, in a tone that actually meant *repulsive*. "The bruises around his eye look worse. Can that happen after death?"

"Not after his heart stops beating." Hiro studied the dead man's face, and agreed with the priest. The bruises did look darker. "This room is better lit than the alley. It might be an illusion."

He laid his hands on Chikao's outstretched arm. "Let's turn him over."

CHAPTER 25

"How did you learn so much about death?" Father Mateo asked as he helped the shinobi turn Chikao onto his stomach.

"A shinobi has to understand the body and how it works," Hiro said.

"Yes," the Jesuit countered, "but the skills required to kill a man aren't quite the same as the ones you use to reconstruct the death of a total stranger. I've wondered this before but never found a good time to ask. How did you learn to read a corpse so well?"

Hiro shifted his gaze to the body. "You do not want to know."

"If I didn't want to know, I wouldn't ask."

Hiro glanced at the priest. "Then I choose not to tell you."

He bent forward and touched the flattened area at the base of Chikao's skull. The fractured bone moved beneath his fingers as he palpitated the injury.

"The lower left side of his skull is shattered." Hiro withdrew his hand. "I can't tell exactly how badly, but the extent of the injury doesn't matter. This is the one that killed him. The first blow probably knocked him unconscious. It might or might not have cracked his skull. Chikao fell to the ground, and the killer struck him several times—substantially more than necessary to kill him."

"That probably rules out bandits," the Jesuit said.

Hiro nodded. "Only an angry killer does this much damage."

"Or, possibly, someone who hated him?" Father Mateo asked.

"Perhaps, but hatred tends to express itself in calculating ways." Hiro gestured toward Chikao's broken skull. "It's fury that doesn't know when to stop attacking."

"What can you tell about the weapon?" Father Mateo asked. "Could Ginjiro's stoneware flask have caused this damage?"

"The flask is a problem," Hiro said. "I can't be sure."

Father Mateo considered this. "Could the killer have known how to swing the flask in a way that prevented its breaking long enough to kill Chikao?"

"Perhaps," Hiro said. *Which looks bad for Ginjiro.*

He indicated the tear in Chikao's scalp. "Look closely. What do you see?"

Father Mateo leaned forward. "Not as much blood as I would expect from a head wound. He died before the cut occurred."

Hiro smiled. "Yes, but we already established that in the alley. This suggests another fact as well. Would you like to guess?"

Father Mateo thought for a moment and shook his head, defeated. "Nothing comes to mind, except that only a coward attacks a man from behind."

"Exactly," Hiro said. "I've seen what I needed. Let's turn him over."

"We haven't seen anything new," Father Mateo protested as he helped return Chikao's corpse to its former position.

"We confirmed the killer's rage," Hiro said, "which means the motive probably wasn't debt."

"That eliminates Yoshiko as a suspect," Father Mateo said.

"Not completely," Hiro said, "but, if Yoshiko killed Chikao, it was not because he owed her money."

As Mina walked the men to the door, she asked, "Did your examination reveal anything of interest?"

"Nothing useful," Hiro lied.

"We apologize for troubling you." Father Mateo hesitated.

Hiro recognized the earnest, hopeful look on the Jesuit's face—the expression of a man who yearned to talk about his god.

Mina noticed the priest's expression too. "I see you have something more to say. Please say it."

"Would you allow me to return and speak with you before you become a nun?" Father Mateo asked. "I would like to hear more about your faith and tell you about mine."

"I will consider it." Mina opened the door that led to the street.

Hiro admired her subtle denial. He also doubted that Father Mateo understood her words were a rejection.

"Will you open the Lucky Monkey tonight?" Father Mateo asked.

Mina shook her head. "The shop is closed, at least until after my husband's funeral. People do not drink sake under a roof that shelters the dead."

Hiro and Father Mateo left the alley and walked east toward the Kamo River. As they turned north onto the road that followed the river, Hiro appreciated the late-summer afternoon. The sun felt warm on his head and shoulders. Familiar smells from the river filled the air.

"Do not use my faith as a diversionary tactic." Father Mateo's angry voice interrupted Hiro's reverie.

"What?" It took the shinobi a moment to process the comment.

"You wanted me to tell Chikao's wife I would pray for her husband, as if my efforts could change the fate of the unsaved dead."

"I didn't do it," Hiro said.

"Only because the circumstances made your plan unnecessary." Father Mateo's voice held a warning edge the shinobi had never heard. "If Mina hadn't offered us tea, you would have done it, regardless of my opinions on the matter."

"Is your god so weak that a lie can hurt him?" Hiro asked.

"It isn't God I need to protect," Father Mateo said. "A blasphemous lie is a mortal sin. I worry about your soul."

Hiro raised an eyebrow at the priest. "Well, I suppose that one of us should."

Anger shone in Father Mateo's eyes, though he sounded calm. "I do not require you to share my faith, but if you wish to continue in my company, I expect you to refrain from shaming God—or me— in public in the future."

CHAPTER 26

The genuine anger in Father Mateo's tone left Hiro speechless. The shinobi had lied about Father Mateo's religion before, on several occasions. The priest had done it too. Hiro had trouble understanding what made this incident different.

"Lies cause no shame," Hiro said at last. "I tell them every day. You do, too, when you introduce me as 'translator Matsui Hiro.' You know that isn't my real name or function."

"Your situation is different," Father Mateo said. "Telling the truth would endanger your mission and, probably, your life. I have exactly the opposite problem. Lying about my faith endangers my soul, my honor, and also my work in Kyoto.

"You fail if you tell the truth. I fail without it."

"You have lied about your faith before," Hiro said, "and more than once."

"I have, perhaps, embellished a few noncritical points of doctrine," the Jesuit said, "but I have never denied my God or the foundational tenets of my faith. On matters of any significance I always tell the truth."

Hiro had the uncomfortable feeling that followed mistakes in judgment. Perhaps this Christian god was not so simple after all. Unquestionably, the priest was more complex than he had seemed. Three years into the friendship, Hiro still didn't know the Jesuit perfectly.

"You've said your god despises lies," the shinobi said. "You've never actually claimed he requires the truth."

"I have said it many times." Father Mateo paused in the road. "You haven't heard, because you stop listening when I speak of God."

Pressure rose in Hiro's chest at the pain in Father Mateo's

voice—a pain as sudden and as deep as the Jesuit's previous anger. But now, Hiro understood exactly what he'd done.

Sharing gods and religious customs wasn't a requisite for friendship, but a friend should not ignore the rules by which companions lived. Father Mateo never ignored Hiro's lessons on Japanese etiquette. The priest didn't always agree, but he always listened.

Hiro should have returned that favor.

He had not.

Hiro wished he could disappear, or at least go back in time and correct the error.

Unfortunately, neither was an option.

The ryu had ordered Hiro to protect the Jesuit at any cost. Right now, that cost was admitting his own mistake.

Hiro turned to face the priest.

Father Mateo stiffened, expecting an argument.

Hiro bowed as deeply as possible, then straightened and bowed a second time. "I humbly apologize," he said. "You are correct, and I am wrong. I dishonor myself, and you, by disrespecting beliefs I do not share. Please forgive me for this error. I cannot share your faith, but I won't disparage it again."

Father Mateo blinked, surprised. "You truly mean that."

Hiro straightened. "Yes, I do."

"Then I accept your apology," Father Mateo said with a bow.

Once forgiveness was asked and given, samurai considered a matter permanently resolved. Hiro had noticed, however, that Western etiquette differed from Japanese rules on many points. He waited to see if the priest would say anything more.

The two men stared at each other. Neither spoke.

Finally, Father Mateo asked, "Are apologies always this awkward in Japan?"

Hiro raised an eyebrow. "Only when made to a foreigner."

Father Mateo laughed. "I thought as much."

Hiro and Father Mateo returned to the Jesuit's home on Maru-tamachi Road. The priest went into his private room, but Hiro changed into trousers and a practice tunic and headed into the yard.

The grassy lawn south of Father Mateo's beloved koi pond offered a pleasant exercise ground, and the wooden wall surrounding the yard prevented prying eyes. Hiro knelt and meditated, quieting his thoughts and listening to every tiny sound. A bird sang in a nearby tree. Leaves ruffled in the breeze. One of the Jesuit's koi sucked at the surface of the water.

The door that led to the priest's room rustled open.

Hiro opened his eyes. Father Mateo stood on the veranda, wearing hakama and a surcoat.

The shinobi stood up, surprised. He often offered to teach the Jesuit self-defense, but the priest had never shown any real interest.

"Have you decided to learn to fight?" Hiro asked.

Father Mateo smiled. "A man who lives by the sword will die by the sword."

"Perhaps," Hiro said, "but not as quickly as a man who cannot use one."

Father Mateo raised his scar-covered hands. The injuries had not yet healed completely.

Hiro considered it lucky they healed at all.

"I couldn't fight if I wanted to," Father Mateo said. "Even writing hurts more than I'd like to admit. But physical exercise helps recovery, and I've healed enough to try, if you're willing to teach me defense instead of fighting."

Hiro decided not to mention that, often, they were the same.

He walked the priest through some basic *katas*—exercises so familiar that Hiro no longer remembered when he learned them. With time and practice, the forms became ingrained in the muscles. The body performed them essentially without thought.

After a while, Father Mateo straightened and wiped his forehead. "I thought I was in good condition, but you haven't broken a sweat."

"I did not suffer a serious injury several weeks ago," Hiro said.

"You know I can tell when you're humoring me." Father Mateo smiled.

Hiro smirked. "Only when I let you."

After they finished with katas, Hiro went to the bathhouse while the Jesuit prepared for his evening prayers. Despite his interest in Japanese culture, Father Mateo did not bathe as often as native Japanese.

The samurai guarding the bridge gave Hiro a searching look but didn't demand identification. Either the towel in Hiro's hand made his business obvious, or some of Hisahide's guards could exercise discretion after all.

When Hiro returned to the house, he found the Jesuit reading in the common room. Father Mateo's leather-bound Bible lay open to a page with a missing corner.

"The letter to the Romans?" Hiro asked.

Father Mateo looked up with a startled smile. "When did you start reading the Bible?"

Hiro smiled awkwardly at the priest's misplaced delight. "I haven't. I just recognized the page that Gato chewed."

Gato, Hiro's tortoiseshell cat, bounded in from the kitchen at the sound of her master's voice. Halfway across the room she angled sideways and arched her back. The hair on her tail puffed out on end. She fixed her eyes on Hiro and bounced to the side, inviting play.

The shinobi leaned forward and clapped his hands.

Gato leaped in the air, spun around, and raced from the room, paws pattering the tatami like rain on a rooftop.

Father Mateo laughed but stopped and stared at Hiro's gray kimono. "You don't usually dress so formally in the evening. You have plans?"

"Yes." Hiro nodded. "I'm going to Ginjiro's."

CHAPTER 27

"Is that appropriate?" Father Mateo asked, "With Ginjiro in prison?"

"Patronizing the brewery helps Ginjiro," Hiro said, "though, as it happens, I'm not drinking. I have business there tonight."

"The man Tomiko mentioned," Father Mateo said. "An Iga contact?"

Hiro smiled but said nothing.

The Jesuit took the smile as affirmation. "Please send my regards to your family." The priest looked down at his Bible. As he read, his hand crept up to rub the jagged scar that traced a crimson line from his jaw to the base of his neck.

"Does that hurt?" Hiro bent to examine the scar.

Father Mateo looked up, surprised. "No. But it itches."

"That means it's healing," Hiro said.

"Now that you mention it, my hands ache more than I think they should." Father Mateo looked at his hands as if hoping the words would dull the pain. "I think the bones have mended, but they hurt in the evening, after the sun goes down. I wouldn't complain, but you asked . . ."

"The pain is normal," Hiro said. "Your hands will ache for several months and probably every winter for several years."

If not forever, he added silently.

Father Mateo nodded. "I thought they might."

"Injuries to the hands heal slowly, and hurt, because the hands are unusually sensitive." Hiro glanced toward his room. "Would you like me to give you something to dull the pain?"

Father Mateo shook his head and rubbed the back of his hand. "If you say the pain is normal, I can bear it."

Hiro walked west on Marutamachi Road until he reached the Kamo River. There, he nodded to the samurai on guard. Once again, the guard made no attempt to arrest the shinobi's progress. Either he recognized Hiro's face or the guards had received new orders to stop harassing samurai without cause.

Hiro suspected the former. Matsunaga Hisahide didn't care who he offended.

The shinobi turned south on the road that followed the eastern bank of the river. At Sanjō Road he took a left and headed into a residential ward.

Well-groomed gardens surrounded the houses, which sat on larger lots than those on the western side of the river. A short distance down the road, on the left-hand side of the street, stone dogs guarded a two-story building. The house had a raised foundation and steep peaked roof. Long eaves overhung the wide veranda, and gravel paths led to wooden gates on either side of the building. Fences shielded the yards beyond from public view.

An expensive, hand-painted sign on the veranda read SAKURA TEAHOUSE.

The Sakura looked no different than it had a year before, when Hiro and Father Mateo solved the murder of Akechi Hideyoshi, a samurai who died in one of the private rooms. As he approached the door, Hiro wondered whether Mayuri, the teahouse owner, would respond to his questions about Yoshiko.

Knowing Mayuri, she might not even let him in.

Hiro knocked and waited to speak with the house's servant, but when the wooden door swung open, it was Mayuri who stood in the entrance.

The retired entertainer's flawless hair and makeup complemented her green kimono embroidered with lotus flowers. On another woman, the colors and patterns might suggest a struggle to retain her fading youth. On Mayuri, the years fell away of their own accord.

Hiro disliked entertainers, but understood why men once found Mayuri's company worth their silver. Despite her age, she remained a compelling woman.

Mayuri's painted face adopted a frozen smile. "Good evening, Matsui-*san*. I don't remember your name on this evening's list of guests."

Only a person trained to read faces would notice the concern that flickered through Mayuri's eyes before she spoke. Unfortunately for Mayuri, Hiro was that kind of person.

He said nothing, hoping discomfort would make her talk.

"To what do I owe this unexpected pleasure?" Mayuri asked.

"I hoped to speak with you privately," Hiro said.

Mayuri's smile faded. "Does this relate to last year's business?"

"It relates to an Akechi," Hiro said, "though not the one who brought me here last summer."

"I understand." Mayuri nodded. "Follow me."

She led him through the entry and into the room where entertainers waited for their guests. The teahouse smelled of lotuses and other strange perfumes, as if haunted by the ghosts of forgotten blooms. Shoji along the walls led into private rooms on either side. Murmuring voices and the wavering notes of a *shamisen* told Hiro some of the evening guests had arrived already.

An entertainer entered the room from a sliding door to the north. She wore a blue kimono painted with a scene of crashing waves, a patterned obi, and a hairstyle featuring several jeweled pins. Despite the costume's weight, she moved with ease and confidence. Her face looked barely twenty, though Hiro knew her real age was almost twice that number.

The entertainer crossed her hands and bowed in greeting. "Good evening Matsui-*san*. It is nice to see you."

"Good evening, Riko," Hiro said. "You look well."

The woman covered her surprise. Entertainers memorized the

names of everyone they met but didn't expect a man to return the favor—especially not a samurai who never patronized the woman's house.

"Matsui-*san* has come on a business matter," Mayuri said. "Please ask Okiya to answer the door until we finish our conversation."

Riko bowed. "I will, Mayuri."

"Do not open the door yourself." Mayuri raised a hand like a mother admonishing a willful child.

Riko blushed. "He wouldn't mind."

"I mind." Mayuri's tone allowed no argument.

"I understand." Riko bowed in acceptance and stepped aside as Mayuri led Hiro through the door in the northern wall. Beyond the waiting room lay a private *oe* and a narrow passage that led to Mayuri's office. Hiro remembered the way, and also the office. The white tatami and hardwood writing desk looked just as he remembered.

Mayuri slid the shoji closed behind them, crossed the room, and knelt on the opposite side of the wooden desk.

Hiro didn't like to turn his back on the only entrance, but etiquette didn't give him another option. He knelt facing Mayuri but angled his body just enough to see the doorway from the corner of his eye.

To his surprise, Mayuri didn't wait for him to speak.

"Forgive my presumption," she said, "but I have a busy evening, and we are well enough acquainted to dispense with needless formalities. Whatever you have to say about Yoshiko, please speak plainly."

"I understand that Akechi-*san* has acquired an interest in this house and serves as its debt collector," Hiro said.

"That is neither a question nor a complaint," Mayuri said.

"Very well," Hiro said. "A question: Do you know where Yoshiko was last night?"

"You speak as though her whereabouts are my concern," Mayuri said. "She is a business partner, not a servant."

"Yes," Hiro said, "but the law holds you responsible for crimes she commits in the course of collecting your debts."

"Have you left your job as a translator and joined the Kyoto police?" Mayuri's eyes widened in a show of false surprise. "If not, I believe you realize I have no obligation to endure this conversation any longer."

Hiro recognized the bluff. Mayuri would not have allowed him in if she didn't intend to talk—at least until she discovered what he knew.

"My authority arises from a private investigation," Hiro said. "But if you would rather answer to the yoriki, I can arrange that also."

Mayuri's face looked carved from stone, like the dogs that guarded her walkway.

Hiro gave her a moment to consider the threat and then continued, "Given your involvement in General Akechi's murder, the yoriki might prefer to take a detailed look at your establishment."

Mayuri said nothing.

Most samurai would have repeated the threat, or followed up with a stronger one, but Hiro simply waited. Eventually, his silence and Mayuri's fears—or guilt—would prompt an answer.

"I cannot tell you what Yoshiko may have done," the teahouse owner said at last, "but I do not condone violence. Not even in debt collection."

"Interesting," Hiro said. "I didn't mention violence."

CHAPTER 28

"What have you heard about Yoshiko's collection tactics?" Hiro asked Mayuri.

"Lies and rumors, nothing more." The teahouse owner waved her hand as if to dismiss the topic. "No man likes an aggressive woman, and some would rather make up lies than pay an honest debt. Wise people put no trust in debtors' words."

"Did you see Yoshiko last night?" Hiro asked.

"Briefly," Mayuri said. "I didn't speak with her myself. I had a meeting with the owner of the house across the road. You may have seen the ugly lanterns he installed a week ago."

"I didn't notice," Hiro said.

"Clumsy carving, poorly finished . . . a disgrace to a high-class street." Mayuri sniffed. "But you asked about Yoshiko. As far as I know, she picked up a list of debtors and left immediately."

"A long list?" Hiro didn't ask for names. A teahouse owner never revealed her customers' identities.

Not voluntarily, anyway.

"No." Mayuri's lips pressed into a narrow smile. "Most of our visitors pay quite promptly since Yoshiko started work."

"Do you welcome your debtors as visitors, then?" Hiro asked.

Mayuri's smile vanished. "I will not disclose information about my patrons."

"Not to me, perhaps," Hiro said. "You may feel differently standing before the magistrate."

Mayuri matched the shinobi's gaze with intensity, but as the seconds passed her expression wavered.

"I will not reveal my patrons' names," she repeated at last, "but men who refuse to pay their debts will find no welcome here."

Hiro lowered his voice. "I need to know if Yoshiko's list included a man named Kaoru."

Mayuri straightened. "You know I will not answer that. However, I have heard that name, and the man it belongs to is not welcome here."

She spoke with a finality that indicated the end of the conversation.

Hiro stood. "Thank you for your time."

Mayuri's forehead furrowed, sending shadowed lines across her features. "What has happened to the man of whom you speak?"

"To Kaoru? Nothing." Hiro paused in the doorway. "His father is dead."

"And you think Yoshiko killed him." Mayuri narrowed her eyes. "You believe it, without evidence, because she dares to call her life her own."

"On the contrary," Hiro said, "I have no objection to independent women. I do, however, take offense when the guilty blame the innocent. I will find this killer, as I did in General Akechi's case, and if the trail leads back here, I promise, you will not escape unscathed."

"You may leave," Mayuri said. "Our talk is over."

"At last, we agree." Hiro slid open the shoji. "There is no need to escort me out. I know the way."

Hiro headed for the river, regretting his decision to see Mayuri. The teahouse owner essentially confirmed that Kaoru owed her money, but her words had offered little else of note. Worse, Hiro hadn't found an opening to ask what Mayuri knew about Yoshiko's other employers, and he doubted he would have a second chance.

As he reached the Kamo River, Hiro saw a samurai approaching. He slowed, loathing the thought of another confrontation with Matsunaga Hisahide's obnoxious guards.

A lantern lit the samurai's features, revealing not a guard but Akechi Yoshiko.

She wore a masculine blue kimono and an obi of smoky silk. Her wakizashi hung from her sash and a long katana stretched upward behind her back. The longsword waggled when she walked like the tail of a happy dog.

Or a she-wolf, Hiro thought.

Yoshiko bowed. "Good evening, Matsui-*san*. Or, perhaps, I may call you Hiro?"

Hiro returned the bow. "Good evening, Yoshiko."

His use of her given name gave her permission to use his also; Hiro saw no way to refuse without causing offense.

"This is a pleasant surprise." She looked past Hiro up the street. "Are you coming from the Sakura?"

"Yes. I was looking for you." Hiro smiled to cover the lie. He doubted the woman could see his features well in the gathering darkness but knew the smile would carry into his tone.

"For me?" Yoshiko's voice revealed delight.

Hiro swallowed his distaste and smiled more broadly. "I hoped you would help me."

"Of course I will. I can walk with you, and you can explain on the way." Yoshiko inclined her head toward Hiro as she spoke. Most of the time, the shinobi thought that particular feminine gesture unduly subservient. On Yoshiko, it looked absurd.

"No need," Hiro said. "I do not want to interrupt your errand."

"Please, it would be my pleasure." She turned and stood at Hiro's side.

He accepted the inevitable and started across the bridge.

"Where are we going?" Yoshiko asked.

"Ginjiro's sake brewery."

"Ginjiro brews the best in Kyoto," Yoshiko said. "As it happens, I need to visit there myself. Ginjiro's daughter, Tomiko, asked to speak with me this evening. I intended to see her later, but this works just as well. Better, really, because I can walk with you."

She lowered her face as if embarrassed, but the light of a passing lantern lit the smile that touched her lips.

For the second time that day, Hiro wished he could disappear.

CHAPTER 29

Yoshiko matched Hiro stride for stride, with a confident pace that belied her awkward attempts at femininity.

He noticed her stealing sidelong glances at him as they walked. He wondered—not for the first time—what he'd done to encourage her affections. Their previous interactions, shortly after her father's murder, were not the sort that usually sparked romantic feelings.

He remembered telling Mayuri that he didn't mind an independent woman. That was true. Hiro preferred aggressive women to wilting flowers. Even so, something about Yoshiko put him off.

He had barely finished the thought when Yoshiko asked, "Have you made any progress with your murder investigation? I would gladly offer assistance, if I may."

Hiro expanded his earlier lie to encompass a partial truth. "I am glad you decided to see Tomiko. She and her mother need someone to guard the brewery during the evening hours, at least until Ginjiro returns from prison. I believe she intended to ask you, though I do not want to presume."

"I'm sure she won't mind your asking," Yoshiko said. "I know I don't."

Only Hiro's years of training kept his expression neutral.

"I know what it is like to lose a father," she continued. "I would be honored to help Tomiko, doubly so because the work helps you as well."

"Guarding the brewery won't take too much time from your other duties?" Hiro asked.

"No." She shook her head. "Last night alone I collected two debts—and made arrangements for a third—and finished them all two hours before the temple bells rang midnight."

"How fortunate," Hiro said. "I'm sure your mother was glad you came home early."

As they passed by Pontochō, a ripple of feminine laughter fluttered toward them on the air. Yoshiko turned. Hiro followed her gaze.

Dozens of colorful paper lanterns lit the alley that held the entertainment district. More lights blazed in the teahouse windows, flickering gaily behind the paper panels.

Samurai thronged the street, their darker tones offsetting the brilliance of the painted entertainers whose silk kimono shimmered with every imaginable hue. *Kanzashi* sparkled in the ladies' hair, but stark white makeup turned their faces into phantoms.

Fitting, the shinobi thought, an entertainer's love has all the substance of a ghost.

"I did not go home." Yoshiko's voice jarred Hiro back to the moment.

He gave the samurai woman a curious look.

"When I finished collecting debts," Yoshiko said. "I did not go home. I returned to the Sakura and guarded the teahouse until the last of the guests departed."

Yoshiko's story contradicted the one Mayuri told, which meant that one—or both—of the women lied.

For the moment, Hiro let the story pass. "I've considered taking on extra work as a debt collector. Do you find the jobs unpleasant or hard to find?"

"Not particularly." Yoshiko glanced over her shoulder as another stream of laughter echoed out of Pontochō. "Most of my work, of course, is for the Sakura."

"But you work for other clients too?" Hiro asked.

"On occasion." Yoshiko seemed more comfortable with this topic than with flirting. "Once you build a reputation, work finds you."

"Do you work for samurai, or just for merchants?" To his surprise, Hiro found himself truly interested in her answer.

"I do not call on samurai, for work or for debt collection."

Yoshiko spoke firmly, but without anger. "Samurai suffer embarrassment if a debt collector appears at their homes, and, as you know, it violates the law for samurai to engage in business."

Hiro nodded. "A law you honor in the breach."

Yoshiko smiled, this one genuine rather than simpering. "True enough, and, as you know, I'm not the only one. In truth, I do not think our kind would tolerate a female debt collector. Not all men share your willingness to overlook my choices."

Hiro smiled. *I wish that you would overlook me in return.*

Just before the pause grew awkward, Yoshiko continued, "Collecting from merchants is easy. Take last night, for example. The men I sought are known in Pontochō. I found them quickly—"

"In Pontochō?" Hiro asked. "You collect in the pleasure district?"

"Why not?" Yoshiko asked. "Men don't forego entertainment just because they owe a debt."

"Why confront them in Pontochō and not at home?" the shinobi asked.

Yoshiko's smile grew more confident and decidedly less feminine. "Men pay more quickly in public places. Wives get angry for a night. Teahouse owners have much longer memories."

They turned onto the road that led to Ginjiro's. People thronged the narrow street despite the evening hour. Vendors' braziers filled the air with the scented sizzle of grilling meat.

Hiro still had not confirmed whether Yoshiko tried to collect a debt from Kaoru or Chikao the night before. He had time for one more try. "You said you collected two debts, but not a third? What happened there?"

She shrugged. "I couldn't find the debtor. Not a total failure, though. His father agreed to pay."

"You asked the father?" Hiro feigned surprise. "Is that permitted?"

"The law holds a man responsible for the debts of every person under his roof," Yoshiko said. "The debtor lives with his parents, so I had the legal right to approach the father."

Ginjiro's brewery lay two shops away.

"You asked him," Hiro said, "or you demanded that Chikao pay?"

Yoshiko startled but recovered quickly. "Why did you use that name?"

"You know as well as I do why I used it," Hiro said.

She stopped and stared at Hiro coldly. "You mean, did I threaten him. I didn't have to threaten. Chikao offered to pay the debt to keep his son out of prison." She leaned toward Hiro and spoke more slowly. "And to be clear, before you ask, I didn't kill Chikao."

She turned away and walked off toward Ginjiro's.

Welcoming light streamed from the brewery storefront. Just inside, a group of merchants sat on the pale tatami. A samurai in a dark kimono huddled near the honey-colored counter. He had his back to the street, but his posture indicated tension.

Tomiko stood behind the counter. She seemed nervous, too, but her gestures looked too calm for real trouble.

Hiro didn't trust Yoshiko's words but couldn't risk her anger either. Not until he knew the reason for her sudden change in attitude.

"Wait," he called.

Yoshiko stopped and turned.

"How could you believe that I suspected you of murder?" Hiro walked to meet the female samurai.

She took a step back toward him. "How could I think it? What else should I think your accusation meant?"

"Accusation?" Hiro feigned surprise and then embarrassment. "I'm sorry . . . I never intended . . . I asked the question to clear you of suspicion. I needed to hear you say the words, to establish them as fact. You, of all people, could not commit this murder."

"I—of all people—could not kill?" Yoshiko's fury grew. "You don't believe I could take a person's life?"

Hiro hated when women asked a question that had no decent answer. But, usually, these no-win questions involved a clothing choice or beauty, not a murderous intent. He considered his answer carefully but quickly.

He knew from experience, masculine pauses only made the situation worse.

CHAPTER 30

"Not without cause." Hiro infused his voice with unfelt warmth. "Not over money. I know you better than that, Yoshiko. You wouldn't stoop to such an act."

A flush rose in the samurai woman's cheeks, but not from anger.

Hiro startled as someone grabbed his arm. He turned, fist cocked, but relaxed when he recognized Suke at his side.

"Do not grab me," Hiro said. "I almost hurt you."

A smile lit Suke's face. "You wouldn't hit me, Hiro-*san*. I need your help."

"Just a moment," Hiro said.

"I need you now," Suke insisted. "Urgent business."

Yoshiko gave Hiro the smile a woman gives her husband when their children play at mischief. "Please, do not make him wait on my account. I apologize for misunderstanding your intent. I was not aware you knew my heart so well."

Hiro gave her a smile that he remembered from the days when he actually cared to understand a woman's heart. From the look in Yoshiko's eyes, he faked the feeling well.

"Please excuse me," Yoshiko said with a dip of her head and a genuine smile. "We can continue our conversation later. I don't know any more about the matter you mentioned, but I will gladly help you investigate if I can."

Yoshiko knelt up onto the brewery floor.

The samurai at the counter stood up and turned to leave. His eyes widened at the sight of Yoshiko approaching. As soon as Tomiko returned his sword, the samurai hurried out of the brewery and scurried into the night. Hiro wondered whether the man thought Yoshiko frightening on her own account or whether he owed a debt and was afraid she had come to collect it.

Suke tugged on Hiro's sleeve and dragged the shinobi toward the alley. Hiro lengthened his steps to keep the pace. He didn't want his kimono torn, and Suke's grip seemed strangely tight for a man of advancing age and drunken tendencies.

When they reached the relative privacy of the alley, Hiro asked, "What's going on?"

In the dim light, Hiro saw the whites of Suke's eyes grow large. "I found important evidence—of the crime!"

The monk peered around the shinobi, as if to see that no one followed them from the street. Satisfied, he leaned toward Hiro and whispered, "The woman you arrived with is a debt collector. She beats up men who do not pay. Chikao was beaten to death—I think she did it!"

"You think so?" Hiro asked.

"That's why I rescued you," Suke said, "before she could attack you too."

"She might attack me," Hiro said, "but not the way you're thinking."

Suke tilted his head in confusion. "What?"

"Never mind," Hiro said. "The fact that Chikao was beaten to death does not mean Yoshiko killed him. We have to connect the killer with the crime."

"But how?" Suke asked.

"With evidence," Hiro said. "Facts that put the killer in this alley at the time Chikao died."

Suke frowned. "I think she did it. I will keep an eye on her and find the evidence we need."

"Be careful," Hiro warned. "A suspicious killer hides his tracks."

"Don't worry." Suke nodded. "I am sneaky. She won't even know I'm watching."

Hiro doubted Suke's form of stealth could fool a child. "Good. Remember, the less you watch, the better."

"I did well, though, figuring out she's a debt collector?" Suke looked anxious.

Hiro smiled. "Yes, you did. That's very helpful."

"Good enough, perhaps, to merit payment?" Suke asked.

Hiro grinned at the monk's transparency. "Of course. A flask of sake?"

They left the alley as Yoshiko stepped out of the brewery and tucked a stoppered flask in her kimono. Hiro only saw the flask for a moment, but its color and lacquered surface indicated it hadn't come from Ginjiro's stock.

"Is that a wooden flask?" he asked.

Yoshiko frowned. "I can afford a stoneware one. I carry the wooden type by choice. It doesn't break as easily."

And, also, makes a better weapon, Hiro thought.

She gave the shinobi an awkward smile. "Speaking of which, you were correct. Starting tomorrow, after dinner, I will guard the brewery until Ginjiro . . . well, until the magistrate hears his case."

Before Hiro could reply, a voice behind him said, "Good evening, Matsui-*san.*"

He turned to see a commoner, a man in his early forties with wiry, muscled arms and a slender build. The man wore the clothes of a carpenter, and his cropped hair glittered with silver that he didn't bother to hide with colored oils.

Hiro nodded in recognition. "Good evening, Master Carpenter Ozuru."

He used the man's official title, though Hiro knew this carpenter was more than he appeared.

Ozuru's gaze shifted to Yoshiko. He bowed. "Good evening."

Hiro noted the omission of gender-specific honorifics. Ozuru knew better than to offend by choosing poorly.

"Good evening," Yoshiko said. "I will not delay you further, Hiro. I look forward to seeing you at dinner tomorrow night."

A slow smile crept over Ozuru's face as he watched Yoshiko stroll away. He turned to Hiro. "Charming woman."

Hiro didn't return the smile. "You might think differently if you knew her well."

"I'll trust your judgment." Ozuru glanced at the brewery. "We need to talk. Not here."

"I need a minute." Hiro caught Tomiko's eye, withdrew a coin from his kimono, and held it high. "Give Suke a drink, and see that he eats tonight?"

Tomiko nodded.

Hiro handed the coin to a customer at the near end of the counter. The man put the silver into Tomiko's hand.

Suke gave Hiro a one-toothed grin as he climbed into the brewery. "A thousand blessings on you, Hiro-*san*. The *kami* will remember your generosity forever."

Hiro faced Ozuru. "Shall we walk?"

The shinobi matched the carpenter's rapid pace through the crowded streets. Neither spoke, though Hiro didn't wonder why. Ozuru clearly intended his message for Hiro's ears alone.

The men had met two months before, when Hiro investigated the death of a ranking shogunate clerk. The carpenter—a shinobi from the rival Koga ryu—was neither Hiro's ally nor his enemy. As a result, Hiro followed Ozuru with a mixture of curiosity and caution.

When they reached the Kamo River, Ozuru turned south as if to follow the path along the riverbank. Hiro turned the other way and headed north.

Ozuru paused, then altered course and fell in step at Hiro's side. Hiro relaxed a fraction. Compliance with a change in plan suggested Ozuru didn't intend an ambush.

As they walked along the river, Ozuru said, "Your actions have enraged the shogun. Matsunaga Hisahide wants to know what made you break your word."

"Matsunaga Hisahide is not the shogun," Hiro said. "More importantly, what promise have I broken?"

"You know which promise," Ozuru said. "Luis Álvares, the Portuguese merchant who shares a house with your Jesuit friend, has sold a shipment of firearms to the Miyoshi. You promised Hisahide you would prevent this."

Hiro remembered his promise, and the circumstances surrounding it, with clarity. He made the bargain with Matsunaga Hisahide on the night the shogun died. The promise saved at least two lives, one of them Father Mateo's.

"That wasn't the agreement," Hiro said. "I promised Luis wouldn't sell to Lord Oda. The deal did not include the Miyoshi clan."

Ozuru gave Hiro a sideways look. "Shogun Matsunaga has changed the deal."

"Matsunaga-*san* is not the shogun," Hiro repeated. "The Ashikaga clan retains the shogunate."

"For now." Ozuru paused. "You know as well as I do that the Ashikaga heir is still an infant. You also know how easily a child can meet an accident."

"Especially with men like Matsunaga-*san* around." Hiro changed the subject. "Why does he object to the Miyoshi buying firearms? The last I heard, he swore allegiance to their clan."

"Not anymore," Ozuru said. "Matsunaga-*san* broke his oath and declared his intent to keep Kyoto, and the shogunate, for himself. Daimyō Miyoshi did not take this news well."

Hiro understood. "The Miyoshi want the foreign firearms to start a war."

Ozuru paused beneath a tree. "This sale will have unpleasant consequences, for the city, for the merchant, and for the Jesuit you guard. Do not deny your function. I know a hired guardian when I see one."

"This does not concern the priest," Hiro said. "Luis is a merchant. He sells to whomever he wishes—with the admitted exception of Lord Oda. You tell Matsunaga-*san* I reject his expansion of our agreement and will not tolerate threats to the foreign priest."

Ozuru lowered his voice. "You fail to understand. Matsunaga Hisahide did not send me here. I came to warn you—brother to brother—a dangerous wind is blowing."

"Perhaps," Hiro said, "but the Portuguese merchant is not a kite. He does not have to obey prevailing winds."

"You must see that he does," Ozuru said, "or the coming storm will tear the merchant and the priest to shreds."

Hiro said nothing.

"Heed my warning," Ozuru hissed. "You may not get another."

CHAPTER 31

Hiro returned to the Jesuit's home. As he opened the door, he inhaled the tantalizing aroma of grilling fish. His stomach rumbled. The afternoon's noodles seemed a distant memory.

He hoped that Ana had cooked enough and that Luis and Father Mateo hadn't eaten it all already.

Father Mateo knelt beside the common room hearth with a half-empty dinner tray before him. Gato sat to the Jesuit's right, staring at the priest. The cat's ears swiveled as Hiro entered, but she didn't take her eyes off Father Mateo.

The Jesuit studied his bowl intently.

Gato studied the priest.

Hiro grinned. "Tasty fish?"

Father Mateo looked up. "You should have some. It's delicious. Have you already finished your business at Ginjiro's?"

Gato caught the shinobi's eye and gave a plaintive mew.

"She is not hungry," the Jesuit said. "Ana fed her less than an hour ago."

"Apparently, she's not happy with innards and tails," Hiro said.

Ana, the housekeeper, bustled into the room. "Hm," she said indignantly. "As if I'd force this dear to eat the scraps!"

She scooped the cat into her arms. Gato purred.

Ana glared at Hiro. "She had a fish of her very own."

"You bought a fish for the cat?" Hiro asked.

Gato's purr crescendoed as she kneaded her paws in Ana's kimono sleeve.

"I didn't have to," Ana said. "The fishmonger found a little fish in a bigger fish's belly. Not fit for a person, but Gato didn't mind."

A shoji on the eastern side of the room slid open, revealing a sleepy-looking Portuguese man with a bearded chin and a rounded belly.

"That cat eats better than me," he grumbled.

Luis Álvares wore a lace-necked doublet in an uncomplimentary shade of purple. Dark brown leggings stretched over his meaty thighs. Together, the garments put Hiro in mind of a lace-crowned plum swollen far too large for its twig.

"Good evening, Luis." Father Mateo gestured toward the hearth. "Would you like to eat?"

"That depends," the merchant said. "Is there any the cat hasn't licked?"

Ana smiled, but her eyes revealed displeasure. "Of course, Luis-san. I saved you the best of the fish."

Hiro wondered whether the merchant knew that, to Japanese, the head was the choicest morsel. He doubted it, almost as much as he doubted Ana would really save that part for Luis. The housekeeper disapproved of the merchant only slightly less than she did of Hiro.

"Fetch it." Luis thumped his ample rear to the floor and crossed his legs.

Despite having watched the merchant sit this way for several years, Hiro didn't understand why Luis preferred such an ugly and awkward position. Then again, the merchant favored habit over comfort.

In Hiro's experience, difficult people often did.

Ana bowed and carried Gato from the room.

"Luis," Hiro said, "I hear the Miyoshi placed a weapons order."

He didn't bother with subtlety. The merchant had no manners and didn't care about Japanese etiquette anyway.

Father Mateo gave Hiro a curious look. The shinobi met the Jesuit's eyes and shook his head a fraction. The priest appeared to get the message. At least, he didn't ask any questions.

"You heard correctly." Luis swelled with pride. "The largest single order I've had since arriving in Japan. Two thousand arquebuses now, and more if they like the first ones."

"Two thousand?" Father Mateo asked. "Have the Miyoshi gone to war?"

"Not my business." Luis shrugged. "I'll make a nice profit from it, war or no."

The Portuguese merchant rubbed his tiny beard. "But, if I can find out who they're fighting with, perhaps I could double the order."

"Two thousand firearms means hundreds, or thousands, of people dead." Father Mateo set down his chopsticks. "Doubling that means twice as many graves."

"You can't have it both ways, Mateo," Luis chided. "You know these sales support your work. Without them, you'd be sailing home tomorrow."

"The necessity of an income does not mean I support a war," the Jesuit said.

"You're overreacting, Mateo," Luis said. "This isn't any different from other sales."

"The others you sold for self-defense," Father Mateo said. "Daimyō and samurai lords protecting their castles. It is different when men seek to start a war."

"Tell yourself whatever you like, if it helps you sleep at night," Luis said. "War or not, these Japanese squabbles are none of our concern."

"The lives of the Japanese people are precisely my concern." Father Mateo leaned forward, preparing to stand.

"I agree with Father Mateo," Hiro said. "Sell firearms to the shogunate or samurai nobles in and around Kyoto. Those sales will generate sufficient wealth. Do not choose to facilitate a slaughter."

Luis frowned. "You agree . . . with him? Where did you find a conscience?"

Hiro looked down at Luis. "No daimyō needs two thousand foreign firearms. No one in Japan controls so many."

"Since when do you object to violence? I expect that sort of talk from him"—the merchant gestured to the priest—"but not from a samurai."

"Self-preservation is not the same as objection," Hiro said. "The Miyoshi want those weapons to seize Kyoto and the shogunate."

"Nonsense," Luis said. "Their man's already on the shogun's throne."

"Matsunaga Hisahide is not the shogun," Hiro said. "And also, the shogun doesn't sit on a throne."

"Hisahide's in control," Luis retorted. "That's what counts."

"Hisahide no longer answers to the Miyoshi," Hiro said. "He breached his oath. That is why the Miyoshi march to war."

"When did you hear this?" Father Mateo's voice revealed alarm.

Hiro shifted his gaze to the priest. "Earlier this evening, at Ginjiro's."

"So?" Luis shrugged. "Who cares if they fight? A war just means more profits for us all."

CHAPTER 32

"You do not understand." Hiro glared at the merchant. "Matsunaga-*san* will consider you a traitor for selling firearms to his enemies."

"Lord Matsunaga doesn't even know me," Luis said. "I'm Portuguese. I'm not his subject. I've permission to do business in Kyoto, and that means I'll sell my weapons to whatever lord I please."

"You prove yourself both foolish and shortsighted," Hiro said. "If you anger the acting shogun, you will put us all in danger."

Ana returned with a tray of food, which she set in front of Luis.

The merchant surveyed the roasted fish and heaping bowl of rice with hungry eyes. "I appreciate your opinion, Hiro, but if you've finished foretelling my doom, I'd like to eat in peace."

The following morning, Hiro woke before dawn and spent an hour in meditation, though not the inward-style reflection Buddhists favored. Instead, he stilled his thoughts and focused on the scents and sounds around him, sharpening his ability to "see" without his eyes.

A croak and a splash near the koi pond indicated a leaping frog. In the trees, a bird chirped sleepily. She set the nest to crackling as she stirred.

A breeze filled Hiro's nostrils with the scents of grass and dew. A hint of sewage followed, as the nightsoil collector passed the house on his morning rounds.

Hiro opened his eyes, returned to the house, and donned his favorite gray kimono and his swords.

When he left his room, he found Father Mateo waiting in the common room. The priest wore a brown kimono fastened at the waist with a dark blue obi. A wooden cross hung from a braided thong around his neck. The pale light from the firepit highlighted the jagged scar on his neck.

"Good morning," Hiro said.

Father Mateo nodded. "Shall we eat before we leave?"

"I'd rather have noodles." Hiro paused. "Wait . . . you're coming with me?"

"I am," the priest replied, "and do not argue. I spent most of our last investigation recovering from that attack. I've no intention of missing this one too."

Hiro nodded. The interviews he had in mind would go more smoothly with the Jesuit along to ask the awkward questions.

"Did you learn any new information yesterday evening?" Father Mateo asked. "Aside from Daimyō Miyoshi's plans to start a war?"

"Not much," Hiro said. "I'm confident that Kaoru owed the Sakura Teahouse money, but I still don't know if Ginjiro hired a guard or how Yoshiko learned about Chikao's death."

"So we haven't eliminated anyone," Father Mateo said.

"Not yet."

They left the house and headed west on Marutamachi Road. The air felt muggy and far too warm for Hiro's taste. He thought wistfully of autumn's colder nights and cleaner air.

As he passed Okazaki Shrine, Hiro shifted to taking shallow breaths. In the mornings, braziers just outside the shrine emitted clouds of cloying incense, and the smoke clogged Hiro's lungs like lacquer vapor.

Father Mateo nodded to the priestess selling amulets beside the temple's tall *torii* gate. She returned the nod and also smiled.

Father Mateo turned to Hiro. "Where are we headed first?"

Hiro briefly related his conversation with Mayuri and the relevant parts of his talk with Yoshiko.

"Almost everyone on our suspect list spent time in Pontochō

that night." Father Mateo counted off names on his fingers. "Kaoru, Yoshiko . . . well, I guess Bashō is not a suspect."

"He might be," Hiro said. "I'd like to know more about what he did there, anyway. But before we head to Pontochō, I have a few more questions for Tomiko."

CHAPTER 33

Tomiko stood in front of Ginjiro's, sweeping the street with a wooden broom. The merchants along the street took pride in keeping their storefronts clean.

Ginjiro's daughter looked up as Hiro and Father Mateo approached. She stilled her broom and bowed. "Good morning, Matsui-*san* and Father-*san*."

"Good morning," Hiro said. "Have you seen your father?"

"I took him food this morning," Tomiko said. "He seemed well. At least, as well as any man could seem, in prison."

Father Mateo looked confused. "The guards allowed you to take him food?"

"How else would a prisoner eat?" Hiro asked.

"In Portugal, the prison feeds them."

Hiro stared at Father Mateo and tried to imagine a prison where the guards gave the prisoners food. "Who pays for the meals?"

"The people do," the Jesuit said. "The taxes we pay to the king are used, in part, to pay for prisons."

"Why should law-abiding people have to pay for feeding criminals?" Hiro asked. "Let the prisoners' families care for their own—or not, as they may choose."

Before the priest could initiate an argument about the proper treatment of prisoners, Hiro turned to Tomiko and said, "We need more information about Kaoru."

"Kaoru?" Tomiko repeated. "Why ask me?"

"He owed your father money, so he must have spent some time here," Hiro said.

Tomiko raised her shoulders in what might have been a shrug. "My father always sent me out of the shop when Kaoru came. And

yes, before you ask, he had a reason. Kaoru made . . . comments . . .
some of them about me."

"Why didn't Ginjiro throw him out of the shop?" Father Mateo
asked.

"He did, on at least two occasions," Tomiko said, "but he
decided not to ban Kaoru permanently, at least for now. You see, my
father wanted to help Chikao and Ren. The za would never admit a
man whose son was banned from entering a brewery. Father didn't
want to hurt Chikao by making an issue of Kaoru's conduct."

"Instead, he made you leave," Hiro said. "I take it Kaoru's comments went beyond a compliment on your appearance?"

Tomiko looked down at her broom and didn't answer.

"You don't have to tell us," Father Mateo said.

Hiro frowned at the Jesuit. They needed the woman to talk.

Tomiko's cheeks flushed pink as she raised her face. "It happened only once, when he was drunk. Kaoru grabbed my wrist. He
wouldn't let go. He said . . ."

Her words trailed off into embarrassed silence.

Hiro didn't think Tomiko would complete the thought, but
after a moment she drew a breath and continued, "He said, 'When
you're my wife, I'll know how you feel inside as well as out.'"

Tomiko met Hiro's eyes with an unusual resolve. Few women,
aside from prostitutes, could have said such words at all, let alone
to an audience of males. The words made Hiro marvel that Ginjiro
hadn't been arrested sooner.

Father Mateo shifted the subject slightly. "Did your father want
you to marry Kaoru?"

"My father would never force me into such a disgraceful match."
Indignation flared beneath Tomiko's civil tone.

"Then what made Kaoru think he could marry you?" the Jesuit
asked.

"I can't imagine," Tomiko said. "My father never encouraged
him and never discussed the matter with Chikao. I assure you, my
father would never consider such a thing."

"Could someone else have given Kaoru that idea?" Father Mateo asked. "Chikao, perhaps?"

Hiro wondered what made the priest believe Chikao would consider such a union possible. By all accounts, the brewer knew his son a worthless match.

"Anything is possible," Tomiko said, "but no one mentioned marriage to me, and my father knows my views on the topic."

Tomiko's tone confirmed what Hiro had long suspected: Ginjiro's daughter did not intend to marry. Though rare, some artisans' daughters did inherit shops as sole proprietors—a lonely life, but not a bad one in its way. Either that, or she intended to delay her marriage while her parents lived, to ensure Ginjiro and her mother always had her help.

"Chikao would want his son to marry," Father Mateo said, "especially if he found a wife with business sense and skills to run a brewery."

"Perhaps," Tomiko said, "but I suspect Chikao knew better than to cast me in that role. He understood the nature of his son."

Hiro admired her restraint and changed the subject. "What made your father want to help Chikao join the guild?"

Tomiko bit her lower lip in thought. "He never told me, and I never asked. Helping people is my father's way."

"Did Chikao ask for help, or did Ginjiro make the initial offer?" Father Mateo asked.

Hiro glanced at the Jesuit, surprised the priest had thought to ask the question.

"It was Ren who first approached us," Tomiko said.

"Chikao's business partner?" Hiro asked.

Tomiko nodded. "Father met him at the New Year's Festival this year. Ren said he wanted to join the guild, and Father agreed to help. I think he felt sorry for Ren—as he would for any working man who didn't possess a wife or a growing business."

"Indeed," Hiro said. "Do you know Ren?"

"Not to speak of." Tomiko shook her head. "My father

introduced him once, but I only really know what my father told me, which isn't much."

Hiro thought of the night Chikao died. "Did you hear the fight between your father and Chikao? I know he sent you out of the shop, but voices sometimes carry through the walls."

And women sometimes listen behind the noren.

Tomiko blushed, understanding the implication. "Arguments upset my mother—she lives in fear of angry ghosts, and shouting also frightens her. She has many fears these days, all unfounded but very real.

"When Father told me to leave the shop, I understood that Kaoru might cause trouble. I took Mother upstairs, made her tea, and sat with her until she fell asleep. No, I didn't hear a thing that night."

"What time did your father come upstairs?" Hiro asked.

"I don't know exactly. Late. He closed the shop and locked the shutters. Then he came upstairs." She thought for a moment. "I don't remember if I heard the temple bells.

"I asked him what happened with Chikao. He told me not to worry. But he did say something strange. He said to wake him if I heard a noise of any kind."

"Did you ask him what he meant?" Hiro asked.

"I did." Tomiko gripped her broom. "He told me it was nothing. At the time, I trusted him. Now I wish I hadn't."

CHAPTER 34

Hiro asked Tomiko, "Did your father go downstairs again that night?"

Ginjiro's daughter didn't answer.

"I need the truth," he said.

Tomiko nodded. "I woke and heard his footsteps on the stairs."

"Did you follow?" Hiro asked.

"Why would I?" Tomiko shifted her broom from one hand to the other. "Father often had trouble sleeping. When he did, he went downstairs to keep from waking Mother. I didn't follow, but I wish I had. I might have saved him."

"Saved your father or Chikao?" the Jesuit asked.

"Maybe both." Tomiko shook her head. "I mean, if I had followed, perhaps I could prove my father didn't do this."

Hiro and Father Mateo said farewell to Tomiko and headed for Pontochō. As they approached the narrow alley, Hiro considered how different the pleasure district looked in daylight hours. At night the district blazed with colored lights and shimmering silk, a vibrant dream made touchable and real. In the morning, passion faded into scents of human waste and old perfume.

A block down the alley, Hiro saw a tiny, handmade sign beside a doorway. Smoky grime obscured the writing, but the faded letters read THE GOLDEN BUDDHA.

A portly, smiling statue sat cross-legged on the stones beneath the sign. The hands of countless visitors had worn away the bronze atop the figure's rounded head, leaving Buddha with a crown of brownish-gray.

"This doesn't look much like a teahouse." Father Mateo gestured toward the Buddha.

"Not much of a teahouse, anyway," Hiro agreed.

The businesses of Pontochō displayed as much variety in wealth and reputation as the men who frequented the pleasure district. High-end houses catered to samurai and wealthy merchants. Places like the Golden Buddha served a poorer class.

Hiro stepped to the teahouse door and knocked.

The door swung open immediately, revealing a girl of eight or nine. She wore a blue kimono with a red and white striped obi. Her hair fell down her back in a long, thin braid.

Her eyes grew wide at the sight of Hiro's swords. Without a word, she dropped to her knees and bowed her forehead to the ground.

"We wish to see your mistress," Hiro said.

The girl stood up, bowed, and disappeared into the house without a word.

She left the door ajar.

Hiro thought about entering, but changed his mind when he caught a whiff of the air inside. It reeked of male sweat and stale sake, with an undercurrent of greasy food that hadn't been good when warm.

He took a step backward, seeking the slightly fresher air of the street.

Footsteps approached, and a middle-aged woman appeared in the doorway. The tired wrinkles around her eyes suggested a life of hardship that her callused hands confirmed. She wore her graying hair pulled back in a tidy bun, and her blue kimono showed faded spots where cleaning removed the dye along with the stains.

She bowed to the samurai and the priest. "Good morning. My name is Eba. I own this establishment. How may I help you?"

Hiro noted her lack of surprise at the sight of a foreigner on her doorstep. Then again, in a place like this, she'd probably seen quite few surprising things.

"Good morning," Hiro said. "We have come on official business."

"At this hour? I'd imagine so." Eba didn't sound hostile, but she didn't seem curious either.

"Two nights ago, a murder happened several blocks from here." Hiro made a gesture that indicated no real direction. "We believe the killer came to your establishment that night."

"Before or after he took a life?" Eba sounded strangely calm, considering the news.

"Before," Hiro said, noting the woman's use of the masculine pronoun.

Eba nodded once. "You want Kaoru."

"How did you know that?" Father Mateo asked.

Hiro wished the Jesuit hadn't revealed the answer, though he couldn't fault the reaction. Eba's words surprised the shinobi too.

She shrugged. "He has a temper and won't control it. That kind always comes to no good. Also, he owes everyone money, and trouble finds a man when his debts grow high."

"Did you see Kaoru that night?" Hiro asked.

"Sure." Eba nodded. "He was here. He drank too much, stayed too late, and didn't pay for his sake. Who did he kill?"

Hiro ignored her question. "Did he drink alone that night, or did he have companions?"

"Couldn't tell you," Eba said. "On busy nights, I don't have enough tables to go around. The patrons sit together, whether or not they arrived that way. I never know who's who unless I happen to see who pays, and, as I mentioned, Kaoru didn't pay at all.

"I can tell you, though, that he's not a regular patron. He drinks here only when everyone else has cut him off, and then only until his father pays his bills."

"Why would you serve him under those circumstances?" Father Mateo asked.

"Because his father always pays the bills," Eba said. "Sometimes cash, other times in kind, and though his sake's mediocre, most of my customers don't know good from bad."

"Did you notice a female samurai here that evening?" Hiro asked.

"Akechi Yoshiko?" Eba laughed without humor. "She won't show her face here again. Not after the last time."

"What happened?" Hiro asked.

"She came in here a few weeks back, trying to collect a debt from one of my regular customers. And no, before you ask, it wasn't Kaoru." Eba shook her head. "Most samurai aren't welcome here, and Akechi Yoshiko made it worse by breaking every rule of polite behavior. She confronted the man at his table and threatened him loudly enough to silence the room. When he told her he didn't have the money, she threw his flask to the floor and pulled him right up out of his chair. I think she would have beaten him on the spot, but other patrons intervened."

"They had a fight? Inside the teahouse?" Father Mateo asked.

"No." Eba laughed. "I wish they had. Bashō would have taught that uppity samurai a thing or two." She glanced at Hiro. "I'm sorry if that offends."

"Just tell us what happened," Hiro said. "By Bashō, do you mean the rice merchant?"

"You know him?" Eba asked. "He can throw a punch."

Hiro found it interesting that Bashō drank sake at the Golden Buddha. A man of Bashō's standing could afford a nicer place.

"Three men escorted Yoshiko out," Eba continued. "I followed them into the street. I told her if she returned to my house, for debt collection or otherwise, I'd have her arrested and dragged before the magistrate. I won't have samurai threatening my patrons and starting fights in my shop without a cause."

Hiro found the woman's confidence impressive. Few commoners would dare to confront a samurai in anger, and fewer still would admit it without remorse.

"Did she agree to stay away?" Hiro doubted Akechi Yoshiko would hear such words without a fight.

"No, but she didn't argue either." Eba smiled. "The men who escorted her out were off-duty dōshin. I give them free tea on rounds and complimentary sake when not on duty. My establishment isn't large, or fine, but it's one of the safest in Pontochō."

So much for samurai not being welcome, Hiro thought. Apparently Eba only objected to the wealthy kind.

"Then you didn't see Akechi Yoshiko two nights ago," the Jesuit said.

"Better than that," the shopkeeper said, "I can say with certainty that woman wasn't here."

CHAPTER 35

"What time did Kaoru leave two nights ago?" Hiro asked. "At closing," Eba said, "about three hours after midnight."

"Did he stay in the teahouse all evening?" Father Mateo asked. "Did he leave alone?"

Eba considered the questions. "He might have come and gone—I wasn't watching. Sometimes he does, sometimes he stays all night. As far as leaving, I think Bashō and a couple of others stayed that late. Half a dozen of them left at closing time."

"Did they leave together?" Father Mateo asked.

"Not that I noticed, but then, I don't pay attention unless there's a fight."

Hiro nodded to end the conversation. "Thank you. We appreciate your help."

"If I helped." Eba looked from Hiro to Father Mateo. "You never did say who it was that Kaoru killed."

"I did not," Hiro confirmed, "and I don't intend to."

"Fair enough," Eba said. "Killer or no, Kaoru isn't welcome in my teahouse anymore. Not after this. I'd appreciate your telling him so, when and if you see him. Again, no offense intended."

"None taken," Father Mateo replied.

After Eba closed the door, the Jesuit turned to Hiro and said, "I guess the apprentice told the truth about where Bashō went."

"About the teahouse," Hiro said. "I'm still not sure he took the travel road."

He had more to say, but the words died out on his lips when he saw Akechi Yoshiko step out of a building across the street.

She noticed Hiro a moment later.

Yoshiko squared her shoulders and stalked toward Hiro, wearing the glare of a furious tiger. Her left hand gripped the hilt of her katana.

"Matsui Hiro!" she declared. "You stop right there!"

Hiro sensed no immediate danger, though Yoshiko's disposition indicated the conversation would not be pleasant.

"What does she want?" Father Mateo whispered in Portuguese.

"No idea," Hiro replied in kind. "She does look angry."

"What did you do?" Father Mateo asked, but Yoshiko reached them before the shinobi could answer.

She didn't bow.

"How dare you?" she demanded.

"Good morning, Akechi-*san*." Hiro kept his expression neutral. "I am sorry, I don't understand your question."

"You lied, and you betrayed me!"

Hiro suspected the samurai woman had talked with Mayuri but feigned ignorance until he knew for sure. "In what way do you believe I have betrayed you?"

"I can't afford to lose this job." Yoshiko gripped her katana far too tightly for someone intending to draw it. "My father's stipend ended upon his death, and my share of the Sakura's profits does not cover my family's bills."

Her nose turned red as she added, "I considered you a friend."

Hiro hoped she wouldn't cry. He hated it when women cried, especially in public.

Fortunately, she controlled herself before any tears could fall.

"Matsui-*san*," Yoshiko said, "you accused me of attacking innocent men—and committing murder. Do not deny it. Mayuri told me everything."

I doubt that, Hiro thought. Aloud, he said, "I did not accuse you of murder."

"I only strike the men who refuse to pay," Yoshiko said. "Recalcitrant debtors are not innocent men."

Her glance flickered over Hiro's shoulder toward the Golden

Buddha. "What are you doing in Pontochō?" She paused. "You do believe I killed Chikao. You lied to me last night."

Father Mateo gave Hiro a startled look, but to his credit the Jesuit didn't speak.

Hiro chose his next words carefully. "I did not tell Mayuri that I thought you killed Chikao."

"How could you, of all people, believe me guilty of murder?" Yoshiko's lower lip trembled.

Hiro caught the injury in her voice.

Silence stretched between them.

As it grew awkward Hiro said, "You do not know what I believe. You make an assumption."

Yoshiko straightened and raised her chin. "A reasonable one, I think. You made me trust you, and then you lied to me and betrayed my trust."

"That can't be true." Father Mateo stepped forward. "Hiro would never betray a woman's trust."

"This is not about trust," Hiro said. "And it's not about you, Akechi-*san*. We are merely using logic to solve a crime. Exactly the way we did with your father's murder."

"Then seek logical answers, which don't involve me." Yoshiko removed her hand from her sword. "I have nothing to gain from Chikao's murder. In fact, it disadvantages me severely."

"Disadvantages you?" Hiro repeated.

"Kaoru will never pay his debt. He's never paid a debt in his life." Yoshiko made a frustrated gesture. "You didn't have to go to Mayuri. I would have told you the truth if you asked. Yes, I saw Chikao the night he died. And yes, we spoke of Kaoru's debt."

"His blackened eye suggests he refused to pay." Hiro spoke with candor. He doubted Yoshiko would ever speak with him again anyway.

On the positive side, he had finally rid himself of her affections.

"Yes, I struck him," Yoshiko said, "but he had no serious injuries when I left him."

"Why did you strike him?" Hiro asked.

"He said he didn't have the money, too many other debts to pay. I didn't believe him, but when he didn't change his story after I hit him . . . I decided it must have been the truth."

"What changed your mind?" Hiro asked.

Yoshiko shrugged. "Most men pay up to avoid a second strike."

"How did you learn about Chikao's death?" Hiro watched her carefully, expecting her to lie.

Yoshiko smiled, though her eyes revealed regret. "I saw you in the prison yard. The dōshin told me who you'd come to see and why. I feigned surprise because I didn't want to admit to asking about your business."

To Hiro's chagrin, he couldn't tell if Yoshiko spoke the truth.

"I would not have killed Chikao," she continued. "Losing a father is not a thing I would wish on any man. Not even such a worthless one as Kaoru. Chikao would have paid the debt, in time, but even if he refused to pay I would not kill him—or any other man—over money."

She met Hiro's gaze without faltering.

"What brings you into Pontochō this morning?" Father Mateo asked, a bit too brightly.

Yoshiko turned to the priest. Her eyes went cold. "I'm afraid that's not your business. Please excuse me. I have matters to attend to."

Hiro and Father Mateo bowed as Yoshiko turned away and started off toward Sanjō Road. After half a dozen paces she turned back. "My mother and I will not be able to host you at our home. Regrettably, it appears our plans have changed."

CHAPTER 36

After Yoshiko disappeared, Father Mateo said, "Well, that went poorly."

"It could have been worse," Hiro said, "and might have actually helped us."

He examined the building Yoshiko had emerged from just before their confrontation. The two-story structure stood almost directly across from the Golden Buddha. No sign hung from its narrow entrance. Without the indigo noren that displayed the shop-keeper's name during business hours, the barren storefront offered no clue to the business's name or purpose.

Hiro stepped to the door and knocked.

No one answered.

Hiro hammered his fist against the door. The knocking loosened a shower of detritus from the rafters, dusting Father Mateo's hair with thatch and one extremely indignant spider.

The Jesuit brushed the debris away and flicked the arachnid to the ground.

"We're closed," said a female voice from behind the door. "Go away until evening."

"No," Hiro said. "You opened this door for Akechi Yoshiko. You will open it now for me."

Father Mateo gave the shinobi a startled look, no doubt caused by Hiro's breach of etiquette.

"Are you a friend of Yoshiko's?" the woman asked, though the door stayed closed.

Hiro weighed the cost of a second lie and decided it couldn't hurt—as long as the woman hadn't been watching the argument in the street.

"I am," he said.

The door swung open, revealing a woman about Yoshiko's age, but far more lovely than any Hiro had seen in Pontochō. She wore no makeup, and when she smiled, her teeth showed no sign of the blackening favored by women who mimicked the courtesans' style. Many men liked blackened teeth, but Hiro thought they looked as if their owners lost a fight.

"What do you want?" The woman's tone counteracted any advantage her beauty offered.

"What manner of business do you run?" the shinobi asked.

"If you do not know, you don't belong here." She started to close the door.

Hiro stuck a foot in the opening.

The woman pressed on the door to force it closed.

Hiro's temper snapped. He laid both hands on the door and pushed with far more force than necessary. The woman stumbled backward with a startled cry and the door flew open.

Hiro stepped on the threshold but didn't cross it. "When a samurai asks a question, commoners answer."

The woman recovered her composure. "Perhaps I do not know the answer."

Hiro raised an eyebrow and studied the woman. She seemed too bold for a servant, but no entertainer answered the door without makeup. Her obi tied in the back, which meant she wasn't a prostitute, yet her smooth hands lacked a merchant's calluses.

He glanced at the front of the building. The narrow frontage and lack of identifying features indicated a business whose clientele did not rely on signage. People came to this door with knowledge and a purpose.

Hiro examined the woman again. The elaborate embroidery on her obi and kimono cost a fortune. Jeweled kanzashi pinned her hair in place.

"You do not know what business your house conducts?" Father Mateo asked.

"My business is not of consequence to samurai or priests." The woman looked from one man to the other. "Samurai visit the Shijō Market. Priests . . . I do not know."

The market gave Hiro the final clue he needed. "You're a moneylender."

"Yes, for the women of Pontochō." The moneylender clasped her hands. "I do not lend to samurai or to men. If you need loans, you go to the rice sellers' street."

"You misunderstand," the shinobi said. "We haven't come about a loan."

"Then what do you want—and how, exactly, do you know Yoshiko?" The woman glanced at the door as if wondering whether she could slam it shut before the shinobi stopped her.

"We saw her leaving and wondered what she was doing here at this hour." Hiro raised his hands, palms up. "As you mentioned, you're not in the business of loaning money to samurai."

"If you know her, then you also know I won't discuss her business, any more than I would tell you of my own." The woman reached for the edge of the door, but didn't try to shut it.

"One last question," Hiro said. "If we did need a loan, who do you suggest we get it from?"

"There is a merchant named Bashō who lends to men of every social class." Her gaze shifted to Father Mateo. "I do not know if he would lend to foreigners as well."

"Thank you," Hiro said as she closed the door.

As they turned away from the house, Father Mateo asked, "Now what?"

"Home." Hiro started north.

"What did you say to Mayuri last night?" Father Mateo asked. "I've never seen a woman as angry as Yoshiko was this morning."

Hiro gave the priest a sidelong look. "It isn't my talk with Mayuri that made her angry—and I doubt you have much firsthand knowledge about angry women."

As Hiro and Father Mateo crossed the bridge that spanned the river at Sanjō Road, a voice beneath the end of the bridge said, "SSSST!"

Hiro whirled, hand on his katana. "Get behind me," he said to Father Mateo.

"Sssst," the voice repeated. "Hiro-*san*, down here."

Hiro peered into the shadows beneath the bridge. A figure moved forward, revealing the spattered hem of a familiar brown kimono.

Hiro shook his head in disgust. "Suke, what are you doing under the bridge?"

"Don't say my name," the monk hissed. "Someone might hear you and recognize me."

"Is that the monk from the brewery?" Father Mateo leaned down for a better view.

"You're attracting more attention by your stealth than you would by talking, Suke," Hiro said.

Suke poked his head into the light and looked around, as if expecting an attack at any moment.

"Is someone chasing you?" Hiro asked.

The monk emerged from under the bridge, smelling of stale sake, unwashed skin, and human waste. He clearly hadn't bathed since leaving prison.

Suke looked over his shoulder. "People shouldn't see us here. Someone might suspect we're working together."

Father Mateo looked from the monk to Hiro. "Working together?"

Suke nodded solemnly. "I'm helping Hiro solve Chikao's murder."

CHAPTER 37

"You're working as Hiro's partner?" Father Mateo asked Suke.

Hiro gave the Jesuit a look that said *don't encourage him.*

Suke nodded, lips splitting into a nearly toothless grin. "I am, and I overheard an important clue the night before Chikao's murder. I'd forgotten all about it until I saw you talking with that *kitsune* in the street the other night."

"Yoshiko isn't pretty enough for a fox spirit," Hiro said.

Father Mateo asked, "What did you hear?"

"The night before Chikao died, I went for a walk in Pontochō." Suke's eyes glazed over with memory. "I like to watch the women . . . shimmering kimono, pretty faces . . . I remember pleasant evenings there, before I became a monk . . ."

Suke faded into silence.

"What did the women say?" Hiro asked.

Suke blinked. "Why did you ask me about the women?"

"You brought it up," Hiro said. "You claimed to have heard a clue."

Suke nodded. "I did. An important clue!" He frowned. "Stop interrupting. You'll make me forget again."

Hiro raised his hands apologetically.

"I was standing outside the Golden Buddha—or was it the Dancing Crane?" Suke scratched his liver-spotted head with a wrinkled hand. "It had to be one or the other."

Father Mateo opened his mouth, but Hiro silenced the priest with a look. Suke didn't need any more distractions.

"From where I was standing, I heard a man say he was going to marry Tomiko. I think he meant Ginjiro's daughter."

"Did you recognize him?" Hiro asked. "Did you see his face?"

Suke shook his head. "Tomiko doesn't have a suitor, so I wondered who he was, but by the time I went around the corner he had gone."

"Another trail leading nowhere," Father Mateo said.

"I wouldn't send you nowhere." Suke looked offended. "I didn't know the man who spoke, but I recognized the voice of his companion."

The monk fell silent, reveling in his secret.

"Well," Hiro said, "who was it?"

"A rice merchant named Bashō. I know, because he bought me sake once." Suke glanced over his shoulder. "I should go before anyone sees us. The killer must not realize I'm a spy!"

Suke hunched his shoulders and scurried away across the bridge.

Father Mateo watched him go. "I don't believe that man is entirely sane."

"Probably not," Hiro said, "but he does remember the men who buy him sake. If he says he heard Bashō in Pontochō two nights ago, Bashō was there."

"We already knew he drank at the Golden Buddha," Father Mateo said.

"And now we know he may possess important information." Hiro resumed his walk toward home. "The other man was almost certainly Kaoru."

"We need to go back to Shijō Market," Father Mateo said, "to speak with Bashō's family and find out where he went."

"They will not tell us," Hiro said. "It seems Bashō's companion is connected to Chikao's murder. There's no other reason for the merchant to disappear."

"Unless he's dead," Father Mateo said. "The murderer might have killed him too."

"I hope not," Hiro said. "But, dead or alive, I doubt Bashō has left the city."

He glanced at a samurai walking south on the opposite side of the river. The stranger strolled at a leisurely pace, watching the sky above and the water below.

The shinobi decided the samurai posed no threat.

"A merchant like Bashō has no excuse to leave Kyoto in the summer," Hiro said. "Without a reason, the Matsunaga guards would never let him leave the city. Bashō would know that, or he should. I think he's hiding in Kyoto, and the story about Edo was a lie."

"He could tell the guards he needed to see sick relatives in the country," the priest suggested. "That would get him past the barricades."

"Unlikely," Hiro said. "Not without his wife along."

"Hiding in the city?" Father Mateo asked. "That's risky, if a killer wants him dead."

"Better than a scene at the city gates," Hiro said. "A samurai in the shogun's service can behead a commoner on a whim. A man who cares about his life won't take unnecessary risks."

Father Mateo frowned. "All right, but where could a merchant hide?"

"The question is, 'Where did he hide?' In this case, I believe he hid at home."

Father Mateo shook his head. "We already checked his home; he wasn't there."

"We asked for him," Hiro said. "We didn't search. We asked, and we left—exactly as Bashō and his wife intended."

"The apprentice came after us . . ." Father Mateo trailed off. "You think he lied."

"Of course he did." Hiro paused. "Hama lied to us too. I simply didn't know what she lied about. Now that I consider it, a frugal man would always hide at home. It costs less money."

"How do you suddenly know he's frugal?" Father Mateo asked.

"Sudden has nothing to do with it. Hama wore a sturdy kimono, cut in last year's style. Her clothes, and the apprentice's, showed signs of careful washing. The household of a moneylender doesn't look austere unless the man is frugal."

"Or in debt," the priest suggested, "which he is."

"True." Hiro smiled. "But while we spoke with Bashō's wife, the apprentice went back into the warehouse behind the shop."

"Filling a customer's order," the Jesuit said.

"I thought so, too, but he returned with empty hands, and gave a guilty glance in our direction," Hiro said.

"You think he went to tell Bashō?" Father Mateo flexed his hand in a manner that suggested it was hurting.

"I do," Hiro said. "It's time to return to Bashō's and find the truth—but this time, I must visit the shop alone."

CHAPTER 38

At home, Hiro and Father Mateo discovered Luis pacing the floor.

"Why can't you people keep your enemies straight?" the merchant demanded as Hiro entered.

"Pardon me?" Hiro reminded himself that the merchant didn't intend a challenge. He tolerated Luis for Father Mateo's sake, but, even so, Hiro often found the merchant's words offensive.

"You heard me," Luis fumed. "You samurai . . . today you're friends, tomorrow mortal enemies. It's like dealing with a bunch of bickering women."

"Is something wrong?" Father Mateo asked.

The Jesuit clearly hoped the obvious question would diffuse the confrontation.

"Of course there's something wrong." Luis made an exasperated gesture. "I asked the Miyoshi, by messenger, if they would mind a delay in the shipment. Apparently, they do, because they need the firearms to go to war."

An answer that surprises only you, Hiro thought.

"To go to war or to threaten war?" Father Mateo asked.

"Does it matter?" Luis demanded. "It's all the same in the end, and they promised it would be my end if I delay delivery. Samurai warriors . . . savages, every one."

Gato trotted into the room and rubbed her side along Hiro's leg in welcome. He bent and scooped the cat into his arms. "Matsunaga-*san* will kill us all if you refuse to stop the sale."

Gato trilled and butted her head against the shinobi's wrist.

"I agree, this is a problem," Luis said.

"I see no problem." Hiro stroked Gato's fur. "Matsunaga

Hisahide represents an immediate threat. The Miyoshi can kill you only if they win and take the city."

"Or if I leave Kyoto." Luis crossed his arms. "I'm disinclined to lose my head at the point of a samurai sword, no matter whose hand holds it."

Hiro raised an eyebrow. "You do know, it's not the point they'll use."

Father Mateo frowned.

"I found a solution, no thanks to you." Luis glared at Hiro. "I sent a message to the warehouse at Fukuda. One of the Portuguese merchants there will fill the Miyoshi order and also pay a nice commission on the sale."

Gato squirmed. Hiro put her down. "Matsunaga-*san* will not approve. He will consider you a traitor anyway."

"Only if someone tells him what I've done," the merchant said. "Lord Omura controls Fukuda. The weapons will ship from there, or from the Portuguese warehouse at Yokoseura, directly to the Miyoshi. We can tell Lord Matsunaga I canceled the order. He'll never know."

"Until the Miyoshi use those firearms to start a war," Hiro countered. "Or until Matsunaga's spies find out the truth."

"Until a month ago, Lord Matsunaga worked for the Miyoshi." Luis brushed away Hiro's words with a wave. "His spies cannot present a real threat."

"Do not underestimate Matsunaga Hisahide," Hiro said. "If you lie to him, his spies will know."

"And if I don't, the Miyoshi will have me killed," the merchant said.

Hiro clenched his jaw against the words he could not say, the ones that revealed his shinobi status and that of Hisahide's hired assassins.

Not that explanations would have mattered. Once Luis made up his mind, an argument would only reinforce his stubbornness. Hiro decided to leave before the conversation tested his patience beyond its limits.

Just before he turned away, loud knocking echoed through the house.

Gato startled and raced away.

Father Mateo looked at Luis. "Do you expect a visitor?"

"No one visits me." The merchant started toward his room. "All this samurai nonsense wears me out. I need a nap."

Ana appeared in the kitchen door and started across the room.

"Don't worry, Ana, I'll answer it," Father Mateo said, but the housekeeper hurried past him.

As she entered the foyer, she looked back over her shoulder. "Hm. Not as long as I'm here and able."

Father Mateo looked resigned.

Moments later, Ana led Tomiko into the oe.

Ginjiro's daughter bowed to Hiro and then to Father Mateo. A woven basket shook in her trembling hands.

"Matsui-*san*," Tomiko said, "I apologize for disturbing you at home."

"It's quite all right," Father Mateo said. "Would you like some tea?"

Tomiko shook her head. "Thank you, but there is no time. Magistrate Ishimaki has ordered my father whipped this afternoon."

"Today?" Father Mateo asked. "He granted us four days to investigate."

Tomiko hung her head. "He changed his mind."

"How do you know this?" Hiro asked.

"I went to the prison to take my father food. I found him tied to a stake in the yard. The guards said Magistrate Ishimaki ordered an interrogation. Worse, the magistrate has changed his mind about my father's trial. He will hear the murder charge tomorrow."

"That makes no sense," Father Mateo said. "We have four days. He gave his word."

Hiro ignored the Jesuit. "Did you ask what changed the magistrate's mind?"

Tomiko shook her head. "I didn't think . . . I turned and ran straight here. I didn't know what else to do. The magistrate won't listen to me the way he would a man. I hoped . . ."

She fell silent. Hiro saw the plea in her frightened eyes.

So did Father Mateo.

"We'll go at once," the Jesuit said.

"Don't let them kill him. Please." Tomiko fought back tears. Hiro wanted to reassure the girl but found he respected her too much to offer false assurances.

"I cannot promise, but we'll do our best."

CHAPTER 39

"I don't understand why Magistrate Ishimaki changed his mind," Father Mateo said as he and Hiro hurried toward the prison.

"Magistrates change their minds for many reasons," Hiro said. "We need to hurry, not to speculate."

A dōshin stopped them at the prison gates.

"What is your business here?" he asked.

"We wish to see a prisoner," Hiro said. "The brewer, Ginjiro."

"Come back later," the dōshin said. "You cannot see him now."

Hiro looked past the dōshin and saw Ginjiro tied to one of the whipping posts in the compound yard. The brewer was naked except for a loincloth. Shackles bound his hands to the top of the post. His body drooped and dark red stains traced jagged lines along his back.

No one stood nearby, suggesting a break in the interrogation.

"The questioning seems to be finished," Father Mateo said.

Hiro appreciated the Jesuit's use of "questioning" rather than "whipping" or "torture." The priest objected to violent punishments, deserved or not, but antagonizing the dōshin now would not advance their cause.

The dōshin glanced over his shoulder as if confirming the Jesuit's words. "He wouldn't confess. We're giving him time to reconsider his lack of cooperation."

"An innocent man has nothing to confess," the Jesuit said. "Besides, the magistrate suspended the brewer's case."

"He unsuspended it this morning," the dōshin said. "New evidence changed his mind."

"What kind of new evidence?" Father Mateo asked.

"How would I know?" The dōshin shrugged. "The magistrate

doesn't share his thoughts with me. I overheard the yoriki telling the prisoner."

Hiro squared his shoulders and laid a hand on the hilt of his sword. "We will speak with Ginjiro now. You have no authority to refuse the shogun's special investigators."

"You're . . ." The dōshin bowed without finishing the statement. "A thousand apologies, noble sir. Of course, you may enter at once."

He stepped aside and bowed again as Hiro stalked into the prison yard.

Father Mateo followed, though without the shinobi's swagger.

When they left the guard behind, Father Mateo leaned toward Hiro and whispered in Portuguese, "What will happen when he learns we're not the shogun's men?"

"We'll be gone before that happens," Hiro whispered back. Father Mateo didn't look reassured.

The brewer stood before the post, head down and trembling slightly. The lines on his back looked darker and angrier, welts and bruises highlighted by streaks of blood.

Hiro smelled the salty scents of human blood and sweat. The odors caused an unexpected ache of sympathy, which made him pause—never once had he felt empathy for the guilty.

Although Ginjiro's innocence remained an open question, Hiro found himself inclined to trust his instincts.

The brewer rested his forehead against the post, eyes shut and lips drawn tight against the pain. He didn't look up as Hiro and Father Mateo approached, though sudden tension in his back revealed he heard their footsteps.

"Ginjiro, listen," Hiro whispered. "Don't reveal you know us."

The brewer winced. "Tell me that my daughter isn't with you."

"No," Hiro said, "but she knows what happened. She's the one who told us we should come."

Ginjiro sighed. "She must not ever come here again."

"Why did they do this?" Father Mateo asked. "What made them beat you?"

"The yoriki claims I lied about killing Chikao," Ginjiro said. "He demanded a confession. I wouldn't give it."

"Did you kill Chikao?" Hiro asked.

"Of course he didn't!" Father Mateo said.

Ginjiro tilted his head, trying to look Hiro in the eye. "I did not, but I did lie to the yoriki."

"Tell us," Hiro said. "We need the truth, and we need it now."

Ginjiro sighed again and nodded. "I might as well tell you, now that the magistrate knows.

"A month ago, or a little more, Chikao and Ren made an offer to buy my brewery. They wanted a better location, and they thought, if I sold them mine, the guild would approve their application on the spot. They wanted to buy my recipes, too, the entire business.

"I told them I didn't want to sell. They left, and then, a few days later, Chikao returned alone. He tried again to make me sell. When I refused, he asked me to let Tomiko marry his son. As if I would consider such a thing . . ."

Ginjiro drew a deep, slow breath and exhaled with a gingerness that spoke of real pain.

"How did that provoke a beating?" Father Mateo asked.

Hiro frowned at the priest. "He hasn't finished."

The brewer closed his eyes and said, "I refused the offer and told Chikao I would never let my daughter wed his son.

"But Chikao and Ren would not accept my refusal. They came again—the last time, just three days before Chikao died. They asked for Tomiko as well as the shop. I told Chikao if he didn't stop, I would withdraw my support for their application to join the brewers' guild, and also do everything in my power to ensure the za refused them membership.

"I lost my temper. I made a foolish threat—but I didn't mean it. Not the way it sounded, anyway."

"How did Chikao respond?" Hiro asked.

"He swore to make me change my mind." Ginjiro looked at the ground. "I told him I would like to see him try."

"Did he fight you?" Hiro asked.

"No." Ginjiro shook his head. "He made an excuse and left."

"Why didn't you explain all this before?" Father Mateo asked.

"I didn't think it really made a difference," Ginjiro said. "I didn't kill Chikao. We argued, spoke unpleasant words. Men argue with each other all the time."

"Perhaps," Hiro said, "but most men's arguments do not end in murder."

CHAPTER 40

"How did the magistrate learn about your problems with Chikao?" Father Mateo asked.

"Kaoru told him," the brewer said, though Hiro had already guessed the answer.

"You there!" A man emerged from the prison house and hurried toward them. The hooked *jitte* in his hand identified him as a dōshin, and he wore a vibrant, patterned surcoat over dark hakama.

"What do you think you're doing?" the dōshin demanded as he reached them. "You cannot speak with the prisoner now."

Hiro gestured to Father Mateo. "This man is a priest."

"The brewer worships the foreign god?" The dōshin frowned at Ginjiro. "Is this true?"

Ginjiro bowed his head. "I worship the foreigners' god, and Amida Buddha, and also follow the *Shintō* way."

The answer, though contrary to the truth and Father Mateo's theology, didn't sound abnormal. Many Japanese hedged their bets by worshipping all available deities. Hiro was glad the brewer had the presence of mind to go along with the lie.

The dōshin scratched his head. "I don't remember the magistrate granting permission for a priest . . ."

He trailed off, unable to reconcile his respect for religious practices with his duty to follow orders.

Just when Hiro thought the ruse might work, the dōshin said, "I can't allow it. The yoriki could have me whipped for letting you interrupt an interrogation."

"This man has had enough for one day," Father Mateo said. "God restricts the maximum number of lashes a man can receive at once."

"Truly?" Curiosity overcame concern. "How many does your god allow?"

"Forty," Father Mateo said. "No more, regardless of his crime."

The dōshin looked at Ginjiro. "Then he still has a few to go."

"It is a maximum, not a goal." The Jesuit frowned, displeased his plan had failed.

Hiro wondered whether the rule existed or whether the priest had made it up to reduce Ginjiro's punishment.

"Do you intend to beat this man again?" Father Mateo demanded.

"That depends," the dōshin said, "on whether he confesses."

"What if he isn't guilty?" Father Mateo asked. "Surely you wouldn't expect an innocent man to confess a crime."

"The Kyoto police do not arrest innocent men," the dōshin said. "If he doesn't confess before his trial, or during it, the yoriki will bring him here and press him until he does."

Father Mateo looked at Hiro and switched to Portuguese. "Does he mean they intend to place him beneath a stone? They do this in my country, too. It's almost always fatal."

Hiro took a moment to parse the question. The lack of proper names helped keep the conversation secret but made the Jesuit harder to understand.

"Yes," he replied in the Jesuit's tongue, "and they will increase the weight of the stones until he confesses or dies."

Hiro switched to Japanese and told the dōshin, "The foreigner does not speak our language well."

The dōshin nodded, neither surprised nor offended.

"May I speak with you privately?" Hiro asked the dōshin.

They walked a few steps away. As Hiro hoped, Father Mateo remained at Ginjiro's side.

The shinobi lowered his voice as if to keep the priest from over-hearing. "Will the magistrate hear this case tomorrow? And press him immediately afterward?"

"That's what I heard," the dōshin said, "assuming the brewer doesn't confess to the magistrate during the hearing. Why do you care? You can't observe the pressing."

"On the contrary," Hiro said, "we must. The foreign god has different rules than Japanese kami do. If one of his worshippers dies with a lie on his soul, the foreign god will send that man to the hell of everburning flames. The priest must witness the brewer's confession and confirm he died an honest death."

"How can a priest ensure a man is honest?" the dōshin asked.

"How would I know?" Hiro said. "I'm a translator and scribe. I know his rituals. I don't share his faith."

"I don't think the yoriki will allow it," the dōshin said. "You'll have to get the magistrate's permission."

"We will obtain permission." Hiro nodded, the gesture just shy of a bow. "Thank you. Now we will leave, to save you trouble."

The dōshin bowed.

Hiro returned to Ginjiro and whispered, "If you're guilty, confess at once."

"I'm innocent." The brewer spoke so quietly that Hiro had to strain to hear the words. "I swear I am."

After returning home with Father Mateo, Hiro retrieved a towel and headed out for a soak at the bathhouse.

An unfamiliar samurai stood guard at the eastern end of the Kamo River bridge. His lamellar armor bore the Matsunaga crest. His swords hung sheathed at his waist, and he carried an arquebus in his arms. He gripped the firearm like a sword, with the muzzle held much higher than the stock.

As Hiro approached, the samurai stepped forward with the arrogance of a man promoted far above his talents.

"Who are you?" he demanded. "Identify yourself and show your pass."

Hiro stopped and bowed. "I am Matsui Hiro, interpreter for the foreign priest who lives up the road, past Okazaki Shrine. We passed this way, coming home, a few minutes ago."

"I didn't see you." The samurai gripped his firearm more tightly. "I came on duty ten minutes ago, when the temple bells rang the hour. Show me your travel pass and identification."

"I don't need identification." Hiro smiled with a politeness he didn't feel. "I haven't passed any barricades. I don't want to cross the river. I'm going north, to the bathhouse, for a soak."

The samurai scowled. "Okazaki Shrine marks the eastern boundary of Kyoto. If you enter the city from past the shrine, you have to present a pass."

"I left it at home," Hiro said.

"Go back and get it."

Hiro bristled. His desire to avoid attention warred with loathing for this petty bully flexing his authority without cause.

"Fetch your pass," the guard repeated, "or you can explain yourself to the magistrate."

"You're going to arrest me?" Hiro couldn't believe it. "On what charge?"

CHAPTER 41

The samurai took an aggressive step forward. "I have orders to guard this bridge, and to arrest any person who seems suspicious."

He glared at Hiro to reinforce the threat.

The shinobi felt a strong desire to give the insolent samurai a lesson—and a limp. Fortunately, training and the wish to avoid arrest stayed Hiro's hands. Instead, he bowed. "I will go home and retrieve the pass."

The samurai scowled. "I've changed my mind. I'm taking you to the magistrate, on a charge of trying to enter the city without the required documentation."

"That charge does not apply to a man who hasn't passed a barricade," Hiro said. "Do you really want to confess to arresting an innocent man a mile from his home?"

"Enough!" The guard made a grab for Hiro's arm. "You're under arrest."

Hiro stepped away and laid a hand on his katana. "I respectfully decline to be arrested."

The samurai's nostrils flared. "How dare you threaten the shogun's agent?"

"I made no threats," the shinobi said, "I simply refused your invitation to visit the magistrate."

"With a hand on your sword." The samurai lowered the arquebus until its muzzle pointed at Hiro's chest.

"I'm carrying a towel." Hiro waved the strip of cloth across the end of the samurai's firearm. "What kind of man starts trouble with a towel?"

"That might be a ruse," the samurai snapped.

Hiro wondered whether the samurai realized his arquebus wasn't primed and wouldn't fire. "Perhaps you would change your mind if you knew I reside in the home of the Portuguese merchant who sold that weapon to Matsunaga-*san*."

The samurai glanced at the weapon. "The shogun's quarter-master issued this to me this afternoon. I do not know who bought it or from whom." He raised the weapon's muzzle a fraction. "How do I know you're telling the truth? You might be a shinobi in disguise."

"Do I look like a shinobi?" Hiro asked.

The arquebus wavered. "How would I know? I've never seen one. Nobody sees a shinobi and lives."

"Consider this carefully," Hiro said. "If you take me to Magistrate Ishimaki—who, I will add, is a friend of mine—I will have to file a formal complaint against you. Would your record survive the embarrassment of arresting a man for bathing?"

The samurai stared at Hiro's towel. After a minute that felt much longer, he scowled.

"Go on, then, but I'm following you to the bathhouse, and I'll wait outside to ensure you aren't faking."

"You're welcome to follow me all the way in." Hiro shrugged. "It's a public bath. But, just out of curiosity, who will watch the bridge while we are bathing?"

The samurai scowled. "Go away. Enjoy your bath."

"Thank you." Hiro smiled. "I intend to."

As Hiro soaked in the heated water, he considered the samurai guards throughout Kyoto. The presence of the samurai sent a message to the Ashikaga clan, as well as every spy within the city—a message that Matsunaga Hisahide met all threats with force.

However, Hiro suspected Hisahide had a secondary goal. Samurai at the city gates would send a similar message with less effort and expense than posting men in every ward. Hiro wondered what the acting shogun gained by flooding the streets with guards. To his intense frustration, the answer eluded him.

The Miyoshi's threat of war did not explain the city guards. An army on the march moved slowly, giving Hisahide time to secure the city before his enemies arrived. The battle would start outside the Japanese capital, not within it.

Hiro's instincts warned him that Hisahide was up to something. Unfortunately, those instincts couldn't tell him what it was. He hurried home as twilight doused the final flames of the setting sun. As he passed the Kamo River bridge, he nodded to the grumpy samurai.

The guard pretended not to notice.

As he reached the Jesuit's house, Hiro heard the distinctive murmuring of voices raised in prayer. He smiled. Father Mateo held worship meetings almost every evening. With luck, the shinobi could change his clothes and leave again before the Jesuit realized he'd been home.

Hiro laid his hand on the garden gate.

Aggressive barking started in the yard across the street.

Hiro turned.

A giant akita strained against the woven rope that tied it to a stake in the neighbor's yard. Hiro knew the dog did only what its nature called for, but he did not like the beast's near-constant barking in the night—or the memory that this dog had almost killed the Jesuit whose life was tied by oaths to Hiro's own.

Hiro stalked across the road in the gathering dark. Shinobi did not take revenge on beasts, but Hiro wanted to teach the dog a lesson. He stopped three feet from the end of the rope, sending the akita into a frenzy. The barking increased. A line of drool swung from the dog's bared fangs.

The akita lunged against the rope, but cord and stake held firm. In the weeks since the Jesuit's injuries, the neighbor had learned to tie his dog securely.

Hiro snarled, a sound in tone and timbre indistinguishable from the akita's own. The dog stopped barking, momentarily confused. Hiro lunged. The dog leaped backward with a startled yelp.

The akita growled. Hiro growled back.

The akita barked, but with less confidence.

Hiro suddenly realized how foolish he looked and that he had momentarily—and unwisely—let his own emotions off the rope. He didn't actually want the neighbor's dog to quit its barking altogether. He loathed the beast for biting the priest, but as long as the neighbor kept the dog securely in the yard, the dog did make a decent warning system.

"I don't like you," Hiro said as the dog resumed its barking, "but for now your usefulness outweighs the irritation."

Hiro returned to the Jesuit's yard and slipped through the garden gate. He hoped no one had seen his conversation with the dog. He didn't understand why he approached it in the first place— he didn't usually let emotion rule his conscious mind.

The difficulties of this day, and this investigation, must be having more effect than he had realized.

Hiro reminded himself that he must think before reacting from now on.

Gato greeted him at the veranda door with a mew and a patter of paws. He felt the cat rub against his shin and bent to pick her up. Someone—probably Ana—had already lit the brazier in the corner of Hiro's room and unfolded his narrow futon on the floor. Hiro gave the mattress a longing look. Given his plans, he wouldn't be using it very much that night.

Gato squirmed. Hiro set her down and watched her trot into the garden. He left the door ajar for her return, crossed to his desk, and knelt before it. After a moment to clear his thoughts, he walked his mind through his plans for the evening.

He visualized himself avoiding the samurai patrols and reaching Bashō's shop without detection. Once there, he intended to find Bashō and learn what the merchant knew about the murder. He imagined the encounter. Bashō would likely flee. In his mind the shinobi tripped the merchant, who fell to the ground with a thump.

Hiro opened his eyes.

The thump was real.

Father Mateo's worship service had gone silent.

Someone pounded on the Jesuit's front door.

Hiro leaped to his feet and listened. His urge to rush to the priest's defense waged war against the training that required him to hold his ground until he knew the nature of a threat. The visitor might not mean the Jesuit harm. Hiro split the difference. He crouched at the door that separated his room from the common room and listened.

Moments later, a reedy voice called, "Hiro-*san*! Where are you?"

CHAPTER 42

Hiro slid his shoji open as Suke appeared in the doorway separating the narrow foyer from the oe. The monk looked startled by the people in the common room.

Father Mateo walked toward Suke. "Good evening. Welcome to my home."

Suke looked from the priest to the gathered people. "Where is Hiro-*san*?"

Ana stepped into the common room from the kitchen entrance, opposite the one where Suke stood. A dusting of rice flour on her hands indicated a tasty snack in progress, probably for after the prayer meeting. The housekeeper's gaze settled on Suke and dropped to his filthy feet.

Suke shifted nervously. Crumbs of something fell from his kimono to the floor.

Ana slowly turned to Hiro. She caught his eye and shook her head, lips set in a line that boded ill for Hiro's gastronomic future. He wondered how many sweetened rice balls Suke's visit cost him.

He stifled a sigh. He would miss the tasty snacks.

Father Mateo's parishioners stared at Hiro and the monk. One of the older women looked nervous; the others just seemed confused.

Hiro wished that Suke had arrived a little later. The shinobi stayed away from Father Mateo's religious meetings, mostly so the converts wouldn't ask why Hiro didn't care about the foreign god. To his credit, Father Mateo didn't seem to mind Hiro's absence. A decision not to pray was not the same as showing disrespect.

Hiro felt no guilt about rejecting Father Mateo's god and faith. The unknown benefactor who hired the Iga ryu—and Hiro—did not make religion part of the job assignment. All he asked—and paid for—was a man to guard the priest.

Suke noticed Hiro and lit up with recognition. He bowed with such excitement that he almost tumbled over. "Hiro-*san*, we need to speak . . . alone."

Father Mateo's converts shifted. Rudeness made most Japanese uneasy.

Suke blinked and looked around. "Who are all these people?"

Hiro gestured toward his door. "Please come this way. We can speak in private."

Suke surveyed the room. "Is this a meeting?" He bowed to a woman who knelt nearby. "Good evening, Miss. Is this a dinner party?"

The woman wore her obi tied in front, which marked her as a prostitute. She had a narrow face and deep-set eyes. When she smiled, her face showed real kindness.

"No," she said. "We gather here to worship Jesus God. Do you know Him?"

"I'm on a first-name basis with all the kami." Suke straightened proudly, though a wobble drained the dignity from his pose.

The woman gave Suke a sorrowful look. "Kami are evil spirits, trying to lead your soul astray." She patted the floor beside her. "Sit. I will tell you of the real God."

Suke glanced at Hiro, clearly torn between his errand and the prostitute's attention.

"We'll have snacks and tea together afterward," she promised.

Suke's head snapped toward the woman. "Sake?" he asked hopefully.

"Oh, no." She shook her head. "God disapproves of people drinking sake."

"What kind of selfish god keeps all the sake for himself?" Suke demanded. "Never mind. I haven't time. I'm on important business. No distractions."

Suke crossed the floor and entered Hiro's room.

Hiro gave Father Mateo an apologetic look. The Jesuit smiled and nodded.

Hiro stepped back into his room and slid the shoji closed behind him.

Suke knelt beside the open door that led to the veranda. Gato sat on Hiro's futon, staring at the monk. She leaned toward Suke and inhaled, lips apart as if to taste the air.

She sneezed.

Suke laughed at the cat.

Gato stood and shook herself, offended by the laughter. She gave the monk a disdainful look, stalked to the other side of the mattress, and cleaned herself with a vigor that, in a human, would show chagrin.

Hiro knelt. Under the circumstances, he dispensed with formal greetings. "You have news?"

"Urgent news," Suke said. "This afternoon, the jailers whipped Ginjiro!"

When Hiro didn't respond at once, Suke said, "I see your shock. Magistrate Ishimaki changed his mind."

Hiro reminded himself that Suke believed his "news" would help.

"Yes," Hiro said. "I heard about the beating. In fact, I visited the prison this afternoon."

Suke frowned, eyebrows drawn together and lips pushed out like a petulant child's. "How can I help if you learn all the information before I do?"

Hiro struggled not to smile at Suke's genuine disappointment. "I appreciate your help. It's quite important."

"It is?" Suke's smile returned. "I'll find the next clue first."

The smile faded. "Hiro-*san*, we have to help Ginjiro. Never once has he refused me food—or sake—even when nobody pays him for it. Some nights, Tomiko brings food to the alley after closing. Ginjiro watches from behind the door. He is generous and kind. I can't believe he killed a man in anger."

"I agree," Hiro said, "but our opinions will not save Ginjiro. We need proof to show the magistrate."

"I will think of a way to find some proof." Suke closed his eyes. His forehead furrowed as he searched his addled brain.

Hiro contemplated the errand he would run when Suke left. A sliver of moon hung low in the sky, making concealment easier. Hiro appreciated that advantage, especially with nervous warriors guarding Kyoto's streets.

Gato stepped off the bed and approached the monk, ears pricked forward and tail extended. She sniffed the air, nose twitching at the unfamiliar odors emanating from the stranger's robe.

Suke opened his eyes but didn't move. The cat extended her whiskers until they grazed Suke's left knee. The monk's lips twitched as he suppressed a smile. Gato lowered her nose and sniffed at one of the greasy spots that dotted the monk's kimono like fleas on a dog.

Then, to Hiro's horror, Gato licked it.

CHAPTER 43

Suke's face lit up in a gleeful smile. "Cats do like sake!"

Gato continued licking at the spot.

Hiro didn't know what the spot contained, and didn't want to. He grabbed the cat, who flailed her paws in a vain attempt to return to the monk's kimono.

"I apologize for her lack of manners." Hiro tucked the cat to his chest and stroked her fur. After a moment, Gato ceased her struggling and relaxed in the crook of his arm. A rumbling purr rose up in her throat.

Suke leaned forward. "Does it like your rubbing its fur that way?"

Hiro looked at Gato, aware of how unusual his interaction with the cat appeared to others' eyes. Most Japanese people thought of cats as useful vermin hunters but developed no attachment to the beasts. Until he rescued Gato, a little over a year before, Hiro had never known a cat and had no real desire to bring one home.

In the intervening months, his opinion had changed.

He ran a hand over Gato's back, enjoying the feel of her fur beneath his fingers. "She seems to like it."

Gato's purr crescendoed.

Suke raised a gnarled hand. "Can other people touch it? Does it bite?"

Hiro glanced at Gato. "She does bite, sometimes, mostly just in fun."

Suke touched the cat with the tips of his fingers. A smile crept over his face as he stroked her neck and back with a gentle touch. "It has hair like a baby, soft and warm."

Hiro wondered how Suke knew the feel of an infant's hair. He realized how little he really knew about the monk.

Unraveling that mystery would have to wait for another day.

"I have a plan to help Ginjiro," Hiro said.

"Why didn't you say so?" Suke straightened and laid his hands in his lap. "How are we going to free him?"

Hiro resisted the urge to dismiss the question. Suke needed to feel useful, if only to prevent him from unwanted interference.

When Hiro didn't answer right away, the monk stood up and said, "We should go at once."

Hiro thought quickly. "We can't be seen together. You were right—there's too much risk."

Suke leaned forward conspiratorially. "Give me a job. I can handle it."

Hiro stood up. "All right. I need you to watch a suspect." Suke's grin told Hiro the monk had fallen for the plan.

"Go back to Ginjiro's," Hiro said, "and look for Akechi Yoshiko."

"You want me to watch a kitsune?" Suke drew back, aghast. "What if she leads me into the mountains and traps me there forever?"

"Yoshiko is not a fox spirit," Hiro said, "though, if she were, I would think a man of your wisdom could outwit her easily."

Concern warred with pride on Suke's face. At last he said, "I am a dangerous man."

"To foxes as well as to humans, I am certain," Hiro said. "Tomiko hired Yoshiko to guard the brewery tonight."

"Do you think a kitsune might have killed Chikao?" Suke asked.

"Foxes don't strike men on the head with sake flasks," the shinobi said. "Still, I think it wise to use discretion. Akechi-*san* should not suspect you're watching."

Suke nodded. "I will be as secretive as a shinobi!" He furrowed his brow. "I'll need a disguise."

"Pretend to be drunk and sleeping in a corner," Hiro said.

Suke frowned. "That's not a disguise. I do that all the time."

He paused. A smile crept over his face. "But this time, I'll be faking! Hiro-*san*, that might just work!"

The monk had all the subtlety of a swarm of bees in a bathhouse.

Hiro hoped someone would buy Suke enough sake to make the monk forget his assignment altogether. Unfortunately, Hiro couldn't give Suke any more money—the monk didn't usually have any coins, and Hiro had already given him money recently. Someone might notice and ask Suke where he obtained the silver. Hiro didn't trust the monk to remember his assignment was a secret.

Still, he felt fairly certain that someone would offer the monk a drink.

Hiro escorted Suke across the veranda and through the garden. He didn't want to disturb the prayer meeting a second time.

When they reached the street, the monk took off for Ginjiro's at a surprisingly rapid pace, as if determined to reach the sake shop in time to beg a drink before the generous patrons left.

After Suke disappeared, Hiro returned to his room to prepare for his own clandestine mission. He changed from his gray kimono into a pair of dark hakama and a dark blue surcoat that blended with the shadows. As he dressed, he grew aware that the sounds of prayer had ceased again. He paused and listened but heard no voices in the common room.

Father Mateo must have concluded the worship service earlier than usual.

Hiro finished tying his obi and went to the door that separated his room from the common room beyond. He slid the shoji open and looked out.

Father Mateo knelt by the hearth, alone, eating his dinner off a lacquered tray.

Hiro joined the priest at the hearth. "I apologize if Suke ruined your meeting."

The Jesuit smiled. "He caused a stir but did no damage. I needed to end the service early anyway. Some of my converts walk a long way to get here. I didn't want them leaving late, with so many guards in the streets."

Hiro nodded. An arrogant samurai wouldn't hesitate to harass a prostitute, or any other commoner, for that matter.

The front door banged. Heavy footsteps thumped in the entry.

Hiro faced the entrance without alarm. Only Luis Álvares sounded so much like a drunken bear.

Luis stormed into the common room, cheeks red and shoulders heaving. Without a word, he crossed to the hearth and thumped himself down in the seat reserved for the master of the house. As usual, Hiro found the merchant's choice offensive. Father Mateo claimed he didn't care, but the shinobi hated seeing Luis in the Jesuit's rightful place.

After crossing his legs in an awkward manner, Luis declared, "I've sent a message to the Miyoshi daimyō, telling him that a merchant in Fukuda will take over the sale from here. I believe that should resolve the shogun's issue."

He turned his face toward the kitchen and shouted, "Ana!"

Luis leaned forward and peered at Father Mateo's dinner tray. "No meat tonight? How do these people survive on rice and mush?"

Hiro raised an eyebrow but said nothing. Teaching Luis to appreciate Japanese customs was like capturing wind in a bucket, and Hiro didn't waste his precious time on futile acts.

CHAPTER 44

Hiro left home three hours after sunset. He wore dark clothes and left his katana but carried his wakizashi, along with other, less common weapons he concealed within his clothes.

He kept to the shadows along the edge of the street. Not even the neighbor's vigilant akita saw him leave. As he glided from shadow to shadow, he kept a watchful eye on the road. The choice to wear assassin's clothing would not go over well with the shogun's guards.

During other investigations, Hiro wore his samurai clothes on nighttime missions. Until recently, no one noticed a warrior out for an evening stroll. But edgy guards might stop a samurai out late at night, and a search of Hiro's person would reveal forbidden shinobi weapons.

Hiro passed the torii gate in front of Okazaki Shrine, silent as a shadow and ephemeral as the incense smoke that drifted upward in the starry night. He crossed the road and sneaked through private yards until he reached the final residence before the Kamo River.

The arrogant young samurai marched back and forth across the bridge, doubtless to combat his rising boredom.

Hiro smiled. Guards who sought to amuse themselves created opportunities for spies to pass unnoticed.

At the near end of the bridge, the samurai guard turned around on his heel and marched away with his back to Hiro. When the guard passed the middle of the bridge, Hiro dashed across the open space between the end of Marutamachi Road and the line of sakura trees that shaded the path along the eastern side of the river. By the time the guard turned back around, at the far end of the bridge, the shinobi had disappeared into the shadows.

Hiro headed south along the path beside the river, hoping to cross unchallenged at Sanjō Road. That bridge sat close to Pontochō. With luck, the allure of beautiful women and glowing lanterns would distract the guards assigned to watch the Sanjō bridge.

Hiro slowed his pace as he approached the river crossing. A samurai stood at the eastern end of the bridge, interrogating a peddler. The peddler knelt, head bowed, and clutched a sack of goods before him. Lanterns on the bridge illuminated the poor man's frightened face.

The samurai shouted a question and slapped the back of the peddler's head. The poor man cringed away from the blow, which made the samurai strike him a second time.

"What are you doing out after dark?" the samurai bellowed. "Identify yourself and state your business!"

The peddler lowered his face to his hands and moaned.

Hiro stopped in the shadows beneath the trees.

"What's in there?" The samurai kicked the peddler's sack. It rattled. "What's in the bag?"

The samurai kicked the sack again, and the peddler lost his grip. The sack fell over. Wooden bowls spilled out into the dirt.

The samurai grasped the sack by its bottom and shook it, sending a shower of wooden objects into the road.

"Worthless." The samurai dropped the empty sack. "Nobody sells wooden junk after dark. What are you doing? Are you a Miyoshi spy? Speak up!"

The peddler shook his head and pressed his face to the dirt.

"I said, speak up!" The samurai kicked the peddler in the ribs.

The man fell onto his side. He raised his knees to his chest and curled his arms around his face. As the samurai kicked him again, he whimpered softly.

Hiro's temper flared. Any fool could recognize a pauper heading homeward for the night.

The samurai kicked the peddler's shins. "I asked you a question! Answer me."

Conflict sliced through Hiro's chest like a sword through silken cloth. His hatred of bullies prompted him to intervene on the ped-dler's behalf, but Hiro knew the samurai would only arrest them both. He briefly considered assassinating the guard. Unfortunately, that could create more problems than it solved.

Hiro looked around for another solution.

A pair of carved stone lanterns flickered brightly in a yard to the east of the bridge. They sat about four houses up the road, across the street from the Sakura Teahouse.

Hiro heard Mayuri's voice in his head.

Clumsy carving, poorly finished . . . disgrace to a high-class street.

Hiro smiled. Perhaps he could solve two problems in one evening.

While the samurai yelled at the peddler, Hiro scaled the wall that separated the river path from the private home beyond. To his relief, the house was dark and shuttered.

He hurried through the darkened yard with no more sound than a pine tree shedding needles. When he reached the street, he looked back toward the bridge. Distance and foliage made the samu-rai's anger less distinct, but his posture, and the peddler's quivering, told the shinobi the harassment hadn't ceased.

When the samurai bent over the peddler, Hiro dashed across the street and into the shadows on the far side of the road. He made his way through the darkened yards until he reached the veranda of the home with the flickering lanterns.

Light seeped under the cracks in the house's entryway and glowed behind the oiled paper windows. The family who lived there was awake.

Hiro retrieved a pair of stoppered bamboo segments from a pouch concealed within his tunic. He double-checked the thickness of the segments and the stoppers. Then he checked the street and all the houses. He saw no one.

A final glance toward the bridge confirmed the samurai remained preoccupied with the peddler. Hiro raced to the lanterns— which were, in fact, as ugly as described—and dropped a bamboo segment into each.

He returned to the shadows, but didn't pause beside the house. He raced along the edges of the houses toward the river, counting off the seconds as he ran.

Just as Hiro reached the final house before the bridge, the bombs exploded.

The explosion split the silence, setting Hiro's ears to ringing. Pieces of the broken lanterns clattered on the ground. Hiro didn't waste a moment looking back. He knew exactly what the bombs had done.

Ahead, by the bridge, the samurai leaped away from the peddler.

"Run!" he yelled. "Kyoto is under attack!"

But instead of running toward the explosion, the samurai guard ran away across the bridge.

Hiro heard shouts behind him and risked a glance. The owner of the ugly lanterns ran into the yard and tossed a bucket of water on the wreckage. The shattered lanterns hissed and sent up plumes of acrid smoke.

"Water!" the man yelled toward his house. "Hurry, before it catches the house on fire!"

Hiro knew the house was in no danger. He had used small charges, packed with just enough explosive force to cause a nice distraction—and destroy the ostentatious lanterns.

The homeowner ran for another bucket.

Hiro hurried across the road to the place where the peddler lay.

"You need to get up and run," the shinobi said.

The peddler's moan explained why the poor man hadn't answered the samurai. He was mute.

Hiro grabbed the peddler's arm and helped the quivering man to his feet.

"If you can understand my words, you need to run—right now."

CHAPTER 45

The peddler shielded his face with his hands.

"Do you understand me?" Hiro asked.

The peddler nodded and gestured toward the empty sack.

Hiro picked it up and shook it open. "I will help, but hurry. You need to leave this place at once."

And so do I.

The peddler grasped the nearest wooden bowl.

Hiro and the peddler gathered up the scattered wares. When they finished, the poor man bowed, making sounds that indicated gratitude.

"Go," Hiro said, "and from now on, make sure you're home by nightfall."

The peddler nodded, bowed, and hurried off. Hiro noted with approval that the poor man stuck to the shadows near the edge of the river road.

Busy listening to the patter of the peddler's feet on the earthen path, Hiro almost missed the hiss of steel behind his back.

Almost.

The shinobi ducked. A swish of wind brushed past his head. The attacker's blade had missed by only inches.

Hiro drew his shortsword as he spun to face his foe—the samurai guard who kicked the peddler and fled when the explosion shook the street.

He must have recovered his courage and returned.

"Shinobi," the samurai hissed as he advanced and struck again.

Hiro blocked the attack with his wakizashi and backed away to the shadows of the trees. He didn't want the people up the street to see the fight and raise an alarm.

The samurai followed, slashing the air with strikes that made up in force what they lacked in accuracy. Hiro continued to back away, dodging the body-level strikes and ducking when the samurai aimed for his neck.

Without a katana, Hiro lacked the samurai's reach. He couldn't get in range to attack. He could only defend himself and wait for an opening.

When they reached the shadow of the trees, the samurai paused, sword high. "You are a disgrace," he said, "you honorless, beggar-loving shinobi dog. You and all your kind deserve to die."

Hiro gripped his wakizashi. "The only dog I see in this street is you."

With a growl of rage, the samurai raised his katana, lunged . . . and impaled himself on the blade of Hiro's shortsword.

Hiro grasped the samurai's shoulder with his free hand as he shoved his sword into the samurai's stomach. He had dodged beneath the guard's attack and angled his wakizashi upward, piercing the guard beneath his ribs and thrusting the point toward his heart.

The samurai gasped and dropped his sword.

Hiro shoved the blade even deeper, feeling the warmth and wetness of the samurai's blood flow over his hand. He stopped when the hilt stuck fast.

The guard coughed and choked on the liquid flooding his lungs. He sputtered, coughed again, and sent a spray of bloody spittle down his chin.

Hiro stepped away, withdrew his sword, and pressed the blade against the samurai's neck.

"You're a dead man," Hiro said. "The question is, do I end this fast or let you bleed to death on the riverbank?"

This time, there was no priest to stay his hand.

The samurai spit a mouthful of blood in Hiro's face and reached for his wakizashi. Hiro wrenched the weapon from his hand.

The samurai fell to his knees, struggling to breathe as his lungs filled up with blood.

"Enough." Hiro dropped the samurai's shortsword in the road and wiped his own sword clean on the dying man's robe. He grasped the man's topknot and pulled it back.

He bent to look the guard in the eye. "Unlike you, I do not want a man to suffer."

Hiro sheathed his sword, grasped the samurai's chin with his free hand, and snapped the man's neck.

He felt the samurai go limp, life ended with merciful speed.

Hiro released his grip, and the body crumpled forward on the road.

He wiped the blood from his face and hands as best he could and looked around. No one had seen him. The trees along the river path were out of sight of Sanjō Road, and no one walked the path that night—most likely to avoid the samurai guards. Even the peddler had disappeared, though Hiro doubted the mute would turn him in.

Hiro needed to vacate the scene but didn't want to leave a body lying in the road. He had an errand to complete and didn't need the shogun's guards discovering a samurai corpse before he finished his mission. In truth, he would rather they never found it at all.

Without a witness, no one could tie Hiro to the crime, but he still preferred to dispose of the body.

He looked at the river. The current near the banks ran slow, but farther out the water flowed with better speed. He hoped it was enough to move a corpse.

Hiro sheathed his sword and raised the samurai's limp arm. Slinging the arm around his shoulders, Hiro grasped the dead man's waist and lifted the samurai to his side. With one arm around the samurai's waist and the other holding the dead man's lifeless arm around his shoulders, Hiro started toward the bridge. From a distance, they looked like a poorly dressed samurai helping a friend stagger home after too much sake.

When they reached the bridge, Hiro risked a glance up Sanjō Road toward the ruined lanterns. A cluster of people stood in the road, faces lit by the flickering glow of a handheld lantern carried by a woman who might—or might not—have been Mayuri. Angry voices pierced the night. The words didn't carry as far as the bridge, but Hiro didn't care what they said. They hadn't noticed him or the corpse.

Hiro started across the bridge, carrying the samurai at his side. When they reached the middle of the river, Hiro checked to make sure that no one was looking and swung the samurai over the railing.

The body hit the water with a muffled splash.

As Hiro hoped, the current carried the dead man's body away, the corpse already starting to sink as water soaked his heavy silk kimono.

Hiro glanced in both directions. The bridge was empty. No one had seen him dump the body. Sooner or later, the samurai's corpse would wash up on the bank or catch on a bridge, but at least no one would discover it here tonight.

After retrieving the samurai's fallen swords and tossing them into the river, Hiro hurried across the bridge and continued west, though not on Sanjō Road. He wove through narrow side streets to avoid patrolling guards. Not only was he dressed as a shinobi, but his clothes were now stained with samurai blood.

CHAPTER 46

Hiro doubled back from the south and reached the rice sellers' street as the temple bells began to ring hour.

As Hiro expected, a samurai stood guard at the intersection of Sanjō Road and Karasuma Street. Hiro paused and observed the guard from the safety of the shadows. Unlike the samurai on the bridge, this one didn't pace or seek distractions. He watched the road, bored but alert.

Hiro pulled a stoppered bamboo segment from his tunic. As he weighed the explosive in his hand, he considered its effect. The bombs had served their purpose at the bridge, but after dark, in a silent ward, another explosion would lead to trouble Hiro didn't need.

He returned the bamboo tube to his tunic and bent to untie the thongs that held his trousers against his ankles. Once released, they fell into a standard hakama shape. Hiro hoped they would pass for normal trousers in the dimly lighted street.

He stepped from the alley and headed toward the guard, affecting the purposeful gait of a man on an errand.

The samurai turned as Hiro's footsteps reached his ears. Light from a nearby lantern shimmered on his graying hair. The slenderness of his lower arms revealed advancing age.

Hiro hoped the guard was new and didn't know the neighborhood too well.

When the shinobi drew within speaking distance, the samurai said, "Come no farther, sir. Please state your name and business on this street."

Hiro stopped and bowed, encouraged by the samurai's politeness.

"Good evening," he said, "I am a physician on an urgent call."

The samurai looked suspicious. "I didn't see anyone go to call a physician." He took a closer look at Hiro and frowned. "Is that blood on your clothes?"

Hiro looked down at his clothes as if just noticing the spray of bloody droplets down the front. The dark fabric muted the color, but, as he expected, an experienced samurai recognized it even so.

"I was called to a fight in a teahouse. A cook and a brewer, fighting over a girl. I didn't even have time to put on proper clothes." He hoped his tone was sufficiently nonchalant. He didn't want to kill another samurai that night.

"Who won?" the samurai asked, suspicion giving way to curiosity.

Hiro shrugged. "The cook had a knife, but I think both men will live."

"Who called you here?" the samurai asked.

"They sent a boy—he found me at the teahouse," Hiro said. "I don't remember the patient's name. The shop lies two doors past the one of a merchant named Bashō."

The guard shrugged. "No idea who that is, but before you go— my wife has a problem with a recurring toothache. The physician we consulted couldn't cure it."

"Toothache?" Hiro asked. "Have you tried mint tea? Any apothecary should have mint leaves. Buy the fresh ones—they work better than the dried. Your wife should chop a handful of leaves, boil them in water for ten full minutes, strain the liquid, and let it cool. She can drink two cups at a time, three hours apart, until the ache subsides. If that doesn't work, the tooth will have to come out."

"Thank you!" The samurai reached for his purse. "May I pay you? I don't want to take advantage."

Hiro shook his head and bowed. "Not many men would treat a physician with courtesy and respect. I consider your generosity more than sufficient compensation."

"I wish you great success with your other patient." The samurai stepped aside.

Hiro continued down the street, pleased that the samurai's personal needs played into his ruse so well. At the same time, his heart thudded in his chest and his stomach swirled with anxious tension.

As he approached Bashō's warehouse, he slowed and moved to the side of the street.

Lights flickered in the upper floors of half the merchants' houses. Wealthy men could afford the oil to stay up after dark. Unfortunately, wakeful neighbors made the errand far more dangerous. Hiro would have to wait for them to sleep before he entered Bashō's shop.

Wooden shutters covered the front of Bashō's warehouse, blocking the light from within. The upper story had no windows on the front and angled slats across the windows on the sides. Hiro wouldn't know for certain when the merchant's family went to sleep.

Narrow alleys separated Bashō's building from the ones on either side. Hiro stepped into the alley on the east side of the warehouse. Squinting up, he thought he saw a light between the slats of the upstairs window. Unfortunately, he couldn't tell for certain.

Hiro returned to the edge of the alley and looked out into the street. He saw no one in the road and heard no sounds except cicadas and, more distantly, the hoot of an evening owl.

Halfway along the alley, a pair of barrels sat outside a door that probably led to a private storage room behind the shop. Hiro lifted the lid of the closest barrel. The grassy scent of rice hulls wafted out, along with a hint of dust.

Hiro reached inside and found the barrel empty. It seemed solid and smelled clean, but merchants rarely left undamaged barrels out unguarded overnight. Faulty or no, this one would serve his purpose. Hiro climbed into the barrel and returned the lid to its place above his head. The space was dark and cramped but smelled far better than many places Hiro had spent the night.

As he crouched in the barrel, Hiro considered Chikao's murder, and why Ginjiro felt the need to hide the truth about his interactions with the brewer. Omissions seemed suspicious from a man who claimed he had nothing to hide.

208 · FLASK OF THE DRUNKEN MASTER

Yet Ginjiro wasn't the only suspect.

Kaoru's temper, combined with his love of money, gave Chikao's son a motive, too. However, in Hiro's experience, laziness trumped avarice when a murder required work.

Yoshiko claimed innocence, but Hiro didn't know how to interpret the samurai woman's denials. He needed more information about her whereabouts at the time of Chikao's death.

The lack of a clear investigative path made Hiro peevish. In both of the previous murders he solved—the one at the teahouse and the more recent one at the shogunate—specific facts had pointed the way to the killer. This time, the evidence didn't point in any clear direction.

Hiro hoped he could find Bashō and that the merchant's information would prove useful. If not he had killed a man, and spent a night in a barrel, for no good reason.

Temple bells rang. An hour had passed. Hiro stretched his muscles as well as he could to keep from cramping in the tiny space. His foot and ankle went to sleep, sending painful tingling up his leg. Hiro wiggled his toes until the unpleasant sensation went away.

No sooner had he managed this when the other one started prickling.

The temple bells marked the passage of another hour.

Hiro lifted the lid of the barrel and listened. He heard no human sounds in the alley. All the houses he could see were dark. A cricket chirped near the base of the barrel, but only once. Then silence fell.

Hiro left the barrel. As he replaced the lid, he heard footsteps in the street. He crouched behind the barrel and pressed himself against the warehouse wall.

A shadowed figure passed the alley. Hiro saw a scabbard sticking up behind the shadow's back and caught the faintest gleam of moonlight off the oiled *chonmage* on a samurai's head.

Hiro pulled a strip of cloth from beneath his obi and secured it over his nose and mouth.

The thump of geta echoed on the porch of Bashō's shop, followed by the hollow bang of a fist on wooden shutters.

"Bashō!" yelled a female voice. "Get up and open this door at once!"

The voice belonged to Akechi Yoshiko.

CHAPTER 47

Hiro crept along the alley toward the street.

Yoshiko pounded on the shutters. "Bashō! I know you're in there—open up! Quit hiding in your rice like a frightened rat. Get out here now and pay your debt like a man!"

A muffled female voice came through the shutters. "Bashō isn't here."

"You're lying," Yoshiko replied.

"It's after midnight," Bashō's wife complained. "Come back tomorrow."

Yoshiko gave a derisive snort. "Why, so you can claim he isn't here? We've played that game long enough. No more."

"We haven't got your money," Hama called. "Come back tomorrow."

"No," Yoshiko growled. "Open this door, or I'll break it down." Hiro jumped as the shutters banged and rattled.

He peeked around the corner just as Yoshiko stepped back and kicked the wooden shutters hard. Hiro didn't know many women capable of breaking down a door, but Yoshiko had the strength—and the determination too.

Hiro looked at the upper floors of neighboring houses. He saw no lights or movement. No one cried alarm, although that fact did not surprise him. Merchants often worked together to protect their wards from fire and natural dangers, but no one wanted to confront a thief or debt collector in the dark of night. Unless Matsunaga Hisahide's guards investigated, Hama and Bashō were on their own.

Hiro doubted the samurai would come to save the merchant,

either. Hisahide's guards weren't paid to intervene in debt collections. More importantly, the guard on duty let Yoshiko down the street.

She kicked the door again, and Hiro heard a cracking underneath the shuddering bang.

"Stop it—please!" Hama's voice revealed an edge of fear. "I'll open up. Don't break it down!"

Hiro heard the click of a latch and a rattling sound as the shutters opened.

This time, Hama's voice was clear. "I told you, my husband is not home. You have no right to harass us in the middle of the night."

"Your husband owes a substantial debt to the Sakura Teahouse." Yoshiko's response held no remorse. "Over a month ago, he asked for mercy, and I granted him additional time to pay. He hasn't paid a single copper coin. I'm finished waiting."

"Bashō went out of town on business," Hama said. "He'll pay when he returns."

"No rice merchant leaves Kyoto at this time of year." Yoshiko's voice sounded slightly farther away, as if she had stepped inside the shop. "He's hiding, trying to avoid his debt."

Hiro wondered whether Yoshiko was bluffing.

"You have no authority to threaten this family," Hama said. "I'll report you to the magistrate!"

"Go ahead," Yoshiko said. "In fact, I'll stand right here and wait. Your husband owes a legitimate debt. I have the right to collect it. Who will the magistrate punish if you wake him in the night?"

"Only a wicked woman would use her status in this way," Bashō's wife hissed. "You disgrace your family and your class."

Hiro expected Yoshiko to kill the older woman on the spot. No commoner could legally insult a samurai. Instead, he heard a heavy crash and the shimmering hiss of rice against the floor.

"No!" Hama gasped.

A second barrel crashed to the floor.

"No, please," Bashō's wife moaned, "I'm sorry—I apologize!

Please stop, before you ruin us. We cannot sell the rice once it's been soiled."

"Give me the money," Yoshiko said.

Hiro clenched his fist at his side.

Yoshiko would destroy the shop in her search for Bashō's money. The law protected her right to collect a debt, but her bullying tactics turned the shinobi's stomach. Unfortunately, Hiro could not intervene without Yoshiko's wanting an explanation and also recognizing that he wore assassin's clothes.

The samurai woman would not forgive his interference, either way. Any intervention would embarrass Yoshiko in front of Hama. Hiro knew how quickly infatuation could shift to loathing, and he didn't want to think about the emotional outburst that might follow if he pushed Yoshiko over that razor's edge.

Inside the shop, another barrel crashed onto the floor.

Hiro looked around the street, hoping someone would appear.

He thought he saw a shadow move in a darkened upstairs window, but it didn't move again, and no one came into the street.

He cringed at the sound of Yoshiko's geta crushing the merchant's rice. His training told him to stay in the alley, silent and unobserved, but a deeper instinct revolted against the unjust injury the woman caused.

At times, a sense of justice proved an inconvenient traveling companion.

Just as Hiro drew a breath and prepared to intervene, a high-pitched cry and the patter of footsteps echoed in the street.

A shadow darted across the road and into Bashō's shop. Moments later, a human body hit the floor. Wooden scabbards clattered and Yoshiko's voice cried out in startled pain.

"I will not let you hurt these people!" Suke yelled. "You bad kitsune!"

The female samurai tried to speak, but her words sounded muffled, as if someone pressed her face against the floor.

Hiro longed to look but didn't dare expose himself to view.

"The law grants you the right to collect," Suke said, "but not to ruin a merchant's rice without good cause!"

"Get off me!" Yoshiko's words were clearer but sounded strained.

"No," Suke replied.

Hiro leaned around the corner.

Hama stood inside the entrance, holding a lantern that illuminated a startling scene.

Akechi Yoshiko lay facedown on the wooden floor. Suke perched atop her back like the monkey king on his golden throne. He twisted the female samurai's arm in a way that caused significant pain if Yoshiko moved at all.

Grains of rice and overturned barrels lay on the floor around them.

"Let me up right now," Yoshiko snarled.

"If I do," Suke said, "will you leave this shop alone?"

"Her husband—OW!" Yoshiko's words became a yell as Suke pulled her arm a little higher.

"We will pay you," Hama said, "I promise. But we haven't got the money now. Matsunaga Hisahide raised our taxes just this month. We had to call in all our loans, and even then we couldn't pay the bill."

"Not my problem." Yoshiko turned her head and glared at Suke. "Get off my back, old man!"

"I should break this arm," the bald monk mused.

"If you try, I'll have you dragged before the magistrate and executed." Yoshiko struggled slightly, then lay still. "You've already earned a whipping, if not more, for laying hands on a samurai."

CHAPTER 48

"Swords do not make you a samurai, any more than the smell of my robe makes me a sake flask," Suke told Yoshiko. "The magistrate will not flog me, either. You see, I was born a samurai, which makes this a legal fight."

A door slid open somewhere in Bashō's shop.

Hiro stepped back into the alley and listened as heavy footsteps crossed the floor. The footsteps stopped. Something metallic bounced and jingled on the wooden floorboards.

"There's your silver," a deep voice said. "Now go away and leave my family in peace."

"Bashō," the merchant's wife exclaimed, "where did that money come from? I thought you loaned everything we had to the man from the Lucky Monkey."

"The guild has emergency funds. I took a loan." He paused. "I'm sorry, Hama."

Hiro glanced around the corner just as Suke released Yoshiko's arm.

The samurai woman pushed herself to a kneeling position and scooped the pile of coins into her hands. She counted them quickly. "This is only half of what you owe."

"You agreed to take half to start with," Bashō said.

Yoshiko stared at the merchant. After a long, uncomfortable moment she closed her fist around the coins. "Very well. This much will do for now."

She stood up and straightened her kimono.

"You got what you came for," Suke said, "now go."

Hiro slid out of sight around the corner.

"I expect the rest in a month," Yoshiko said. "Do not make me track you down again."

"I will pay as soon as the farmers deliver the harvest," Bashō said. "Sooner, if the men that I've loaned money pay their debts."

"See that you do," Yoshiko snapped.

Hiro pressed himself against the wall as Yoshiko's departing shadow crossed the street and disappeared.

"Please excuse me," Suke said from inside the shop, "I need to go!"

The monk followed the samurai woman down the road. To his credit, and to Hiro's surprise, Suke moved almost without a sound.

Hiro shook his head. He hoped Suke wasn't crazy enough to let Yoshiko see him again that night.

"Go back upstairs," Bashō said, presumably to Hama. "I will clean this up and join you. There's no point in hiding anymore."

"I'll leave the lantern," Hama said. Her footsteps faded away toward the back of the shop.

Hiro looked up and down the silent street. Suke and Yoshiko had disappeared. The buildings remained dark and shuttered, though Hiro felt certain some of the neighbors had watched the scene from upstairs windows.

He hoped they had turned away when Yoshiko left.

After a check to ensure the cloth remained securely tied across his nose and mouth, Hiro rounded the corner and stepped up into the shop.

Bashō had started to close the shutters, but startled and jumped backward. The merchant's jaw fell open as Hiro entered and pulled the shutters closed behind him.

"Take anything you want—just please don't hurt me," Bashō whispered, clutching the lantern in both hands as if it might protect him from attack.

As Hiro hoped, the merchant took him for a bloodstained bandit.

"I have no silver," Bashō said, "I gave it all to a samurai—you probably saw her leave. But you can have all the rice you want, and anything else I have."

Hiro pitched his voice as low as he could comfortably speak. "I do not want your rice. It's information I desire."

"Information?" Bashō echoed. "I don't understand."

"My friends and I drink sake at a brewery not far from here. Two nights ago, an unknown person killed the brewery owner. Rumors say you know the killer. I want to know his name."

Bashō's eyes went wide with terror. "No. I don't know anything!" His hands trembled. Light from the lantern danced across the walls. "I don't even know what you're talking about. I swear!"

"My sources say otherwise," Hiro said. "They saw you with the dead man's son the night the murder happened."

Bashō started to shake his head but stopped as recognition lit his features. "You mean Kaoru? I saw him at the Golden Buddha two nights ago, but I know nothing about a murder."

Hiro remembered Hama's mention of the man from the Lucky Monkey. "My sources say you also loaned him money."

"Kaoru? No—he asked for a loan, but I never gave him money."

"Let me tell you how this works," Hiro said. "If you tell me what you know, and tell the truth, I let you live. If you lie or pretend ignorance—you die."

Bashō slipped on the rice-strewn floor and staggered backward several steps. He recovered his balance and shook his head. "I made a loan to the Lucky Monkey and haven't been repaid, but I don't know anything about a murder. Sir, I swear it!"

"Then you are of no further use to me." Hiro reached for his wakizashi.

"Wait!" Bashō pleaded. "I—I do know something. Not a name, but it might help you find the man you seek."

"Speak carefully," Hiro said. "Your life depends upon your memory."

"I didn't intend to go out that night." Bashō gripped the lantern hard enough to turn his knuckles pale. "My wife didn't like my spending money—especially when we already owed so much and our debtors didn't pay—"

"I care nothing about your debts," Hiro growled, "and even less about your wife. Unless, perhaps, she's attractive? Is she here?" He glanced at the ceiling as if considering a trip to the upstairs living quarters.

"No, she's not attractive," Bashō said, then added, "well, only to a fat old man like me."

"Then get to the point," Hiro said, "I have no patience for rambling stories."

"I stopped at the Golden Buddha for a drink," Bashō said. "I didn't want to sit with Kaoru—he always leaves his bill for someone else—but the only seat in the place was at his table. After we shared a couple of flasks, he started bragging that soon he'd have lots of money and a pretty young wife as well."

"Get to the point." Hiro stepped forward.

"I'm sorry!" Bashō raised the lantern to shield himself. "Kaoru said his father intended to buy a bigger brewery and that he—that Kaoru—would marry the brewer's daughter as part of the deal."

"How does that help me?" Hiro demanded.

"There's more to the story," Bashō said. "A lot of dōshin drink at the Golden Buddha. They laughed and said no man would let his daughter marry a good-for-nothing drunk. Kaoru took a swing at one and missed."

"A fight?" Hiro asked.

"No," the merchant said, "I stopped it. I don't like Kaoru much, but I didn't want to see him arrested, either. I asked him to take a walk outside and tell me about his newfound fortune."

"Why do you care if dōshin arrest a drunk?" Hiro asked. "More importantly, why should I?"

Bashō glanced over his shoulder, as if to ensure his wife had not returned.

"Get to the point," Hiro growled, "and quickly, if you want to live."

CHAPTER 49

Bashō looked at his lantern and murmured, "I didn't want Kaoru arrested . . . because of his mother."

That wasn't the answer Hiro expected. "What do you mean? Explain yourself!"

"I knew Mina—Kaoru's mother—before she married." Bashō gestured toward the shutters. "Her father owned the shop across the street and two doors down. I wanted to marry her, but her father chose Chikao instead of me."

"You stopped an arrest because you care about some drunkard's mother?" Hiro asked.

"You don't have to believe me," Bashō said. "But it's the truth."

"What did you learn on your little walk?" Hiro narrowed his eyes at the merchant.

"Kaoru talked about calling upon the angry ghosts of Ginjiro's ancestors and how a selfish man would always pay for his selfish ways. He said, 'We'll see how big Ginjiro feels when he's lost everything.' Ginjiro is another sake brewer."

"I know who he is," Hiro hissed. "Enough delay. Tell me who killed Chikao."

"I swear, I do not know." Bashō looked desperate.

"If you truly knew nothing, you wouldn't have guessed that he was the man I meant." Hiro drew his wakizashi. "Would you remember more with a blade at your neck?"

"Please," Bashō whimpered. "I don't know who killed him. I swear. I was told that he died but nothing more. Please, I have a family . . ."

Hiro believed the merchant but needed to ensure his silence. He placed the point of his sword on Bashō's stomach. "You will never mention this conversation. Not to anyone, including your wife."

"I won't breathe a word." Tears spilled over Bashō's eyelids, but the merchant didn't dare wipe them away. "I swear I won't."

"I hope not," Hiro said, "because I will know, and even a word is more than your life is worth."

He sheathed his sword, slid the shutters open, and dashed away into the night.

When he reached the opposite side of the road, he hid in the shadows and watched Bashō close up the shop. He didn't leave until the locks slid into place with a click that echoed through the midnight silence.

Hiro didn't worry about Bashō discussing his visit. Kyoto's bandit clans showed mercy to people who held their tongues, but none to those who talked. Bashō would never risk his family's safety, or his own, by telling tales.

Unfortunately, the merchant's words had not revealed as much as Hiro hoped. The shinobi considered the story as he made his way home through the darkened streets and alleys.

Even if ghosts existed—and Hiro did not believe they did—the dead would not obey the commands of the living. Father Mateo's religion claimed that people could speak with a holy ghost, but the priest didn't say he could bend the ghost to his will. On the contrary, the Jesuit claimed it worked the other way around.

However, the part about Ginjiro's losing everything suggested a real threat and also implicated Kaoru. Hiro might have dismissed the story as a drunken flight of fancy, but the words meshed well enough with the facts to make him wonder why Chikao returned to Ginjiro's brewery the night he died—and whether or not he truly returned alone.

Someone in Kyoto knew what happened in that alley. Hiro had to find out who and make that person talk—and he had less than half a day in which to do it. He wished he could have asked Bashō what time Kaoru left the Golden Buddha on the night Chikao died, but the question would have sounded too suspicious coming from a bandit's lips.

He would have to learn the answer another way.

When he reached the bridge at Sanjō Road he found half a dozen samurai standing guard. Given the explosion and the missing guard, he expected more. Hiro waited in the shadows until the guards distracted themselves in conversation. When they did, he scurried off to cross the river farther north.

Only a single samurai guarded the bridge at Marutamachi Road. The guards must have decided Hiro's bombs were an isolated incident, worthy of extra guards at that location but nothing more.

Hiro slipped under the western end of the bridge and considered his options. He doubted his physician act would work so close to home. The guards who patrolled this bridge had seen him in the past, or else would see him in the future, making the lie too great a risk.

Explosive charges wouldn't help him either. One exploding lantern was coincidence. Two explosions in one night meant sabotage. Hiro wanted to get across the bridge, but not enough to generate a citywide alert.

A shadow moved in the street to the west of the bridge. Hiro watched it from his hiding place among the pilings. The shadow didn't move like a tree or with the measured pace of a human being or a horse. The movements came at intervals, and without repetition, in the manner of a spy who wanted to remain unseen.

Nervous excitement loosened Hiro's joints and pooled in his stomach. Whoever approached the bridge did so with the stealth and speed of a highly trained shinobi.

Hiro took a long, slow breath to counteract the energy that lit his veins on fire. Many shinobi worked in Kyoto, rivals as well as those from his own ryu.

Unfortunately, a shinobi heading east on Marutamachi Road at night suggested only two potential targets—and only one if the assassin crossed the bridge. If that happened, Hiro would have to kill the spy before he reached the house where Father Mateo lived.

The other shinobi approached the river slowly, with the subtlety of a master. Hiro tracked the assassin's movements with interest, wondering how the rival shinobi planned to cross the bridge. He doubted the assassin would swim the river. Not only would the samurai guard see someone in the water, but soaking clothes would leave a trail—a fatal error no trained spy would make.

The shadow reached the final house before the bridge and disappeared into the yard. Hiro fixed his eyes on the spot and waited. Nothing moved.

Perhaps the assassin wasn't after the Jesuit after all.

Hiro breathed a sigh of relief and reprimanded himself for the assumption.

As the surge of excitement left his muscles, Hiro wondered who lived in the house at the end of the street. He stared at the building but saw no clues to the owner's identity. He saw no sign of the assassin, either. No light shone through the latticed windows. No foliage moved in the yard.

Hiro turned his thoughts to the river and how to cross it safely.

A woman's scream shattered the silence.

Hiro tensed. The scream came from inside the final house before the river—the one the shinobi assassin entered.

"Help!" the woman screamed again. "Help me! Help! A thief!"

Geta thumped on the wooden bridge as the samurai guard responded to the cry. Footsteps pounded the earthen road, and Hiro peeked from beneath the bridge to watch the samurai race to the darkened house.

Hiro crouched, preparing to run across the bridge the moment the guard disappeared from view. He knew he could get across and hide before the samurai returned. He took a breath, prepared to run . . .

. . . and ducked back into his hiding place as the strange shinobi broke from the shadows and raced across the Kamo River bridge.

CHAPTER 50

Asecond surge of adrenaline shocked Hiro's system as the assassin's footsteps pattered overhead. When they faded into silence, Hiro hurried out from his hiding place and pursued the strange shinobi across the bridge.

As he ran, he caught a glimpse of the assassin disappearing into the shadows on Marutamachi Road.

Hiro didn't stop running until he reached the torii gate at Okazaki Shrine. There, he paused in the shadows to listen. He heard crickets and cicadas, nothing more. He hoped his race across the bridge alerted the assassin to his presence. Most shinobi abandoned a mission, temporarily at least, if someone saw them approaching the target's home.

He moved along the street, staying in the darkness when he could. Although he hoped the assassin had disappeared, Hiro didn't trust his hopes any more than he trusted assumptions.

Lights flickered behind the oiled paper windows of Father Mateo's home. The sight released a bit of the tension binding Hiro's chest. A shinobi would wait for the lights to go out before infiltrating the residence.

Hiro paused and watched for movement in the shadows. The house on the opposite side of the street from the Jesuit's was dark and silent. Hiro found himself suddenly grateful for the neighbor's akita. The assassin could not approach from that direction without triggering a fit of angry barking.

Something moved in the shadows near the fence that circled Father Mateo's yard. Hiro watched with horror as the strange shinobi approached the gate and slipped into the garden without a sound.

As Hiro started toward the fence, he realized that Matsunaga

Hisahide might have sent the assassin after Luis Álvares, believing the merchant's death would stop the weapon sale to the Miyoshi. That left Hiro with yet another ethical dilemma. He loathed Luis on a personal level but didn't think the Portuguese merchant deserved to die. Not unless his death would save the priest.

The Iga ryu didn't care about the merchant, and the unknown client who paid for Hiro's services had never mentioned Luis Álvares. Even so, no other shinobi would harm the Jesuit's household on Hiro's watch.

A shout would send the assassin running, but he would return, perhaps at a time when Hiro did not expect him.

Hiro didn't intend to let his enemy slip away.

A shinobi would notice someone following him through the garden gate, so Hiro slipped into the neighbors' yard and climbed an ancient cherry tree that sent its questing branches across the wall. From the relative safety of the tree, he peered into the Jesuit's yard.

A shadowed figure stood on the veranda outside Father Mateo's room. The Jesuit's silhouette flickered on the paper panels, separated from the assassin by only a flimsy shoji.

The strange shinobi reached for the Jesuit's door.

Hiro retrieved a *shuriken* from a pocket inside his sleeve. He preferred to use the metal stars as fistload weapons, not projectiles, but he had no time to close the distance now. He measured the distance carefully. In daylight, and without obstructions, Hiro could strike a fatal blow to the man on the porch with ease. Tonight he had to make the throw in darkness and through branches, and he didn't know how quickly this assassin would react.

Hiro drew a preparatory breath.

The strange shinobi pivoted, and Hiro saw his opponent's face. It was Ozuru.

Hiro threw the shuriken but knew as he released it that the star would miss its target. He leaped from the tree and hit the ground as the metal star embedded itself in the porch with a silent thump.

"Don't move." Hiro jumped to the veranda and drew his sword. "I missed the throw on purpose. I will kill you if you run."

Ozuru raised his empty hands. "We have no dispute, Matsui-san."

"We do," Hiro said, "if you attempt to kill a man that I protect."

Ozuru lowered his hands to his sides. "I came to warn you, not to kill the priest."

Hiro didn't believe him—not yet, anyway. "Deliver your warning."

Ozuru's gaze flickered from Hiro's blade to the spots on his clothing. His eyes narrowed. He met Hiro's gaze and nodded, accepting Hiro's decision not to lower the sword.

"Hisahide has refused the Miyoshi daimyō's demand to surrender Kyoto. War is now inevitable. If the Miyoshi start that war with Portuguese firearms, Hisahide will declare this household guilty of treason. He will execute the merchant and the priest."

"The Miyoshi weapons order has been canceled," Hiro said. "Hisahide has no cause to blame the Portuguese. Not the ones in this house, anyway."

Ozuru drew back in surprise. "Canceled? When?"

"Yesterday," Hiro said. "The merchant does not want to start a war."

"My sources claim the sale proceeds on schedule," Ozuru said, "and that your merchant simply arranged for a different Portuguese to deliver the firearms to the Miyoshi stronghold."

Hiro hid his chagrin behind an innocent expression. "You cannot blame Luis if another merchant revives a canceled sale."

"Matsunaga Hisahide will not consider that a cancellation," Ozuru said.

"I appreciate the warning." Hiro wondered what the Koga ryu would gain from helping Hiro save the Jesuit and Luis. The respect and passive truce between the Iga shinobi and Ozuru's Koga ryu did not explain the other man's behavior. Somehow, the priest's survival—or the merchant's—benefited Koga's plans.

Hiro sheathed his sword.

Ozuru's expression softened. "Koga desires stability in Kyoto. Foreign deaths will divide the city, creating opportunities for enemies far more dangerous than the Miyoshi."

"You mean Oda Nobunaga," Hiro said.

"And others." Ozuru paused. "Ashikaga Yoshiaki has left Nara."

"The former shogun's brother?" Hiro frowned. "Can a monk lay claim to the shogunate?"

"Yoshiaki renounced his vows when he left the temple," Ozuru said. "Rumors say he does intend to claim the shogunate."

"How much truth do these rumors hold?" Hiro asked.

Ozuru shook his head. He would reveal no more. "You should leave Kyoto quickly, with the merchant and the priest. This city is no longer safe for you."

"I understand." Hiro bowed but kept Ozuru's hands in sight. "And thank you."

"Do not thank me. I was never here." Ozuru sprinted to the wall and disappeared over the top without a sound.

Hiro hoped he would move as smoothly when he reached Ozuru's age.

The door behind Hiro slid open. Father Mateo stepped onto the porch.

"I heard voices." The Jesuit looked around the yard. "Where did he go?"

"I don't know what you mean," Hiro said. "It's only me."

CHAPTER 51

Father Mateo gave Hiro a knowing look. "Just you, you say."

The priest stepped into his room and beckoned. "I don't suppose you'll tell me where you've been the last few hours?" He frowned. "What's on your clothes?"

"Three years ago, I promised I would not lie to you," Hiro said. "It is better you don't know about my clothes."

The Jesuit frowned but didn't press the issue.

"As for the other half of your question, Bashō has made a miraculous reappearance." Hiro explained about his conversation with the missing merchant, though he left out all the details of his journey there and back.

Father Mateo shook his head at the thought of Suke tackling Yoshiko. He frowned when Hiro mentioned Kaoru's words about angry ghosts.

"Phantoms don't exist," the Jesuit said. "Not in the sense you mention, anyway."

"I agree," Hiro said.

"You do?" Father Mateo looked surprised. "I thought all Japanese believed in ghosts."

"Most do," Hiro said, "but I do not. If vengeful ghosts existed, I'd have seen them."

Father Mateo slid the shoji closed. "What makes you say so?"

Hiro didn't answer.

The Jesuit gave him a searching look. "Do all shinobi think this way?"

"My training is not the reason." Hiro didn't intend to say more, but found himself continuing. "When I was nine years old, I spent a night with a murdered man."

"You what?" Father Mateo ran a hand through his hair, too startled to prevent the nervous gesture. "What kind of parent leaves a child alone with a corpse?"

"My parents had nothing to do with it." Hiro knelt, facing the priest. He had never told the tale but felt the Jesuit should hear it. "In fact, I doubt they even know it happened."

Father Mateo knelt and waited for Hiro to continue.

"The spring I turned nine," Hiro said, "a spy infiltrated the Iga ryu. My elder brother uncovered the truth, and my father interrogated the spy until he confessed his mission. It took four days, despite my father's excellent skills at persuading men to talk.

"The enemy died of his wounds within a day of his confession. Hanzō ordered the body moved to an empty, defiled storehouse in the woods about a mile from the ryu."

"They kept the body?" Father Mateo asked.

Hiro nodded. "Iga doesn't miss a chance to make a point. Hanzō wanted the body stored until the stiffness that follows death had ended. After that, he planned to return the body to the enemy's lord—in several pieces."

"That's barbaric," the Jesuit said.

Hiro raised an eyebrow. "Civilized people would nail him to a cross?"

Father Mateo pressed his lips together.

Hiro stifled a smile and continued, "That morning, while exploring in the woods, I saw a group of older boys on the path that led to the storehouse. The rules forbid our going there, but some boys do not care so much for rules. I followed at a distance."

Hiro paused. "I did not think they would notice me."

"But they did," the Jesuit said.

"Not right away," Hiro answered. "They dared each other to enter the storehouse and look at the dead man's corpse. I moved too close, drawn by curiosity and overinflated pride in my own skills. The oldest boy saw me and called me forward. He dared me to enter the storehouse too. Refusing would brand me a coward, so I did it."

"You were nine." Father Mateo shook his head. "No one would call you a coward."

"You are not shinobi," Hiro said. "You cannot understand."

The Jesuit leaned back, lips tight with disapproval but unwilling to start an argument. "They locked you in with the body, didn't they?"

Hiro hadn't expected the priest to guess. "Correct. They did."

"No one noticed you missing?" Father Mateo asked. "No one heard your cries for help?"

"I did not call for help." Hiro considered the Jesuit's furrowed brow and downcast eyes. "I did not tell this tale to cause you sorrow—and even less to earn your pity. I speak because it proves a vital point about the dead."

Father Mateo folded his hands in his lap, as if to demonstrate a willingness to listen without any further questions.

"At first," Hiro said, "the terror felt like fishbones in my throat. I breathed too fast, grew dizzy, and sat down on the wooden floor. As my eyes adjusted, I noticed little slivers of light coming in through cracks in the storehouse walls. I saw the spy's defiled body, barely out of reach across the floor.

"I thought I saw the body move. I thought I heard him breathe. I pushed my back against the wall, too terrified to move or make a sound.

"I sat that way for many hours. Evening came, and darkness, and I passed the night in silent terror, listening for the vengeful ghost I knew would come for me. I heard a rustling noise and screamed— just once—when a rat ran across my toes. But it was only a rat. No ghost appeared. The body did not move.

"By morning, terror left me. As the cracks around the door grew gray with dawn, I realized I need not fear the dead. My father tortured that spy to death. If a man could return as a ghost, to take revenge, he would have done so.

"I do not know where the life inside a man may go when the body dies. But the corpse of a man is just like that of a fish, or a bird, or a dog. It is dead, and only dead, and nothing more."

After a pause Hiro added, "Since the dead cannot return, no man can persuade a ghost to do his bidding, which means Kaoru had some other plan to force the sale of Ginjiro's brewery."

"Perhaps some kind of trick?" Father Mateo asked. "A trick that went wrong and killed Chikao?"

"I don't know," Hiro said, "but I know who does."

The Jesuit nodded. "Kaoru."

"No," Hiro said, "Mina, Chikao's wife. She mentioned a need to atone for her husband's wrongful acts but wouldn't give details."

"That could refer to anything," Father Mateo said. "Husbands and wives have many private conflicts."

"True," Hiro said, "but Mina's words suggested something serious, and judges of the afterlife don't bother much with trifles. Men don't endanger their souls by minor quarrels."

"Don't be so certain," Father Mateo said. "Still, it can't do any harm to try and find out what she knows."

CHAPTER 52

The following morning, Hiro and Father Mateo walked to the Lucky Monkey brewery. Father Mateo carried his travel papers to ensure they met no samurai delays. Hiro disliked obeying Hisahide's protocols but acknowledged that cooperation ended better than spiteful argument.

They crossed the river at Shijō Road. Only a single samurai stood guard on the river bridge. He seemed relaxed and didn't ask to see their travel papers.

Apparently, the missing samurai's body had not been found. A short distance past the river, Hiro turned into Pontochō.

"Where are we going?" the Jesuit asked. "This isn't the fastest way to the Lucky Monkey."

"We need to make an intermediate stop," the shinobi said. As they walked down the narrow, shuttered alley, Hiro inhaled the distinctive smells that meant the morning's nightsoil collection hadn't occurred on time.

He stopped in front of the moneylender's shop across the street from the Golden Buddha. As he raised a hand to knock, the wooden door swung open before his fist.

Hiro lowered his hand and nodded to the familiar, beautiful woman in the doorway.

"What do you want?" she asked. "You already know that I don't help your kind."

"We haven't come for a loan," Hiro said. "We want to know about the debt Akechi Yoshiko collected for you."

"That is a private matter," the woman said.

"Between you and a man named Kaoru?" Hiro asked.

The woman seemed to consider closing the door in Hiro's face.

"I won't discuss my loans, or the names of my clients."

"So, if I wanted to repay that loan, you wouldn't let me?" Hiro asked.

The moneylender crossed her arms. "That trick won't work with me. Also, I told you, I don't make loans to men."

Hiro nodded. "Very well, I'll speak with Mina. Thank you anyway."

"Mina?" the woman looked confused.

"Kaoru's mother," Father Mateo said.

The moneylender's eyes revealed no recognition. "I have never heard that name, Matsui-*san*."

Hiro caught a subtle shift in the woman's tone. He also noticed something else. "When did you learn my name?"

"After you left, I went to the Golden Buddha," the woman said. "Eba didn't know you, either, so I asked around. Your foreign friend has a good reputation, which is the only reason I opened the door for you today."

Hiro gambled on the truth. "We're investigating a murder, and believe Akechi Yoshiko has information about the crime. Did you see her in Pontochō two nights ago? Perhaps at the Golden Buddha?"

"The Golden Buddha?" The moneylender laughed. "She wouldn't cross the threshold. But I did see her that evening. She was here."

"Which shop did she visit?" Father Mateo asked.

"This one." The woman gestured toward the ceiling. "She was here. She wanted to collect a debt from one of the Buddha's patrons, but she knew if he saw her coming, he would run. She asked me to let her watch for him from one of my upstairs windows."

"And you agreed?" Hiro asked.

"In a manner of speaking." The moneylender crossed her arms again. "She made a request I could not refuse.

"A little over a year ago I brokered a deal to move an entertainer from the Sakura Teahouse to a brothel here in Pontochō. There were lies involved, although I didn't know them at the time. I learned about it only after the girl's lover died.

"Two nights ago, Yoshiko said she knew about the lies and that the brothel paid far less than the girl's real value. She threatened to call me before the magistrate on a claim that I conspired to help the brothel cheat the Sakura Teahouse on the purchase price. That is, unless I let her use my house to wait for the man she sought."

"Yoshiko didn't work for you, then." Father Mateo frowned. "Why didn't you call the dōshin?"

"To what end?" the moneylender asked. "Akechi-*san* is samurai. I am not. The dōshin may not like her, but her rank would still prevail."

A smile crept over the woman's face. "I handled the situation a different way. I allowed Akechi-*san* to watch . . . and also sent a boy to warn the debtor."

"So Yoshiko never saw her target leaving," Hiro said.

"I don't know," the moneylender said. "She was watching from the window when I went to sleep a few minutes before midnight. When I woke, at dawn, she had gone. I sleep soundly. I didn't hear her leave."

"Why did she come here yesterday?" Hiro asked.

The moneylender smiled. "Much the same reason you're here now. She threatened to shut my business down if I spoke to anyone about her waiting here that night."

"Then why are you telling us?" Father Mateo asked.

"As I said, you have an unusual reputation." The moneylender nodded toward the far side of the street. "People say you intervene to stop the poor from suffering without cause. I'd say that merits help when I can give it."

"We appreciate your assistance." Hiro retrieved a handful of silver coins from his purse and dropped them into the moneylender's palm with a gentle clink.

She closed her hand around the coins. "Do not call on me to testify before the magistrate. If I ever see your face again, I'll swear you are a stranger."

Hiro and Father Mateo left the moneylender's shop and headed south toward Shijō Road.

"What made you think to speak with the moneylender?" Father Mateo asked.

"A guess, though as it happens, an incorrect one. I wondered why Yoshiko would visit a shop that didn't make loans to samurai. I guessed—inaccurately—that the moneylender had hired her as a debt collector."

"She said she didn't make loans to men," Father Mateo pointed out. "Why would she make an exception for Kaoru?"

"I didn't think she made an exception," Hiro said. "I thought she lied to us about the nature of her loans."

"Still, we learned that Yoshiko might be the killer," Father Mateo said. "We can't account for her whereabouts at the time the murder happened."

"Yes," Hiro said, "though whether she killed Chikao remains to be seen."

As they approached the Lucky Monkey, Father Mateo asked, "What will we do if Mina refuses to see us?"

Hiro ignored the question, stepped to the door, and knocked.

Footsteps approached on the opposite side. The door opened a fraction and Mina's face appeared in the crack. When she recognized the visitors, she opened the door the rest of the way and bowed. "Good morning, sirs."

"Good morning," Hiro said.

Mina bowed again. "I humbly apologize for my son's demand that Magistrate Ishimaki shorten the time for the brewer's trial. I asked him to show mercy, but he refused." She closed her eyes and shook her head. "I am sorry you have come. I cannot help you."

CHAPTER 53

"I think, perhaps, you can help us more than you realize," Hiro said. "May we explain?"

Mina stepped away from the door. "Of course. May I offer you tea or sake?"

"No, thank you." Hiro followed her inside. "We can't stay long."

When they reached the drinking room, Mina made a gesture that invited the men to sit.

"Forgive my directness," Hiro said, "but we need to leave in time for the brewer's trial.

"During our previous visit you mentioned a need to atone for your husband's sins—to ensure the heavenly judges pass his soul to paradise. What, precisely, threatens your husband's spirit?"

Mina looked at the floor. "Chikao was not a wicked man."

"We believe that," Father Mateo said.

"I suppose it cannot hurt to tell you." Mina looked up. "My husband planned to do an evil thing. The kami required his life in recompense."

"God did not take Chikao's life," Father Mateo said. "A person did."

Mina shook her head. "It was his karma. Evil plans bring evil consequences."

The Jesuit opened his mouth to argue, but Hiro cut him off. "Tell us the evil thing your husband planned."

"Chikao and Ren wanted to buy Ginjiro's brewery," Mina said, "but Ginjiro would not sell at any price. They picked Ginjiro's largely because of Tomiko—Ginjiro's daughter. A wife who could run a brewery could help my son in ways no partner could."

"But Ginjiro refused to sell, and refused the marriage," Hiro said.

Mina nodded. "After they realized that neither money nor words would sway him, my husband and Ren—along with Kaoru—planned to vandalize the brewery and, thereby, force Ginjiro to sell."

"Vandalize it?" Father Mateo asked. "How would that force a sale?"

Mina's cheeks flushed red. "They planned to break the brewery doors and urinate into the casks. They thought if they ruined Ginjiro's stock, he wouldn't have the money to make repairs and cleanse the brewery—he would have to sell and allow my son to marry his daughter, Tomiko.

"I told them I disapproved of the plan and even threatened to tell Ginjiro. After that, Chikao agreed to abandon the idea. I believed him—he had never lied to me before.

"But then, the evening before Chikao died, I heard him talking with Ren and Kaoru. My husband had changed his mind. They were making final plans to vandalize Ginjiro's brewery.

"I confronted my husband and told him what I heard. He explained that Kaoru owed more money than we knew—far more than this small brewery could pay. Without a successful place like Ginjiro's, we would never pay off Kaoru's debts. And without a wife who could run the business, Kaoru could never succeed once we were gone . . ." Mina trailed off.

After a brief silence she continued, "That very evening, a debt collector threatened to throw our son in prison unless we paid his debts at once."

"So you agreed to go along with your husband's plan," Father Mateo said.

"I did not." Mina straightened. "I love my son, but he made his own decisions, and no innocent man should suffer in his place. Unfortunately, Kaoru seemed determined to force his father to turn to vandalism."

A creak behind them made Hiro shift position to watch the doorway.

Mina continued, "The last time we talked, Chikao promised to stop the plot, but since he died in Ginjiro's alley, on the very night they planned to vandalize the brewery, I have to believe he did not keep his word."

"Correct." Ren appeared in the doorway. "Which is why Ginjiro killed him."

Ren bowed to Hiro and Father Mateo. "Forgive my interruption."

"How do you know what happened?" Hiro asked. "Did you go with Chikao that night?"

Ren shook his head. "I already told you, I was home in bed. Chikao tried to persuade me to attempt the vandalism, but I didn't want to risk Ginjiro's ruining our chances with the guild. The chance of someone seeing us or connecting us to the acts was far too high. I tried to persuade Chikao of that. Like Mina, I believed that I succeeded."

"What about Kaoru?" Hiro asked. "Could he have changed his father's mind?"

"He must have," Ren said. "I know he tried. Kaoru said he would spend the early part of the evening in Pontochō, so people would see him there, and no one would suspect that he and Chikao committed the crime. He thought the customers here would vouch for his father."

"So Kaoru planned to meet Chikao at Ginjiro's that night, after closing?" Hiro asked.

"I didn't know any of this," Mina said, "but I don't believe my husband went to vandalize the brewery. He took the money with him, which he wouldn't do unless he meant to pay off Kaoru's debt. At least, I want to believe that was his plan and that he changed his mind about the vandalism before he died."

Father Mateo glanced at the service counter lined with wooden flasks. "You must have had a successful evening if the profits allowed a payment toward the debt."

"We didn't make that much," Ren said. "Enough to make the initial payment Ginjiro demanded, but nothing more. Even for that, I had to give my half of the evening's profits too."

"I thought you disapproved of helping pay off Kaoru's debts," the shinobi said.

"I did," Ren said, "but we couldn't risk Ginjiro giving the brewers' guild a bad report."

"Chikao must have given up the plan," Father Mateo said. "Otherwise, he wouldn't have taken the money. Maybe a bandit killed him after all."

"I don't think so," Ren replied. "Bandits use swords and daggers, not sake flasks."

"True," Hiro said. "But tell me: why didn't you confess the plan to vandalize Ginjiro's brewery sooner?"

"Would you have mentioned it in my place?" Ren asked. "To tell the truth, I'm ashamed we even considered it. I'm glad that Mina heard of it and stopped us. I got caught up in wanting something I didn't have. When she made us stop and think, I realized it wasn't worth the risk. I thought we could make this brewery work until we joined the guild, and then the guild could help us find a better place to purchase."

"It didn't occur to you that Kaoru might not have surrendered the plan?" Hiro asked.

"He said he agreed to abandon it," Ren said, "and he sounded convincing."

"We appreciate your honesty," Hiro said. "We need to go."

"I will escort the visitors out," Ren said, turning toward the entry.

Mina bowed and started for the room where her husband's body lay.

Hiro followed Father Mateo through the passage to the door. After the Jesuit left the building, Hiro turned to Ren. "Do you plan to attend Ginjiro's trial this afternoon?"

"Someone should," Ren said. "Kaoru is not reliable, and Mina doesn't want to—"

"I will be there." Kaoru stepped into view.

Hiro wondered where Chikao's son had been during their

conversation and how much he had overheard. Based on the angry look on the young man's face, he had heard it all.

Kaoru scowled at Hiro. "I intend to watch my father's killer die."

Hiro and Father Mateo left the Lucky Monkey and turned north on the road that paralleled Pontochō.

The Jesuit shook his head. "We're out of time. I really thought we'd find the killer and save Ginjiro."

"We found the killer," Hiro said.

Father Mateo stopped in the street. "But how? We don't know for sure who killed Chikao."

"I do," Hiro said, "and now, I think I can prove it."

CHAPTER 54

Hiro and Father Mateo stopped by Ginjiro's brewery on their way to the magistrate's compound. Tomiko stood in front of the shop, sweeping the street with a broom. She bowed as the men approached.

"Matsui-*san*," Tomiko said, "please tell me you found a way to save my father. The magistrate's hearing starts an hour from now."

"Will you attend it?" Hiro asked.

"I wanted to, but I cannot." Tomiko gripped the broom. "I cannot take my mother there and cannot leave her here alone."

"Don't feel bad," Father Mateo said. "Your father did not want you to attend."

"I still feel like a coward," Tomiko said.

"Attendance is no reflection on your courage," Hiro said, "and Ginjiro will worry less if he knows that your mother is safe. However, if you can manage it, I think your father would draw strength from your presence at his trial."

Father Mateo shot Hiro a look. The shinobi hoped the priest wouldn't argue. He wanted Tomiko present at the hearing. She deserved to hear the truth.

Ginjiro's daughter blinked back tears. "If I don't go, I will not get to say good-bye." She set the broom against the wall and bowed. "I will find someone to watch my mother. Matsui-*san*, please save my father. I will be forever in your debt."

Hiro and Father Mateo heard the crowd in the magistrate's compound from almost a block away. Inside the wooden palisade, voices chattered and squawked like a murder of crows.

The dōshin guarding the gates allowed the shinobi and the priest to pass in without question.

Hiro paused at the edge of the yard and surveyed the crowd. He never forgot his primary duty was still to protect the priest.

The crowd consisted primarily of merchants and the family members of persons standing trial for various crimes. A dozen armored samurai stood guard along the wall, mostly dōshin, but also several with the Matsunaga crest. Hiro noticed the commoners edging away from the samurai. Not even the innocent ones felt comfortable standing close to the guards.

He scanned the crowd but saw no familiar faces. Ren and Kaoru wouldn't arrive for several minutes more. He hoped Yoshiko would attend as well.

If she didn't, his plan would need adjusting.

Hiro found Suke's absence surprising. He hoped the monk was merely late and not passed out from drinking too much sake.

The magistrate would probably hear Ginjiro's matter first. If the shogun wanted lessons taught, murder trials and executions offered the most persuasive ones.

Hiro caught Father Mateo's eye and nodded toward the front of the crowd. The men moved forward together, commoners parting before them like the panels of a noren blown apart by stormy winds. They stood about a body length behind the sandy pit where prisoners would kneel during hearings.

As the dōshin led a line of sorry prisoners toward the dais, a commotion at the gates made Hiro turn.

"You cannot keep us out!" Yoshiko's voice echoed through the compound. "Let us through!"

The crowd grew silent. People turned.

Hiro left Father Mateo near the *shirazu* and hurried through the crowd. Once again, the packed-in commoners parted as he passed. No one blocked the path of a samurai.

At the gates, Yoshiko stood face to face with the dōshin who guarded the compound. Beside the samurai woman, Tomiko stood as still and straight as an ancient cedar.

"This is no place for a girl," the dōshin said.

"She is a woman, not a girl," Yoshiko snapped. "Her father is on trial today. You cannot bar her entry. Step aside!"

"Is this true?" The dōshin asked Tomiko. "Is your father standing trial today?"

Ginjiro's daughter nodded.

"Go home to your family," the dōshin said. "Why do you want to see your father die?"

"That is not your business," Yoshiko said. "Let us through, or arrest us and let the magistrate decide."

She took Tomiko's arm and started past the dōshin. To Hiro's surprise, he let the women pass.

"Who's next?" The samurai glared at the line of people near the entrance. "Make it quick, the hearing starts in minutes!"

The guard had no authority to keep Tomiko out. Hiro interpreted his words as a vain attempt to save the girl the pain of watching her father's condemnation. Dislike for bullies notwithstanding, he agreed. Ginjiro's daughter didn't need to see her father stand before the magistrate. However, Hiro knew something the other samurai didn't. Tomiko needed to be there, to ensure an innocent person didn't die.

Before Hiro could catch Yoshiko's eye, a yoriki emerged from the magistrate's office, walked to the dais, and glared at the crowd.

Hiro hurried to rejoin the priest before the hearing started.

"Magistrate Ishimaki will hear the afternoon cases now!" the yoriki called above the chattering voices. "Silence! Show respect for the magistrate!"

The commoners knelt and bowed their heads to the ground as Magistrate Ishimaki emerged from the building and made his way to the dais. Ishimaki-*san* wore a black kimono and a pair of expensive swords in decorative scabbards. His bald head gleamed in the midday sun as he climbed the three low wooden stairs and knelt on a white tatami atop the dais.

Hiro considered how different the afternoon sessions seemed from the morning hearings held inside the magistrate's private office. Wealthy men and samurai could speak their claims in private, while the commoners faced justice in the open.

Magistrate Ishimaki arranged his robes and looked at the yoriki, who moved to stand beside the pit of sand.

"Call the first prisoner," the magistrate said.

The yoriki unrolled a scroll. "A capital crime. Ginjiro, a sake brewer, accused of murder."

He looked to the right of the dais, where Ginjiro waited with the other prisoners.

The magistrate nodded. "Bring the accused man forward."

CHAPTER 55

Two dōshin brought Ginjiro to the sand. The brewer walked with his head hung low and his arms and legs bound tightly by elaborately knotted ropes. Ginjiro's stained kimono bore a filthy witness to his time in prison.

When they reached the shirazu, the guards took hold of Ginjiro's arms and lowered the brewer to his knees in the sand.

Ginjiro bowed his head before the magistrate.

"I will read the charge." The yoriki's voice rang out across the yard. "This man, Ginjiro, murdered a fellow brewer during an argument over a debt."

"How do you answer the charge?" the magistrate asked.

Ginjiro raised his head. "I am not guilty."

"Not guilty?" Magistrate Ishimaki looked surprised.

"That is correct," Ginjiro said. "I did not kill Chikao."

The magistrate's forehead wrinkled in consternation. "Can you prove this?"

Hiro stepped forward. "I can prove it."

The magistrate's eyes widened. "Matsui Hiro? You are the man investigating the crime?"

Magistrate Ishimaki looked out at the crowd, but didn't seem to find the face he sought. His gaze returned to Hiro. "The yoriki mentioned seeing you at the murder scene. I should have guessed that you were the one Ginjiro's family asked for help."

Hiro bowed. "Yes, Ishimaki-*san*."

The magistrate leaned forward. "Tell me what you learned."

"I object!" Kaoru pushed his way through the crowd. Ren followed close behind him.

Kaoru pointed at Ginjiro. "That man killed my father. This . . . ronin . . . wants to interfere."

"On the contrary," Hiro said, "I wish to see the murderer brought to justice."

Magistrate Ishimaki shifted his gaze from Hiro to Kaoru as if weighing each man's words. At last he said, "Matsui-*san* will speak."

He looked at Kaoru and added, "You may speak when Matsui-*san* has finished. I wish to hear all the facts before I render a decision."

"May I request a favor?" Hiro asked.

Magistrate Ishimaki frowned. "Do not test my patience. I have granted you a significant favor by allowing you to speak in this man's defense."

"Yes, and I am grateful," Hiro said. "However, I hoped you would order the dōshin to lock the gates until you render final judgment. The real killer is here, inside the compound, as we speak. I would hate to see that person slip away."

Magistrate Ishimaki nodded to the yoriki. "Secure the gates. No one leaves until this matter is resolved."

Hiro waited until the massive wooden gates swung closed with a thump and a rattle.

"You will now reveal the killer," the magistrate said. "But I warn you, falsehoods will result in your sharing the killer's fate."

"I beg the magistrate's indulgence," Hiro said. "I cannot merely state a name. Unless I explain what happened on the night Chikao died, the killer will deny the crime. Ginjiro's innocence will not be proven."

"It's a trick," Kaoru said. "He's stalling for time."

"Silence!" Magistrate Ishimaki glared at Kaoru. "I will decide what is or is not a trick."

He looked at Hiro. "Proceed with your tale."

"Ginjiro owns a brewery in the commercial ward," the shinobi said, "a fine one, with fifty feet of frontage on a trafficked road. Chikao, with his partner Ren, owned a tiny, unlicensed brewery in an unnamed alley south of Pontochō. The only fortunate thing about the Lucky Monkey brewery is its name."

"What does that matter?" Kaoru demanded.

Hiro ignored him. "Chikao made offers to purchase Ginjiro's brewery, but Ginjiro would not sell at any price. At first, I wondered why Chikao would need Ginjiro's shop, and not another. Ginjiro said he'd help the Lucky Monkey's owners join the brewers' guild, and the guilds assist their members when it comes to finding better space.

"The problem was, the brewers' za would not admit a man whose son ran up a debt and did not pay. Not unless that brewer demonstrated some substantial change that would allow him to prevent his son from causing future problems."

Ginjiro's eyes widened. "Like buying a better brewery and marrying that son to a woman with the skills to run the business herself."

"Exactly," Hiro said. "But Chikao ran into problems. He couldn't get a loan to pay the debt. Then, the man who owned the brewery Chikao wanted wouldn't sell and wouldn't consider allowing his daughter to marry Chikao's son. In fact, that man—Ginjiro—wanted only to discuss the payment of the debt that Kaoru owed."

Kaoru scowled but did not deny the words.

"A series of arguments ensued, with threats exchanged," Hiro said. "On the night of the murder, they argued again, and Ginjiro swore to collect on Kaoru's debt at any cost."

The magistrate asked Ginjiro, "Is this true?"

The brewer looked at the sand beneath his knees. "I made some threats, but I didn't mean them. Not the way they sounded."

"Liar," Kaoru said. "You threatened to kill my father, and then you did it."

Ginjiro tried to look at Kaoru but his bonds prevented him from turning all the way around.

Magistrate Ishimaki frowned. "So far, your tale does not exonerate this man."

"Please indulge me by listening all the way to the end," Hiro said. "After that final argument, Kaoru abandoned his father to go drinking in Pontochō. Chikao started back to his brewery for the night. On the way, Chikao ran into a debt collector seeking payment for another of Kaoru's debts."

Hiro turned to the crowd. "That debt collector is here. She can confirm this."

He wondered whether Yoshiko would come forward without a fight. A moment later, he noticed movement in the crowd. The commoners cleared a path as Yoshiko approached the shirazu. She stopped behind the pit of sand and bowed to the magistrate.

"I am Akechi Yoshiko, the debt collector of whom Hiro speaks."

"You will confirm that you spoke with Chikao on the night he died?" the magistrate asked.

Yoshiko nodded. "I tried to persuade him to pay the debt that Kaoru owed my teahouse."

"Did he agree?" Magistrate Ishimaki leaned forward, curious.

"He did not." Yoshiko glanced at Kaoru. "He refused and walked away."

"But not before you struck him a blow in anger," Hiro said. "You bruised his eye."

Yoshiko rested her hand on the hilt of her katana. "You are wrong, Matsui-*san*. It's true I struck Chikao in the eye, but I hit him in self-defense."

CHAPTER 56

Hiro considered Akechi Yoshiko. Even without her geta, she stood taller than Chikao. A twig had a better chance of frightening a bonfire. Still, she admitted the assault, and Hiro didn't need to prove the reason.

"I apologize for my error," Hiro said. "After Akechi-*san* fended off Chikao, the brewer returned to his shop with a bruise on his eye and a lie on his lips. He told his wife and business partner that Ginjiro hit him. He also said Ginjiro threatened worse unless Chikao made a payment against Kaoru's debt that night."

"My father was not a liar," Kaoru said. "Ginjiro struck him, not this . . . woman."

"This samurai woman says she struck your father," Hiro said.

"Why would my father lie?" Kaoru demanded.

"Would you admit to your wife and son that a woman bruised your face?" Hiro asked.

"I wouldn't," the magistrate said.

A ripple of amusement passed through the crowd.

Hiro waited for the laughter to subside before continuing. "Chikao spent the rest of the evening at his brewery. Didn't he, Ren?"

Ren nodded. "Yes, that's true."

"Thank you," Hiro said. "That night, after the Lucky Monkey closed, Chikao returned to Ginjiro's. Finding it closed, Chikao went into the alley, intending to knock at the private door. Given their earlier argument, Chikao would not have cared about forcing Ginjiro out of bed."

"That's when Ginjiro killed him," Kaoru said.

"You think so?" Hiro asked. "Then tell me: How did Ginjiro,

acting alone, surprise Chikao from behind? The lethal blow was struck on the back of the head."

"He did it somehow," Kaoru said. "Maybe his daughter helped him."

"A valid and intriguing possibility," Hiro said, "and one I did consider for a while. However, Tomiko believed her father would never force her to marry you—and had she plotted with her father to kill Chikao, they would have left a murder weapon implicating bandits or planted a weapon belonging to someone else. That didn't happen.

"In fact, the dōshin never found a murder weapon."

"Yes, they did," Ren said. "A broken flask, impressed with Ginjiro's seal."

Hiro smiled. "Thank you for correcting my mistake."

Magistrate Ishimaki scowled at Ren. "Who told you about the flask and the seal?"

"No one told him," Hiro said. "He knows because he killed Chikao and left the evidence there to ensure that your men would blame Ginjiro."

"I did not!" Ren stepped backward. "That's ridiculous."

"No one knew about the flask except the yoriki and the dōshin," the magistrate said.

"I knew, too!" Suke shouted from the crowd.

Hiro turned as the spectators parted to allow the filthy monk to approach the dais.

Suke bowed dramatically to the magistrate.

"You see?" Ren pointed. "Everyone knew about it, even drunks."

Suke scowled. "I am not everyone. And it was my flask you stole!"

Magistrate Ishimaki shook his head. "I'm sorry, Matsui-*san*. Too many people knew about the flask. This man's knowledge doesn't prove his guilt."

"That's true," Hiro said, "but it does prove more than you think. Ginjiro's flask was not the murder weapon—it was left to throw the dōshin off the trail. The real murder weapon was a wooden flask, presumably from the Lucky Monkey."

Hiro looked at Ren. "It took some time to figure out the truth. I always thought Ginjiro's flask would break before it shattered Chikao's skull. Later, I saw the wooden flasks at the Lucky Monkey Brewery, and Yoshiko mentioned her preference for wooden flasks—because they do not break. That's when I realized Ginjiro's flask was not the real murder weapon, that the killer saw it in Suke's hands and used it to blame Ginjiro for his crime.

"At first I suspected Kaoru, but after listening to everyone talk about him, I realized he lacked the intelligence and the drive to plan the crime. Plus, I doubt he knew about the loan."

"What loan?" Ren turned to the magistrate. "How long are you going to put up with this nonsense?"

Magistrate Ishimaki looked confused. "Loan? What are you talking about?"

"The Lucky Monkey didn't make a measurable profit," Hiro said, "and yet, somehow, Chikao intended to pay Ginjiro on the night he died. Despite my questions, no one actually explained how that was possible. Moneylenders wouldn't loan Chikao and Mina silver to repay the debt, because the Lucky Monkey's profits weren't enough to back the loan. Kaoru couldn't get a loan because of his reputation.

"And yet, just days before Chikao's murder, someone from the Lucky Monkey did secure a loan, from a moneylender named Bashō—a large enough loan that the lender himself had to hide from a debt collector because he couldn't pay his bills.

"Neither Chikao's wife nor Kaoru knew about that money. Mina would have mentioned it, and Kaoru would have spent it. By process of elimination, Ren arranged the loan."

"I don't know what you're talking about," Ren said. "What loan? What money?"

Hiro turned to the magistrate. "When the yoriki searched Ginjiro's, did they find a large sum of money?"

"Not a substantial one," Magistrate Ishimaki said. "Some coins in a cash box, nothing more than a brewery of that size would take in on a normal night."

"Why would I take out a loan, with or without Chikao's knowledge?" Ren raised his hands. "I have no debts. I have no need to borrow money. More importantly, why would I kill my business partner?"

Hiro smiled. "You took the loan because you had better credit than Chikao. You intended to use the money to buy Ginjiro's, but I'd guess you had a backup plan to use it for a brewery of your own if Kaoru's bad behavior ruined Chikao's chance to join the guild.

"When Ginjiro threatened to withdraw his support for your application, you realized you'd never succeed in partnership with Chikao. You went along with the plan to vandalize Ginjiro's brewery, because you'd rather own that shop than buy another. Would you still have killed him if the plan succeeded?"

Ren looked nervous. "I had no reason to kill Chikao."

"Not until the night he died," Hiro said. "That's when he changed the plan and decided to use the money you borrowed to pay off Kaoru's debt instead of saving it to buy Ginjiro's or another brewery. That's why he had the money to make a payment on the loan—he took the coins you were saving, probably without consent. You couldn't let him do that, so you followed him and killed him.

"Don't make Magistrate Ishimaki send his men to search your room—we both know they'll find the money there."

"Why would I steal back my own money?" Ren pointed at Yoshiko. "You said yourself she carries a wooden flask—and she hires herself out as a brewery guard. Ginjiro must have hired her to protect his brewery that night. She must have killed Chikao!"

"The evidence says otherwise," Hiro said. "If she killed Chikao, she would have taken the money and probably credited it toward Kaoru's debt. She could have claimed he gave it to her earlier, before he died. However, she claims the debt remains unpaid."

"The debt has not been paid." Yoshiko glared at Ren. "And I did not kill Chikao."

"She didn't!" Suke jumped forward. "Hiro-*san*, I can prove it! The night you asked me to go to Ginjiro's and listen to the patrons . . . I overheard Tomiko talking with Akechi-*san* about the murder.

"Tomiko said she felt guilty about sleeping through the night. She thought, if she'd stayed awake, she might prove her father's innocence. Akechi-*san* told Tomiko not to blame herself—and then confessed to falling asleep while waiting for a debtor in Pontochō the very night Chikao was killed. She said she should have watched, but she slept all night and missed the man entirely. She said that sometimes people err and that we cannot blame ourselves for our mistakes.

"Akechi-*san* could not have killed Chikao—she was sleeping on the job instead!" Suke looked embarrassed. "That's the important thing that I forgot."

It figured the only useful clue the monk uncovered was one he forgot to reveal.

Yoshiko's cheeks flushed red. She bared her teeth at Suke, furious that the monk had revealed her secret.

For a moment, Hiro thought she might attack.

Yoshiko's anger vanished just as quickly as it came.

"It's true," she said. "I didn't want to admit it, because it makes me seem unfit for my job, but I did fall asleep in Pontochō that night."

Hiro turned to Ren. "Leaving only you to kill Chikao."

Ren's nervousness changed to an angry glare. "Chikao was a stupid fool. He paid off Kaoru's debts long after a reasonable man would have thrown his worthless son into the street. Owning Ginjiro's would make us rich, but wasting that money on Kaoru's debt would ruin us forever."

He turned to the magistrate and raised his hands in a pleading gesture. "Killing Chikao was the only way to stop him."

"Why didn't you keep the loan a secret?" Hiro asked. "Or keep the money where your partner couldn't get it?"

"Thieves break into rooms like mine," Ren said. "The brewery was safer, even though I had to tell Chikao about the money. He understood, or said he did, and agreed to keep the secret from his wife—and from Kaoru. We planned to use the silver to buy Ginjiro's, after we forced the sale. He had no right to change the plan!"

"You killed my father over a bag of silver?" Kaoru drew a dagger and lunged at Ren.

Hiro grabbed the young man's wrist and pressed a thumb between the bones of Kaoru's hand. Chikao's son gave a cry of pain and dropped the dagger.

"Stop," Hiro said. "The magistrate will deal with Ren."

"He killed my father," Kaoru said.

"Silence!" Magistrate Ishimaki shouted. Lowering his voice, he continued, "I declare the brewer innocent. Release him, with apologies for this unfortunate misunderstanding."

The dōshin standing behind Ginjiro cut the ropes that bound his limbs and helped him to his feet.

Ginjiro bowed to the magistrate. "Thank you for your wisdom and your mercy."

The magistrate turned his gaze to Ren. "Seize the murderer and bring him forward."

CHAPTER 57

The dōshin marched Ren onto the sand and forced him to his knees.

"The punishment for murder is death by hanging," the magistrate said. "Have you anything to say before I sentence you?"

Ren raised his face to the magistrate. "I didn't intend to kill him."

"You beat your partner to death with a sake flask." Magistrate Ishimaki's scowl showed no trace of mercy. "Explain to me how that shows no intention."

"When I followed Chikao to Ginjiro's, I intended to persuade him not to use the loan to pay off Kaoru's debt," Ren said. "He refused, so I took the flask from my kimono—the personal one I carry with me—intending to knock him unconscious, take back the money, and leave.

"But once I started to hit him, I couldn't stop. I thought of all the years we suffered because of Kaoru, all that time and money wasted. I kept hitting him, over and over, and when I realized what I'd done Chikao was dead."

Ren glanced at Hiro. "He's right about the broken flask. I saw the monk passed out in the alley, holding Ginjiro's flask in his hands. I thought if I broke it and left a couple of pieces behind, the police would blame Ginjiro and not look into it any further."

"What did you do with the rest of the flask?" Hiro suspected he not only knew the answer, but had used a similar method recently himself.

"I threw the pieces in the river, along with the flask I used to . . . the other one I used." Ren looked at his feet. "If he had only listened to me, instead of always putting Kaoru first."

"No man deserves to die for loving his son," the magistrate said, "regardless of the way that son behaves. Be grateful I allow you death by hanging. I consider the standard punishment too easy a death for the crime you committed. However, you confessed in time to save Ginjiro's life. For that reason, I will show you mercy."

The magistrate looked at the dōshin. "Take this man to the execution grounds and have him hanged at once." He raised his voice. "Unlock the gates!"

The dōshin looped a rope around Ren's hands and pulled the merchant to his feet. The crowd parted silently to allow the condemned to pass.

Hiro released his grip on Kaoru's hand.

Chikao's son bowed to Ginjiro. "I am sorry I accused you." He turned and followed the dōshin through the crowd. As he promised, he would watch his father's killer die.

Magistrate Ishimaki turned to the yoriki. "Call the next case."

As the yoriki read a name from his scroll, Hiro took Ginjiro's arm and turned the brewer toward the gates. Father Mateo joined them, and once again the crowd of commoners separated to let them through.

Near the gates, Tomiko broke from the crowd and threw her arms around her father's neck. Her shoulders shook with sobs. Ginjiro winced as his daughter grabbed the painful wounds on his back and shoulders, but he put his arms around her without comment. Tears welled up in the brewer's eyes and ran silently down his cheeks.

Hiro normally hated when people cried, but under the circumstances he didn't begrudge these heartfelt tears.

At last Tomiko released her father and wiped her face. She bowed to Hiro and then to Father Mateo.

"I can never express my gratitude nor repay the debt I owe you both," she said. "You saved my entire family today."

"I helped!" The crowd parted like scattering roaches before the grinning Suke. "I helped them find the killer!"

Tomiko bowed to the filthy monk. "My gratitude extends to you as well."

"Does it extend, perhaps, as far as a flask of sake?" Suke asked.

"As many as you like," Ginjiro said, "for a month, at least."

Suke's mouth gaped in wonder. "Ten thousand blessings upon your house, Ginjiro-*san*! The kami will reward you a thousandfold!"

"And you?" Ginjiro asked Hiro and Father Mateo. "What can I do for you? Everything I have is not enough to thank you properly, but anything you ask, I'll gladly give."

"I need nothing," Hiro said, "but I'd appreciate your seeing Suke fed—and given a little sake—if a time should come that I'm not here to buy it."

"You know I would do that anyway. Is there nothing you want for yourself?" Ginjiro turned to Father Mateo. "What about you? Could your temple use a contribution?"

Father Mateo shook his head. "My reward, like Hiro's, is in seeing justice done."

"Well, if you ever want a flask of Kyoto's finest sake," Ginjiro said, "just say the word."

Father Mateo smiled. "I will remember."

"There is something I don't understand," Father Mateo said to Hiro as they walked down Marutamachi Road toward home. "How did you know that Ren would confess his knowledge of the murder weapon?"

"I didn't," Hiro said, "but he mentioned the sake flask this morning, back at the Lucky Monkey, and I knew he needed the murder 'solved' as soon as possible. He had the money in his room and couldn't keep it there for long because of the risk of theft. He needed to either repay the loan or purchase another brewery, but he also needed a killer punished so no one would be watching him too closely."

"Surely Mina would ask where Ren got the money to buy a brewery?" Father Mateo asked.

"Mina intends to become a nun. She wouldn't have noticed what

Ren did thereafter." Hiro paused to hold his breath as they passed the smoldering incense at the gates to Okazaki Shrine.

"But how did you know Yoshiko wasn't the killer?" Father Mateo rubbed at the scar on his neck. "Or Kaoru? We never did find out for sure that Ginjiro didn't hire a guard."

"The money tells the tale," Hiro said. "A sum that big will change a person's behavior every time. Kaoru yelled at his mother about money yesterday. He wouldn't have done that if he had taken the money from Chikao. He'd have coins in his purse, and since he didn't consider the future, he wouldn't have felt the need to complain right now.

"Yoshiko would have taken the money to pay off Kaoru's debt. She wouldn't have left it on the body and wouldn't have continued to complain about the debt. She would have made up a story about Chikao paying her before he died.

"In the end, that left only Ren."

A man in a carpenter's tunic and trousers squatted by the side of the road in front of Father Mateo's home. He stood as Hiro and the priest approached.

Nervous excitement loosened Hiro's muscles and warmed his joints. Ozuru would not wait in the open if he intended harm, but the assassin's presence didn't indicate good news.

"Did we hire a carpenter?" Father Mateo asked. "He looks familiar, but I don't remember arranging for any work."

Hiro shook his head. "I know him, a little. He came to see me."

"But you didn't expect him," Father Mateo said. It wasn't a question.

"No," Hiro said. "In fact, I didn't expect to see him again at all."

"I'll wait for you inside." Father Mateo nodded to Ozuru as he passed but didn't speak to the carpenter.

As soon as the door swung shut behind the priest, Hiro said, "This looks a lot like the visit you couldn't ever make again."

"The situation justifies the risk," Ozuru said. "I persuaded Hisahide that the merchant's death, or that of the priest, would prompt the Portuguese to terminate all trade with Kyoto. Hisahide doesn't care about the foreigners themselves, but he does care very much about his access to their firearms. Also, he doesn't want the Portuguese to back Daimyō Miyoshi in the coming war."

Ozuru looked up the empty street. "However, as soon as Hisahide obtains the firearms he needs, he will order the merchant killed—and the priest as well."

"Matsunaga Hisahide would not risk the other Jesuits' anger," Hiro said. "Like the emperor, Hisahide supports the Christians' efforts in Kyoto."

"A ruse designed to destabilize the Ashikaga clan's control of the city," Ozuru said. "As soon as the emperor names him shogun, Matsunaga-*san* will either banish the priests or kill them."

"You're telling me to leave Kyoto now," the shinobi said.

"Yes," Ozuru said, "but not at once. Matsunaga-*san* won't let you leave until he's purchased all the weapons he desires to arm his men. He will need the merchant here at least until the war is over. But the moment the Miyoshi surrender, Matsunaga-*san* will become your enemy."

"He is my enemy already," Hiro said.

"Then we understand each other." Ozuru bowed and walked away toward Okazaki Shrine.

Hiro considered the cloudless sky and wondered how long it would take the Miyoshi to attack Kyoto. If they allied with the former shogun's brother, Ashikaga Yoshiaki, other clans might rally to their cause. However, Hiro suspected the Ashikaga heir would choose a different warlord—one whose name was feared by every daimyō in Japan.

Lord Oda Nobunaga wanted an excuse to seize the capital. Restoring the Ashikaga heir to the shogunate would give him cause and also strong support among the lesser daimyō.

Hiro also wondered, briefly, if the missing samurai's body would be found. The shogunate would call it murder, but Hiro hoped the lack of clues would prevent an investigation. Samurai died all the time, usually by violent means. Hiro would keep his eyes open, but doubted the death would cause him any trouble.

Father Mateo emerged from the house and joined the shinobi near the street. Gato trotted out behind the priest and rubbed herself on Hiro's legs in greeting.

"This day turned out more pleasant than expected," Father Mateo said.

"Not really," Hiro said. "I sense a dangerous storm approaching."

"Are you sure?" The Jesuit scanned the sky. "I don't see any clouds."

"Still blowing in." Hiro picked up the cat and stroked her fur. "But they are coming."

Father Mateo looked nervous. "How will we know when it's time to take cover?"

"I will tell you," Hiro said. "For now, you'll have to trust me."

CAST OF CHARACTERS

(IN ALPHABETICAL ORDER)

Where present, Japanese characters' surnames precede their given names, in the Japanese style. Western surnames follow the characters' given names, in accordance with Western conventions.

Akechi Yoshiko — a female samurai

Ana — Father Mateo's housekeeper

Bashō — a wealthy Kyoto rice merchant

Chikao — a sake brewer; half owner of the Lucky Monkey brewery

Eba — owner of the Golden Buddha teahouse

Father Mateo Ávila de Santos — a Christian priest from Portugal, currently working in Kyoto

Gato — Hiro's cat

Ginjiro — a sake brewer; owner of Ginjiro's brewery

Hama — Bashō's wife

Hattori Hiro — a shinobi (ninja) assassin from the Iga ryu, hired by an anonymous benefactor to guard Father Mateo

Jiro — Bashō's apprentice

Kaoru — Chikao's adult son

Luis Álvares — a Portuguese merchant whose weapons sales finance Father Mateo's work

Magistrate Ishimaki — a judge appointed to oversee justice in Kyoto

Matsunaga Hisahide* — a *daimyō* (samurai warlord) who siezed Kyoto in June 1565

Mayuri — a retired entertainer; owner of the Sakura Teahouse

Mina — Chikao's wife

Oda Nobunaga* — a *daimyō* (samurai warlord)

Ozuru — a shinobi assassin from the Koga ryu, on assignment and posing as a carpenter in Kyoto

Ren — a sake brewer; half owner of the Lucky Monkey brewery

Suke — a Buddhist monk who frequents Ginjiro's brewery

Tomiko — Ginjiro's adult daughter

Yoka — Ginjiro's wife

*Designates a historical figure. (All other characters are fictitious.)

GLOSSARY OF JAPANESE TERMS

B

bakufu: Literally, "tent government." Another name for the shogunate and the shogun's administration.

C

chonmage: The traditional hairstyle of adult samurai males. After shaving the pate, the remaining hair was oiled and tied in a tail, which was then folded back and forth on top of the head.

D

daimyō: A samurai lord, usually the ruler of a province or the head of a samurai clan.

dōshin: The medieval Japanese equivalent of a beat cop or policeman.

E

eta: Literally, "an abundance of filth." A term for members of the Japanese "untouchable" or outcaste class that sat at the bottom of Japan's social hierarchy. In modern times, the term was replaced by the less offensive "*burakumin.*"

F

futon: A thin padded mattress, small and pliable enough to be folded and stored out of sight during the day.

G

geta: Traditional Japanese sandals (resembling flip-flops) with a raised wooden base and fabric thongs that wrapped around the wearer's big toe.

H

hakama: Loose, pleated pants worn over kimono or beneath a tunic or surcoat.

J

jitte: A long wooden or metal nightstick with a forward-pointing hook at the top of the hand grip; carried by dōshin as both a weapon and a symbol of office.

K

kami: The Japanese word for "god" or "divine spirit"; used to describe gods, the spirits inhabiting natural objects, and certain natural forces of divine origin.

kanzashi: A type of hairpin worn by women in medieval Japan.

kata: Literally, "form(s)." A detailed pattern or set of movements used to practice martial skills and combat techniques, performed either with or without a weapon.

katana: The longer of the two swords worn by a samurai. (The shorter one is the wakizashi.)

kimono: Literally, "a thing to wear." A full-length wrap-around robe traditionally worn by Japanese people of all ages and genders.

kitsune: A "fox spirit," often believed to possess superior intelligence, long life, and magical powers. According to legend, kitsune sometimes assumed a human (usually female) form in order to play tricks on people.

koku: a unit of measurement, roughly equal to 150 kilograms (330 pounds), originally used to describe the amount of rice required to feed one adult person for one year.

M

mon: An emblem or crest used to identify a Japanese family or clan.

N

noren: A traditional Japanese doorway hanging, with a slit cut up the center to permit passage.

O

obi: A wide sash wrapped around the waist to hold a kimono closed, worn by people of all ages and genders.

oe: The large central living space in a Japanese home, which featured a sunken hearth and often served as a combination of kitchen, reception room, and living space.

P

Pontochō: One of Kyoto's hanamachi (geisha and courtesan) districts, containing geisha houses, teahouses, brothels, restaurants, and similar businesses.

R

ronin: A masterless samurai.

ryu: Literally, "school." Shinobi clans used this term as a combination identifier and association name. (Hattori Hiro is a member of the Iga ryu.)

S

sake (also "saké"): An alcoholic beverage made from fermented rice.

samurai: A member of the medieval Japanese nobility, the warrior caste that formed the highest-ranking social class.

-san: A suffix used to show respect.

seppuku: A form of Japanese ritual suicide by disembowelment, originally used only by samurai.

shamisen: A traditional Japanese instrument with a long neck and resonating strings strung across a drum-like wooden base. The instrument is played by plucking the strings with a plectrum.

shinobi: Literally, "shadowed person." Shinobi is the Japanese pronunciation of the characters that many Westerners pronounce "ninja." ("Ninja" is based on a Chinese pronunciation.)

Shintō: The indigenous spirituality or religion of Japan, sometimes also called "*kami-no-michi.*"

shirazu: A pit of white sand where criminals knelt during trial and to receive their sentences from the magistrate.

shogun: The military dictator and commander who acted as de facto ruler of medieval Japan.

shogunate (also "bakufu"): A name for the shogun's government and the compound where the shogun lived.

shoji: A sliding door, usually consisting of a wooden frame with oiled paper panels.

shuriken: An easily concealed, palm-sized weapon made of metal and often shaped like a cross or star; used by shinobi for throwing or as a handheld weapon in close combat.

sugi: Also known as "Japanese cedar" (*Cryptomeria japonica*). A type of tree indigenous to Japan, often used for sake casks. The wood imparts a flavor that overpowers the delicate notes of high-quality sake, so sugi barrels are customarily used for ceremonial casks or aging lower-quality sakes.

T

tatami: A traditional Japanese mat-style floor covering made in standard sizes, with the length measuring exactly twice its width. Tatami usually contained a straw core covered with grass or rushes.

torii: A traditional, stylized Japanese gate most commonly found at the entrance to Shintō shrines.

U

udon: A type of thick wheat flour noodle, often served hot in soup or broth.

W

wakizashi: The shorter of the two words worn by a samurai. (The longer one is the katana.)

Y

yoriki: An assistant magistrate, tasked with supervising dōshin and other practical and administrative law enforcement duties.

Z

za: A guild.

For additional cultural information, expanded definitions, and author's notes, visit www.susanspann.com.

ACKNOWLEDGMENTS

No matter how many novels I write, the acknowledgments never get easier. If anything, it becomes even harder to fit an appropriate "thank-you" on the page. So many people help and support me on my writing journey that this page will never suffice to thank them all. Still, I need to thank at least a few by name for their help and support of this paperback edition:

To my husband, Michael, and my son, Christopher—you make me laugh, you bring me joy, and you support me in too many ways to mention. Thank you for every day and every smile.

To my incomparable agent, Sandra Bond: it is an honor and a privilege to work with you, and I look forward to doing so for many books to come.

To my editor, Dan Mayer: thank you for giving Hiro and Father Mateo a home at Seventh Street Books, and for your eagle-eyed help at making these stories better than I could do alone.

To Heather Webb, thank you for your friendship, your eagle eyes, and, most importantly, for being the shoulder I lean on when the writing road gets steep and rocky. But for you, I'd never make it out of the weeds.

To Kerry Schafer, thank you for honest critiques, late-night texts, and being the kind of friend who would even help me fill a carp with bees.

To Chuck Harrelson—thank you for your friendship and for offering the all-important male perspective on my peer-review team.

Thank you to everyone at Minotaur Books who originally helped this novel become a reality.

Thanks to my family: Paula, Spencer, Rob, Lola, Spencer (III),

Anna, Matteo, Gene, Marcie, and Bob—your support, as always, gives me strength and joy.

Thank you to Joe, Master of the Interwebz, for everything from designing and maintaining my website to helping me figure out that the cat has reset my function keys.

Domo arigato gozaimasu to Tomoko Yoshihara for helping with my research about Kyoto and medieval Japan.

Thank you to Wing, Peter, Laura, Michelle, Jacob, and all of the other friends—online and off—who encourage me and support this crazy dream come true.

And last, but certainly not least, thank you to every reader who joins Hiro, Father Mateo, and me for the journey within these pages. Your support is what makes the adventure possible.